Screams in the Forest

Nita Farris

Acknowledgments

As always, there are a million people to thank while writing a book. First off, thank you to my husband and children. It's not easy sharing your life with fictional characters, and you all have been so gracious during my writing sessions and editing rants. Thyler, thank you for believing in me when I wasn't able to believe in myself. I love you with all of my heart.

Thank you to my beta readers, who gave me unapologetic edits, honest advice, and followed the story from the beginning. Kylie, Rose, and Kylee, you all are invaluable to me. Thank you to the author Instagram community for inspiring me and keeping me sane during what felt like an endless editing process. You guys are the best.

Lastly, thank you to each and every person who took a chance on this series and supported me. This would be impossible without you.

For my very own Lenore,
I'll hold you in my heart until I can hold you in my
arms

Chapter 1

Two years ago, I was standing in the same place. I had tried to focus on the beauty of the graveyard. The greenness of the grass contrasted by the flowers in various states of decay. The gleam of the cherry wood that hung precariously before us as we grieved and tried to say goodbye. The deep blue of the preacher's tunic as he tried to put into three hundred words the person that laid inside of that coffin.

Today, the beauty merely seemed to mock the fact that we were here yet again. Everyone wore bright colors to celebrate the life we had lost. We were surrounded by sunflowers. We played music and so many friends told funny stories. Yet, a soul was still gone. We could comfort each other and try to smile through our tears, but it didn't change anything. It didn't change the fact that we would be going home to a house that would be colder than before.

Two years ago, my mother's service had been the very first funeral I had ever had to plan. I was filled with guilt over hurting my mom and sisters so often. Terry was with me today and had primarily planned the service we were attending. Back then, it was all I wanted. I would have done anything to have her lead my mother's service and make all of the decisions. It didn't make it any easier to be here. It didn't make saying goodbye any less painful.

"Mama," Noah twisted in the front carrier so that he was able to wrap his chubby arms around me.

My son was drowsing in Terry's arms and she swung him gently side to side. As he reached for me, she put her head on my shoulder.

I held him close and kissed his powder scented cheek. Having him in my arms and seeing the future

1

in him didn't feel fair. How could I raise him, promising him the world when I couldn't even guarantee him tomorrow? How could I be enough for him when I was so close to falling apart at the seams?

How could I prepare him for the brokenness of this world? How could I tell him it was okay to love if we kept losing pieces of our hearts and members of our family?

I wiped my eyes and turned my attention back to the speaker. My hands clenched as I saw dark wisps dancing behind Pastor Williams. I had seen the shadow figures at my mother's service as well. All of the grief and vulnerability was too much temptation to resist. A graveyard was the perfect place to latch onto another host.

I wondered if anyone here today would unknowingly bring home more than an extra vase of flowers. I looked at Noah again, who was oblivious to the danger that swirled around us. He had lost so much, and he didn't know it. Would I be able to keep him safe? Would I be able to keep myself safe when my unbelievable grief made me the perfect target?

Terry squeezed my shoulder gently, making me jump.

"Are you ready to go or do you need a minute?" she asked quietly, her eyes just as raw as mine.

I wished I was able to reach out to her and give her some kind of comfort. Instead, I stood numbly and soaked up all of the emotions around me. She nodded and told me that she would drive me home when I was ready. She gingerly unsnapped Noah from his front carrier on her chest so that she was able to put him in the car. I kissed his head and watched her latch him into his car seat. As the guests left one by one, I saw my mom standing near the edge of the fake grass draped over the earth waiting to cover the coffin.

During my pregnancy with Noah, I had been able to project my visions so that the people around me were able to see the spirits as well. I could do it now if I wanted to, I could call Terry back over and let Mom give her the consolation I couldn't. Mom shook her head as if reading my thoughts and I joined her.

"I feel like you were calling me," she said simply.

I held her hand, taking a bit of her endless peace.

"You were definitely on my mind today. Were you able to watch your service?" I asked.

My mom shook her head, her red hair swinging lightly in the breeze.

"I guess I could have. You weren't able to see me yet. I couldn't watch you go through that without being able to hold you. That would have been worse than having to leave you in the first place."

"Are you leaving?" I asked her, gripping her fingers even as they wisped through my hand.

She gave me a sad smile.

"Honey, I know you don't want to hear this, but moving on isn't a bad thing. What comes next is the reason why people pray while on earth. It's supposed to be a gift. Moving on is healthy, it's the right thing to do."

"Why does this conversation feel more directed at me than you?" I asked, choking up again.

The coffin was still shining in the late afternoon sun. This wasn't the time to talk about moving on, this was the time to tell me how to survive the next day, hour, second.

"It's not directed at anyone. I am just talking."

I shook free of her and nodded.

"Okay. Thank you for the advice. I think I need some space, so I am going to take a walk."

"Claire…"

3

I didn't turn back. I was able to project my visions and I had just recently learned to push them away if I wasn't ready to deal with it. Today of all days, I was not ready for my mom to talk to me about heaven or hell. But that didn't mean that ghosts couldn't find me if they were persistent enough. My eyes wandered around the cemetery, exchanging glances with the other people lost in their own thoughts.

Seeing a young girl sitting on a squat gravestone by herself was strange, even more so when she seemed surprised to be noticed. She stood, searching my eyes. I realized that she hadn't expected to be seen because she wasn't alive anymore.

Her mouth dropped open as she stared at me.

"Do you see me?"

I nodded, taking in her appearance. She wore a pressed navy dress with shiny black shoes and a pearl headband. Her short brown hair was lightly flipped out at the edges and she had fiery green eyes. Her death must have been quick because she wasn't stuck in a death state.

"Can you help me?" she rushed forward and tried to grab my hands.

I stood back. It didn't matter because her hands went right through me.

She mouth fell open in shock.

"It takes time to learn how to manipulate your surroundings," I told her, wishing that I had walked in the other direction.

"If you can hear me, you can help," she said, not seeming to care about not being able to touch the world around her.

I shook my head and she put her hand up as if to silence me. I wondered how old she was. She only came up to my elbow and already was running the show.

4

"I don't know how long I have been here, and I don't know why I am like this. Where's Kade?"

My skin prickled at her words.

"You don't know why you're like... what?"

Did she mean dead or a ghost? She was so small. I hated the idea of having to tell such a young soul that they were dead.

"I'm stuck," she told me, her eyes filling up with tears.

I nodded, unsure of what to say and feeling completely exhausted.

"Where's Kade?"

"Whose Kade? Is she your sister?"

"Kadence! She's my best friend. We were at a sleepover, and then it all just disappears. She could be hurt. What happened to us?"

My head hurt from crying and I was having a hard time absorbing what she was saying. All I wanted was to remove myself from this situation so I could go home and climb into bed.

I started to back up.

"I don't think I can help you."

Even though she was a ghost, I began looking around for other people. The fact that I was talking to a child made the situation feel like a figment of my imagination brought out by stress. An echo of disappointing Rusty so long ago.

Despite myself, I wondered what could have happened to two young girls. I had never met a spirit who had such a loss when it came to their death. Rusty knew how he died but pushed the memory away as it was too difficult to live with. Was this little girl doing the same thing? Was she hurt in an accident or did someone end her life before she knew she was even in danger? I wished that Macy were here to read her aura. Thinking of her made my heart hurt so much that I could barely breathe.

"You have to help me. It's the only way I can move on, I have to make sure that she is safe wherever she is and able to get to the light."

I believed that the light was the reason I had this gift to begin with. Helping spirits move on was one of the most rewarding things I had ever done. But not every ghost really wanted the directions to the afterlife. Sometimes they just wanted to take sips of the life still walking the earth.

I reluctantly stopped.

"Why should I believe you? Why should I help you?"

She locked eyes with me.

"Kadence was my best friend. Do you have a best friend? I am scared of what comes next; we have never done anything… alone before. I need my best friend. If I am scared, she is out there somewhere alone and even more scared. I can't do that to her."

I thought of my sisters, of Holden holding Noah and singing to him at night. Tears welled up in my eyes and the emptiness inside of me was overwhelming.

"I can't… I can't go to heaven if I know that she isn't there. I will stay stuck here forever if she is stuck here too. That's what friends do."

I looked at her, searching her eyes. I couldn't bring her back to our house. Last year I had been sent a spirit that I thought was a spirit guide. Her name was Barbara, and she ended up being a broken shadow figure who attempted to consume all of the life in the house. After that, we had cast a protection perimeter with tar-water to keep any and all spirits away from Noah. It still felt wrong to leave her here alone.

"Fine. I will help you, but you have to stay here. I will come back with my spirit guide and we will figure this out."

"Do you promise?" she asked, looking so young and somehow fierce.

"I promise."

***

I was so used to the shadowland that I had no idea how beautiful the afterlife could be. Once the shadows were gone, I was able to see my meditation for what it really was and was blown away by it. It felt like something to pray for. I spun around the living room slowly, the light from the windows pouring in and our walls still safe and strong. Sometimes I wished I could stay here forever; somehow hide Noah away with me in this quiet halfway world.

"That's great. Go ahead and come back."

I pressed my lips together, trying not to grind my teeth.

"Claire, it's time."

I reluctantly opened my eyes and came out of my meditation pose. My spirit guide, Lenore, sat across from me on the living room floor. After Barbara was finally gone from our lives, my mom introduced me to my true spirit guide. Barbara had been doing a great job of keeping us apart and I was still a little leery about trusting someone new. As unsure as I was, it was hard not to feel close to Lenore and fall for her a little bit more every day.

Everything about her made me calm, including her grandmother-like appearance. She sported short curly hair that must have been permed when she was alive; it had been dyed, but its copper undertones showed through. She was short, almost as short as Terry. Her smile revealed a little gap between her front teeth and

7

laugh lines that were proof of a great sense of humor. She wore a flowy purple shirt-dress with leggings underneath and never appeared to me with shoes.

She taught me how to meditate and put guards up so that spirits were only able to approach me while I was open or emotionally upset. I put up walls around our house and around my mind so that my view of the afterlife was all light and healing. When she wasn't giving me tips on Southern cooking, she was regaling me with tales of her days as a topless dancer and, later, on her grandchildren. She was somehow an oxymoron and the most secure person I had ever met.

"I can't believe how quickly you have improved. Your inner space looks like a fancy catalog complete with white furniture and custom lights."

I tried to smile at her.

"Thanks. Sometimes it's hard to come back."

She nodded.

"I know sweetheart. But that's not your world. It's not even their world, it's a place to communicate with them so that they can reach their true destination."

I sighed. I was tired of hearing about the "next step."

"Don't sigh at me, missy. You know that it's true."

I laughed despite myself.

"I am not sighing at you. That just feels like such a constant theme of my life right now and I just want to take a breather and figure out what I want before having to worry about the next life. Mine or anyone else's."

"Do you really think that's an option right now?"

I avoided her eyes, refusing to answer.

Now it was her turn to sigh and she changed the subject.

"Did you figure out what you wanted to do about the girl you met at the cemetery?"

We moved over to the couch and I warmed my hands up with a cup of tea Terry had left for me. She was also a huge fan of Lenore and left her a Sunset magazine, one of her favorites.

"We should help her, right? She was so genuine and in so much pain. When I came home, I looked up deaths in the area and a couple popped up immediately. Two eight-year-old girls had died during a sleepover four years ago. The causes of death weren't released. However, the deaths were technically one day apart because one girl passed away after midnight. It was ruled a terrible accident and never in the news again after a few editorials.

"It's up to you, I just work here. You do need to understand that getting involved in a murder investigation, even a closed one, could get tricky. People are not going to want to talk about it. Especially if you are telling grieving parents that the closure that they got from the case wasn't real, that the killer is still out there."

I agreed. My stomach sank whenever I thought about trying to handle something this big. In the past, all of the spirits I had encountered were focused on my family. It was still very dangerous and scary, but this meant coming out to the world as a psychic for the first time. It meant using my gift and needing people to believe me in order to help.

"Something is off. The articles weren't giving the whole story," I told her.

"What do you mean?"

I thought of the online newspaper articles I had found. They were without emotion and very short.

"The girl told me that she and her best friend were at a sleepover and from there her memory trails off. If two little girls were killed, why wasn't it in the news for longer? What happened to them? She was scared, but she also seemed like she needed to find her friend for a specific reason. I think she might feel responsible. Who killed her?"

Lenore nodded.

"This is bigger than just finding her friend."

"Exactly. This is opening up an investigation when it seems like it has been forgotten on purpose."

I rubbed my arms, thinking about what kind of people went after children and wondered what kind of can of worms I could be opening. When I was younger, I was targeted by an older kid in the neighborhood named Len. Over the course of our relationship he victimized me over and over. I thought we were friends and he was a predator all along. I wasn't sure if I was ready to face something like that again.

I was a mom now; bringing this into Noah's life was dangerous and confusing. I didn't want any of this agony to touch my sweet boy. Yet, this was our life, this was his mom. I didn't want him to grow up thinking that we had to hide this part of our lives. I wanted him to face his fears, even if it felt impossible. These gifts were complicated but had so much strength as well.

"I think this is worth it. It would feel good to have something to do. Something that mattered."

Lenore gave me a piercing look. I held her gaze as long as I could before taking a drink of my tea to cover my face.

"Okay, I get that. Just remember that hiding from your grief by trying to fix someone else's broken heart won't make it go away. Your own broken heart will be waiting for you when you are done."

"Lenore, I need to do this," I said, taking her hand.

She gave me one last sad look then squeezed my hand.

"Let's do it, while staying safe."

Terry swung the front door open, her arms full of groceries. She smiled when she saw Lenore, my projection of her strong and clear.

"Girl, help your sister bring those groceries in. I might be beautiful, but I am still as useless as a humidifier."

I put my tea down, satisfied with taking some action. A huge chunk of my life was missing, and I was incomplete. Whenever I imagined my future, I was so afraid and aimless. I needed direction right now, any direction. Even thinking about being able to bring two lost souls back together had me ready to eat dinner for the first time in weeks.

***

Some places live inside of you forever, encapsulating so many memories that the place itself became a living being in your head. This grocery store was one of those places to me. Its where Holden and I reconnected, where we made up after a million fights, where we met after his shifts to take walks and share Blizzards by the lake. This is where Holden made a name for himself and put his footprints down next to his Dad's.

When we became parents, this is where we showed Noah off to the cashiers that became family, where we strolled after midnight to put our fussy little guy to sleep, where we shared newly married kisses during shopping trips that became our naptime date nights. This place was Holden.

Even the smell of freshly baked bread and disinfectant had me reeling and looking around for the life that I had been leading just months ago.

Which is exactly why I had avoided being here.

"In and out, no big deal," Terry said, looking nervous.

She didn't want to be here either and it was the last resort for both of us. We truly had no choice, it was the closest grocery store for miles and Noah was protesting his car seat in a big way. He waved at me from the front pack on Terry's chest, grinning like he hadn't just been screaming his head off.

"You get the chicken, I'll get the milk," I said decisively.

I headed to the dairy section and almost bumped into Holden as he examined the display of coffee creamer.

"Hol."

My feet glued themselves to the ground and my eyes greedily took in his face. It had been forever since we had been in the same room and all of my senses woke up at once.

"Claire," a small smile appeared before he caught himself.

His smile was replaced with a frown before he put on a mask, pretending like I was just another customer. An awkward silence stretched between us as shoppers darted around me.

"How are you?" he asked, shoving his hands in his pockets.

Everything inside of me wanted to reach out to him, to hold him and press my lips against his. Instead, I mimicked his body language. It was physically painful to not touch him.

"As good as can be expected."

"It was a beautiful service," he said gently.

"You came?" I asked, looking up at him. "Why didn't you come to talk to me?"

"I didn't think it was a good idea."

"Why not?" I asked, the last of my composure breaking.

Holden's eyes were stormy and miserable, but still resolute.

"You know why. I can't... you know I can't. I can't be there for you right now."

"So, you are allowed to leave me with a million unanswered questions and a broken heart... you can't *be there for me?*"

As Terry came around the corner, our eyes met. She stilled and held Noah closer. She was trying to shield him from whatever was going on between his Dad and me. Her having to protect him broke my heart even more.

I didn't want this. I wanted to go back to three months ago. To ordering a pizza because we were both exhausted from taking turns waking up, to watching Noah yawn and fight sleep because he wanted just one more kiss, to holding the both of them in my arms and feeling like I could burst from happiness. From the feeling of being more than just yourself because this was my family.

"I've been trying to be there for my mom..." he started, looking like he was trying to find something worth what he was giving up.

"I don't think you are staying away because of your mom. I think that's bullshit," I whispered.

"Claire," he reached out and grabbed my hand.

His skin was electric against mine and made me want to cave in simply because I missed him terribly. My body screamed for him while my mind snapped back, telling me that it wasn't fair. I snatched my hand back and followed Terry to the check stand. Noah twisted in his front pack until Terry unlatched him and gathered him into her arms.

"Banana," he told me, looking serious about the produce on the conveyor belt.

"Of course, sweetheart. We'll have lunch when we get home."

I buried my cheek against his shoulder, his smell centering me.

It felt like it took hours to pay and load the groceries into the trunk. I collapsed into my seat next to Terry.

"Don't say it," I told her, wiping the remaining tears from my face.

"Claire… He doesn't mean it to be cruel."

I nodded.

"On some level, I know that. I just keep thinking of him taking care of his dad when he first got sick again. Seeing his love for him and the way he cared for him day after day. I fell in love with him even more because I knew he wasn't doing it because it was expected of him. He did it because that's who Holden is. Now, I am not getting that same kindness. I just miss him so much."

Terry sat next to me, wringing her hands.

"Do you think it's time to move on?"

I leaned forward and grabbed my sunglasses off of the dashboard.

"Ter, I love you, and we need each other. Especially now that Macy is gone. But please, don't ask me that again. Every morning I get up and have to beg myself to get out of bed. I am barely holding on as it is, I can't think about what comes next."

Terry nodded, wiping tears from her own eyes and starting the car.

"I just think you might be making this hurt more than it has to," she whispered.

I grabbed her arm before she put the car in drive and hugged her tightly.

"I'm sorry. I don't know how else to live."

"By actually living. I did it, you can too."

<u>Terry June 2017</u>

Coming back to work felt like coming home in a lot of ways. This time last year, I thought my career as a counselor was over and that CJ was finished with me forever. Now, I felt guilty for being this happy.

I had hurt CJ so badly and finding myself after sharing my body with Barbara had been incredibly difficult. CJ forgave me but I still had to earn his trust back and build our relationship from scratch.

After months of getting to know each other again, we made it official. It was so right, I regretted not choosing him sooner. I was so stupid to have kept myself from him for so long. I can't even remember the reasons I rejected him back in high school or college, even though they felt very real and important at the time. When we were together, I was whole.

He gave me the strength to go back to work and accept myself for who I am, gift and all. My visions were never going to make my life easy. I was always going to see the parts of people's lives that they wanted to hide the most.

Becoming a counselor allowed me to use this in a way that helped people. It was work that mattered. It gave people hope when they needed it the most. Sometimes, it was the push they needed to save their own life.

"I can't get over how cute he is," Lucy said, cooing over a photo of Noah.

He was splashing in the bathtub with the biggest smile on his face. I beamed just thinking about him. Noah was the brightest part of my life. I never knew I could fall in love this quickly or this hard for someone I had just met.

"I know. He got all the best parts of both of his parents."

Lucy gave me a sympathetic smile, putting the photo back on my desk.

"How is everyone doing?" she asked, sitting across from me.

I shrugged.

"Claire's really hurting. It's hard to allow yourself to accept that that kind of relationship is over. I think it would be easier if Macy were here."

"I keep expecting her to reach out to Claire. She would know how to get through to them."

Before coming back to the center, I had told Lucy everything about my family's background. To come back in good faith meant trying to avoid another Gina situation. She had been such a good friend to me the last year and so understanding of how I had just disappeared. Coming clean with her made me feel a thousand times lighter and more ready for this next leg of my career. If I needed help with another patient or had to leave suddenly to help someone, she deserved to know why. Even though she accepted my gift without question, there were still some things she would never understand.

"I think losing Macy was the one thing Claire can't face. She blames herself. It's not as easy as Macy just picking up the phone."

The door of the center opening brought us both to our feet and Lucy went out to the lobby. After a moment she popped her head back in.

"Your first patient is here," she said, looking unbelievably proud to be saying that.

I took a deep breath and nodded at her.

An older woman in a pantsuit made her way into the office, looking unsure of herself. I could see sweat stains on her thighs from wiping off her palms.

"Hi, I am Terry Shaw. What can I do for you?" I asked, opening the file.

Cheryl Brown, inquiring for her daughter, Kelsi.
Kelsi was a senior and recently tried to commit
suicide. Not someone we would normally see, I
wondered how she was referred to this office in the
first place. A part of me was glad it wasn't something
I had seen before. Something like this might be
perfect for my first case because it was so different
from what I normally dealt with.

"Thank you for seeing me. I am not sure if this is
where I am supposed to be."

I gestured for her to take a seat.

"Just start from the beginning."

Cheryl took a breath, gathering her thoughts.

"We moved here a year ago from Chicago. Kelsi
had so many friends back home, and I hated leaving.
We needed the money though; this was the
opportunity of a lifetime. It was the job that was
supposed to change our life. She had a hard time
fitting in, but one night got invited to a party. She was
so happy… I thought it was finally her finding her
way. And then…"

Cheryl began to cry and accepted a tissue.

"She came back in the middle of the night looking
like she was hit by a truck. Someone beat her up."

My stomach dropped, not an easy case after all. If
she was here instead of her daughter, I had a lot of
emotional walls to break down before I even got to
meet her.

Her eyes welled with tears. I handed her a box of
tissues and our fingers grazed each other. A small
vision filtered through. I froze to keep from showing
it on my face. I was still getting used to receiving
again.

I saw a beautiful teen girl, Kelsi, stumbling into a
doorway. Her shirt was torn, and her mascara was
smeared down to her neck. She was bleeding from her

18

nose and her lips looked raw. My stomach lurched, her mother's misery was so pure and clear.

"Did she tell you what happened?" I asked gently.

"No, she refused. I think she was covering for the guy she was seeing. She swears it wasn't him. Her arm was broken, and her ribs were bruised. It was… awful and brutal. Then a couple weeks later, she tried to kill herself. I found her unresponsive on the bathroom floor. She had taken a bottle of sleeping pills from my bathroom. I have insomnia. She had taken the entire bottle. They pumped her stomach and she was kept in protective custody at the hospital for a couple weeks. We tried counseling a few times already. She is completely shutting us out. I can't get her to go to school. I'm afraid she will try again."

I leaned forward.

"What brought you to the center? If she is resistant to counseling, I am not sure…"

Cheryl leaned forward to meet me, whispering like what she had to say was confidential.

"I have heard about you, Terry Shaw. Good things, strange things. I thought… if you could somehow see what happened to Kelsi, you could help her. You might be the only person who can."

I froze. She had heard of me. How? Was Gina trying to tell people about me in order to begin an insanity case? I wanted to deny what she was implying and couldn't. She looked so hopeful.

Maybe this was my future, something I wanted so much and had never had the guts to wish for. Being able to use my gift without hiding it or making excuses for it, people coming to me because I could help in a way that no one else could. I smiled at her, so happy to be back.

"When can I meet her?"

***

19

It's easy to commit yourself to a tradition when things are going well. Last year Claire, Macy, and I came to Long Beach as a way to reconnect after losing our mom. Claire was pregnant with Noah and life at home was crazy. No matter how bad things became, when we were here, things were perfect. We talked for the first time in forever, rebonding over s'mores and our favorite childhood movies. That weekend finally connected us in a way that made it possible to banish Barbara from our lives and we began to trust each other again.

We promised to come on the anniversary of our mother's death every year, to reconnect and celebrate her life. This year it was even harder. We weren't just trying to accept the fact that our mother had now been gone for two years, we were doing it without Macy. We rented a house with Noah, just the three of us.

We spent the entire first day on the beach, watching Noah bother the crabs and taking turns running into the waves with him while he laughed like a maniac. Walking wasn't a skill he had fully mastered, and he kept falling down into the sand and taking so long to get back up. Sand had become part of him by the time we brought him inside. His laugh made it easier to be here. However, the night came sooner than I wanted it to and as the sunset, the house was quiet with our pain and our grief. How different this trip was from our first trip made my heart hurt so much.

I knew that it was impossible for Macy to join us and her absence ached like a freshly scraped knee that I couldn't keeping myself from touching. Our house was too quiet without her laughing and too-loud pop music. The kitchen was too clean without her snack experiments. My heart missed her. It made missing Mom even worse. I was struggling to fill the silence and make new memories so that I wasn't drowning in the past.

"Do you want to make s'mores tonight? We could sit out on the beach with Noah," I asked Claire, forcing myself to finish my sesame chicken with rice.

She shook her head; she had been zoning out all night and her plate was left untouched. I wanted to believe she was tired from playing on the beach but couldn't quite convince myself. This zombie-like behavior was pretty normal for Claire these days. More and more often, she had been leaving plates untouched. It brought up so many memories from when mom was going through the divorce and I had to force her to eat. I tried not to bug her about it because telling her that she reminded me of those days wouldn't have helped.

"I don't know, do you think the smoke is bad for him? I don't want him to catch a cold," Claire said, running her hands through her hair.

"I think it would be okay. And it would be good for you to get out and get some fresh air. You love the ocean. You could go for a swim."

She smiled.

"That's okay, Ter. I'm kind of exhausted."

I nodded, wishing I knew the opening to the conversation that would bring her back to me. I wanted so much to reach her and get past this weird small talk. She sat up straighter as a small cry from Noah floated over to the dining room. Claire's eyes were dark, and her cheeks were hollow. She has been taking care of him alone for weeks and it was taking its toll on her body. I helped as much as possible, but she was doing it alone as if she had to prove to herself that she could.

"Let me, I'm done eating," I said quickly, pushing up from my table before she could protest.

Claire looked down at her plate, obviously having forgotten that she was supposed to be having a meal.

"Go ahead, I need some auntie snuggles," I said, gently handing her the fork next to her plate.

She gave me a grateful smile and took a small bite. Satisfied, I headed into the second bedroom where Noah was supposed to be napping. The room already smelled like him, a combination of Johnson lotion and Claire's Lucky perfume. He turned towards the door and popped his head above the railing.

"Aunnie," he garbled sleepily, reaching his hands to me.

I smiled at him; his little face always had an immediate calming effect on me. I leaned over to scoop him up and sat in the recliner next to his bed.

"Hello, little one. Did you have a good rest?" I whispered, kissing his cheek.

"Aunnie Terry," he said, nodding heavily.

I rocked him while he slowly woke up. I brushed his dark sandy blonde hair absently; it was so much like his Dad's. I knew that this weekend was supposed to be sisters only and still wanted my brother-in-law more than anything. Holden being able to be here would have been amazing. Maybe the beach could have healed whatever was broken between him and Claire the way that it had helped us last year.

I had given up on them being able to have a future together. It was harder to give up on the idea of a complete family for my nephew. Noah deserved more than this heartbreak. We had lost so many family members already. It was hard to pick up the pieces when Claire didn't know how to make them whole again.

Claire wasn't the only one who missed him. Last year, Holden had held us together in a way that no one else could have. He came into our lives exactly when we needed. He got Claire to fall in love with him despite her best efforts. He was a rock for Macy while she missed her mom and struggled with her identity. He became one of my best friends while I learned to walk again and found my way back to myself. He was my brother. I missed mint mochas and watching *Real Housewives* with him more than I could put into words.

I hid my face in Noah's neck, breathing him in and trying to hide my tears. Knowing that so much of Holden was inside of this little boy was the only thing that made losing him a little bit easier.

***

Claire was finally asleep, her suitcase open next to the couch. I grabbed a blanket from the back of an armchair and covered her gently. A book covered in canvas caught my eye, peeking up at me from underneath a sweater in Claire's luggage. I uncovered it and opened it to the first page.

Photos of the three of us girls were set against colorful paper and protected in clear liners, ranging from our days in elementary school to the year before Claire moved away to Ellensburg. I recognized the handwriting and realized this was the scrapbook Macy made for Claire as a going away present when she got into Central.

Snoozing by the pool. Dance parties with my best friends. Sister by blood, friends by choice.

Her captions jumped out at me and I ran my fingers along her writing, wanting to feel close to her. These photos made Macy so happy, made Claire feel like she wasn't so far away even when she was in another city. I wanted to smile, looking at us trying on hats at the mall or giving each other ill-fated makeovers. But Macy wasn't here and nothing about that was okay.

I shut the book and covered it back up in Claire's suitcase. I wiped the tears from my eyes and headed to the porch, determined to take a walk and soak up the last of the beach before we headed home.

***

"Doesn't it feel like we were just moving you in?" I asked CJ, unfolding a huge box and trying to sneak his DVDs in before he started trying to look through them.

He nodded.

"I didn't have any furniture and we ate gyros on the floor that first night. I think it took me three months to save up the money to buy an air mattress."

I smiled at him. "And now look at you."

CJ sighed. "I still miss my pizzable."

I shook my head, remembering the coffee table he made out of duct tape and pizza boxes. It smelled like cheese and the grease stains were disgusting. However, I got where he was coming from. I would miss this place too. When he first moved in, this apartment was kind of gross; he had really fixed it up over the last few years.

I lived in the dorms in college and I never really wanted to be out on my own. I was never crazy about being by myself. I came home every single weekend and that safety net kept me from feeling like I was alone. Once CJ decided to move out on his own, he made me part of it.

We searched for the right fit for him for weeks, which at the time meant he could afford it with his paycheck from delivering pizzas. He was barely able to scrape enough money together to afford this one-bedroom dump.

We made it home. We saved up for furniture piece by piece. A couch from a garage sale, a bed that he earned by helping a friend move, pots, pans, and appliances that didn't match and were outdated. Posters from his childhood bedroom and shot glasses that he collected when he traveled. It was our home. I thought I wasn't ready for that kind of jump into adulthood. Yet, watching CJ create his own space and spending the night with him made me crave independence in a way I never had before.

As I watched him start to pull his comforter off his bed, a pang of sadness spread through me. There were a million good memories here. Learning to make chicken parmesan, the times we had dance parties in the kitchen, *Dead Files* marathons in the fall, and drinking way more than we should have the year we turned twenty-one.

I was sad to say goodbye to those days. At the same time, I couldn't wait to distance myself from the discomfort of my early twenties. CJ had wanted me to move in and I said no, wanting space from him so I could find myself in school. I had come home to visit and found more than one pair of panties on top of his laundry pile and forced myself to pretend like it didn't bother me. I had been invited over for dinner to meet his latest girlfriend. I had sat on that terrible couch and begged him to come back to me and seen through his hands the way he had cared about his last girlfriend and the love they made in that very room.

This was our history. Finding myself in his arms and being able to be the truest version of myself. It was screaming and knowing how to hurt each other because we knew each other inside and out. It was remembering that first kiss and the night he gave his heart back to me. It was remembering his face each and every time I told him that we were only friends. It had been a long road. A long road that taught me so much about love and life. We needed that balance to truly appreciate the fact that we were standing here together today.

"Hey, you know. Maybe we don't have to pack that up yet," I told him, smoothing his sheet and sitting on his bed.

"Oh yeah?" CJ said, wiping his sweaty face with his arm and smiling down at me.

"Want to make another memory?" I asked.

We had grown up in this apartment, we had always been friends here. Our couplehood had yet to reach CJ's space, even as he prepared to move into mine.

CJ grinned and pushed me back gently.

"I can't think of a better way to say goodbye."

Chapter 2
Terry July 2017

I was always a little unsure of how to introduce myself to people I had already "met" through a vision. I had seen Kelsi at her most vulnerable, with her clothes torn, tumbling through her front door with mascara running down her face. If she knew that I had already been a part of that moment, she would have never agreed to this in the first place. I understood.

In this case, it didn't seem to matter. I was completely new to her and it was clear she did not want to be here.

"What do I say? My mom always came to counseling with me before. I have never done this alone," Kelsi said, wringing her hands and plucking at a loose thread on her oversized sweatshirt.

The bruises on her jawbone and cheekbones were already yellowed, but it was easy to see the damage that had been done. She looked as if she was trying to hide inside the oversized sweatshirt, hiding from herself.

"You don't have to say anything. Did your mom tell you why she wanted you to meet me?" I asked, recrossing my legs.

Kelsi's mother, Cheryl, had told me that she heard rumors about me and wanted me to use my specific gifts to help her daughter. I had no idea what Kelsi knew or how much trust she would place in me because of those same rumors. I didn't even know how much Cheryl knew, and I had been afraid to ask. People always seem really excited about the idea until they witness it firsthand.

Kelsi rolled her eyes.

"She told me that you were a 'special' trauma counselor. I have no idea what that meant. She sounded pretty crazy."

I laughed a little, surprising her.

"Well, why don't we just start from scratch. You are here, we might as well make the most of it. Why do you think she wanted you to come?"

She gave me a forced half-smile, gesturing to her face. I wondered if she found herself unattractive as most teens tend to. The bruises did not hide the fact that she was a beautiful girl.

"I got into a fight. It happens. It's not the end of the world."

I leaned forward. "Okay, I am going to have to stop you right there. This office is a no-bull shit zone. That means you can't lie to me just because it's easier. We both know this was more than a fight."

Kelsi leaned forward as well as if to challenge me. I saw a little bit of her fire and was relieved to see that she hadn't lost it along with her confidence.

"Does that mean you won't lie to me? Adults always say that, and it's the real bullshit."

I nodded. "I promise. I will not lie to you. I also won't sugarcoat the truth to make you feel better. I will be upfront with you because that's what you deserve."

She gave a decisive jerk of the head and relaxed a little bit. I let the silence stretch on until she was ready to break it.

"What kind of people do you normally talk to?"

"I can't go into details; secrets are kind of part of the gig. I mostly deal with people who have experienced some kind of trauma. Rape, domestic abuse, assault."

At the word "assault" she stiffens, and I don't need to be psychic to know that I have hit the nail on the head. I could have guessed as much. I was glad that she truly saw it for what it was. A fight and being beaten is not the same. A fight implies you have a choice and a role, being beaten happens to you regardless of what you want.

"What happens after... they tell?" she asks.

"That depends on the person. Sometimes we just talk, and I help them deal with their feelings. I teach them to try to protect themselves in the future. Sometimes, I help them bring their assailant to justice."

"You can't do that unless the person wants you to?"

My stomach dropped. The truth was, the majority of my patients never reported the person who has hurt them. Escaping is what they want most of all. Asking for justice requires a lot of courage and being able to relive the ordeal by talking about it over and over. A lot of people just want to move on.

"Absolutely. I don't make any of the decisions. You do."

Her eyes filled with tears and I let her process whatever was going on in her head. I waited until she was crying and then gently offered her the box of tissues from the table between us, internally preparing myself for a vision.

I have to stop myself from jumping when I am immediately infiltrated by powerful kicks to my abdomen and chest. I have to force myself to breathe through the pain and try to look through Kelsi's eyes to see who is in the room with me. Blood smudges my vision.

I start to lose control of the vision and slip instead into my own memories of past visions. Cigarette burns sizzling into my forearm and Lucas using a shower curtain to cover my face, feeling my life fade before he ripped it away to make sure I knew who was in control of whether or not I lived or died.

I took a deep breath to ground myself. Gina was gone, Lucas was dead, I was here with Kelsi. I opened my eyes and saw that she was frozen with the tissue still to her face.

"Are you okay?" she asked.

"I'm sorry. Low blood sugar," I said before I could stop myself, the lie reminding me of Gina in a way that almost made me shudder.

I was going to have to keep reminding myself that I was in control, and this wasn't going to be easy. I was special. I had this gift for a reason. Helping Kelsi could help me find my way back to my purpose. I was powerful and could make a difference.

"Where were we?" I asked, sitting up and smiling at Kelsi.

She smiled back. Progress.

***

"Who is in charge of dinner tonight?" Claire asked, coming into the kitchen behind me.

I knew she was asking just to make conversation. It had been weeks since she ate a full meal and was getting tired of me bugging her about it. I had no idea what she expected. Her cheeks were becoming hollow and her wrists were delicate. She knew I couldn't just watch her fade away.

"CJ," I told her, putting away the milk as I made myself another cup of coffee.

She nodded. On the days when she made dinner, she busied herself with it so much that she was able to pretend like she wasn't hungry and instead took a nap after cooking. I was relieved when it was my turn and I could force her to sit at the table.

The front door opened loudly, and I heard CJ shut it with his sneaker.

30

"My loves!" he called.

I smiled and answered him. "In the kitchen."

He walked in with a smile, giving Claire a quick peck on the cheek.

"Are you ready for the best dinner of your life?" he asked.

I stood on my tippy-toes to see into his various brown paper bags.

"Sally's? I think we are familiar with them."

"Oh no, babe. This is something entirely new."

He took three large cartons of fries out of the bag and a small fry that he spread carefully on a plate to cool down for Noah. After that, he grabbed a bag from Wendy's and spooned chili on top of them. Next was a tiny to-go bowl of nacho cheese from Taco Bell. Once it was topped, he turned and grinned at us.

"What is even happening?" I asked, laughing.

"Come on, Claire. You can't say no to this. Its everything you want and more," he said to my sister, raising his eyebrows.

The significance of that sunk in. These were her three favorite fast food places. The fries we ate a million times after school, the chili we celebrated finals with in the winter and the cheese that we once caught her eating with a spoon after a bad breakup. He had created her broken heart trifecta to help her heal.

Claire's eyes watered a little bit. "You're crazy, CJ. You went to all three of these places in one night?"

CJ shrugged. "Best dinner of your life is worth it."

She laughed, the first true laugh in a long time. My heart swelled, and I saw CJ again for who he was and was so grateful that he was mine. Moments like this made me fall for him all over again.

31

Claire grabbed a fork from the drawer under the sink and took a huge bite, closing her eyes as she chewed. When she opened them, she looked like a completely different person.

"Noah is going to love this," she told us, squeezing CJ's shoulder and going to the bedroom to get him up from his afternoon nap.

I wrapped my arms around CJ's neck and kissed him.

"Thank you."

He kissed me back, wrapping his arms tightly around my waist. "No problem. I know how important watching her eat is to you."

I laughed a little and looked at the dinner he created. "We can't eat like this every night."

CJ rolled his eyes. He had always been rail-thin and ate like a behemoth. I couldn't wait until his metabolism caught up with his age. It was so unfair to watch him eat chili fries for weeks without gaining any weight.

Claire came back into the room and served Noah at his highchair.

"Come on, guys," she said, sitting at the table.

***

CJ had been part of my life for as long as I could remember. Last year I woke up from my coma not feeling like myself in the most literal sense. I had all of these other memories dancing around in my head, another self crowding out who I really was. This other woman had another love and I drowned myself in the idea of being able to put another person's life on like a coat. I became lost and this other self, this woman named Barbara, started to take me over completely.

She thought that she loved this man. She had spent years being his little secret as he carved hours out of his married life to sleep with her. When he finally broke it off to make it work with his newly pregnant wife, Barbara went off the deep end. She killed him and she killed herself. When she became attached to me, she thought that she would get a second chance to find whoever his soul was now in and start over.

I found him and I chose him over CJ, chose Barbara over myself. I had hurt CJ so much, I told him that I never belonged to him. I stopped belonging to myself.

When Barbara was finally gone, my feelings came back to me with intense clarity. What I had done was almost unbearable. CJ welcomed me back and we tentatively began a true relationship.

It was hard for CJ to forget his pain, though. I caught him looking at me out of the corner of his eyes sometimes like he was waiting for the other shoe to drop. Like he was waiting for me to change my mind again. When we touched, I caught snapshots of him crying alone, tearing up photos of us, wanting to take out his heartbreak on a punchbag and going to the bar instead. I had broken so much inside of him and received that injury back even though he had forgiven me, and we had moved on.

Being hurt that badly didn't just go away; we had to pave over it with happier memories. I had so much to make up to him. I wanted to begin our real life; I wanted to put as much distance between Barbara and me as possible.

"Terry?"

CJ pushed my bedroom door open gently, searching the wall for the light switch.

I took a deep breath, gathering all of my courage.

CJ flicked the light on and cursed under his breath when nothing happened. I had taken out the lightbulb to achieve my starry night idea. I pressed the button on the globe in front of me, projecting a million pinpoints of lights onto the ceiling.

"Hey, babe," I said from my place on the floor.

CJ jumped and I laughed softly.

"What are you doing in the dark, creeper?" he said, sitting across from me.

I watched him take in the picnic blanket, the wicker basket I had just gotten from Home Goods, and the caramel milkshakes and fries from Sally's.

"I was in the mood for a picnic. Fry?" I said, my hands shaking a little.

He leaned in and stole the fry from my hand, kissing me on the neck.

"Thank you, I love it. Did I forget anything? What's the special occasion?" he asked.

I took my time sipping from my milkshake. This morning I had tried to put everything I felt onto paper. Right now, I couldn't even begin to be able to put it into words. It was too big. It was so much that I felt like I was bursting with it and would never be able to do it justice.

"CJ, you have been my favorite person for over fifteen years. My best friend, my first everything, my absolute heart. When I think about what happened last year, it kills me," I began, choking up way faster than I thought I would.

He stilled, surprised. "Babe, we've been over this. It wasn't you…"

"Please," I said, wiping my cheeks and smiling. "I have a point, somewhere."

CJ nodded, watching me gather my thoughts.

"We need something big; I need something big. To prove to you that you are and always have been my forever. It was always you, it was always going to be you. The only time I want a second lifetime is when I think about our eternity being limited to right here and right now. I love you, CJ."

He grinned his lopsided grin, making my heart skip the way it had been doing since middle school.

"I want to start that eternity as soon as possible," I slipped a small velvet box out of my pocket and pulled out a white gold band.

"Will you marry me, CJ? Will you be my forever?"

CJ stared at the ring. "These Shaw girls. Can't let a guy propose, huh?"

I laughed. "Is that a no?"

CJ stood up in order to dig in his pocket. "I bought this that night before going to Sally's. Do you remember? I told you that my birthday was always special. I felt forever that night, I have felt it since that night we first slow danced, since our first kiss on my swing set."

He dropped to his knees in front of me, holding his own velvet box. The lid was open and a princess-cut emerald jewel glinted up at me. My breath caught in my throat.

"You've always been my forever. I would love to make it official," he said, holding my gaze.

He slid the ring on my finger, and I did the same, wrapping my arms around his neck and falling back on the blanket. Those poor milkshakes always seemed to go forgotten.

***

"When is the right time to plan a wedding after… everything," CJ said, sitting up. His bare chest sparkled with the starlight projection still slowly spinning around the room.

I took a deep breath of his fading cologne, wanting to stay locked in this moment before having to come back to reality. That was the first thing that came into my mind when I decided to propose and I had refused let myself dwell on it.

I sighed. "I was thinking the same thing when I bought the ring. I know that Claire will be excited for us and knew this was coming. But it still feels like the worse timing. It feels selfish to be this happy."

He kissed my bare back, trailing up my spine. "I wish Macy was here. She would be the first person we would tell. I can just imagine her squeal. It would probably break the windows. She would be planning an engagement party before we could announce it ourselves."

I laughed, my heart squeezing a little bit, and it was hard to breathe.

"Are you going to ask your dad to walk you down the aisle? How traditional are we going with this?" CJ asked.

I laid back against the blanket, grabbing some fries from the basket between us.

"I have to ask, for Claire. I wish Holden could do it, or even one of my sisters. But Claire wouldn't understand and I can't fight with her right now. It feels like something I can't compromise on. Maybe it will feel right at the moment."

"Church?"

I thought about the last time I had gone to church. It was right after the conversation where my dad had told my mom that our gifts were proof of us being too far from God. That nothing this supernatural could be right with God. I had found my way to forgiving my Dad, at the same time, there was no way in hell I would get married on his turf. It was our way or no way.

"No church. What about outdoors? A garden?"
"Perfect."

I rolled towards CJ, feeling complete at this moment. Feeling whole.

"I love you, CJ."

He smiled back at me and I could feel that he was experiencing the exact same fullness.

"Love you more, Ter."

***

There were a lot of reasons to be mad at my Dad. For a long time, I blamed him for my mom never finding love again. When we were growing up, he hated her gift and wanted her to hide it from us so that we could be "normal." Instead of allowing us to be who we were, he made us choose, and I always felt broken and unwanted. My mom chose us, and it almost killed her. She loved us, and we were worth it. As wonderful of a mom as she was, how could she teach us about marriage and relationships when hers only worked when she was the worst version of herself?

Love didn't ask you to pretend and it didn't make you less of who you were. After the divorce, both of my parent's kind of went into their own shell. My mom threw herself into work and became the last beacon of light for her dying patients. She loved us fiercely. The same fierceness and her determination to teach us about the supernatural parts of life robbed her of her relationship with Claire. I hated my Dad for putting Claire in that position in the first place.

My dad threw himself into being "normal," and eventually, Claire went to live with him. They were in this little bubble that we had nothing to do with and little by little, he stopped reaching out. He stopped raising us. He stopped being my dad.

There were also a lot of reasons that I loved my dad. I remembered who he was when I was growing up. He was the complete opposite of my mom's bubbly personality, and that kind of calm was welcomed when I was stressed out. I loved reading the comics next to him while he perused the Sunday paper every weekend. I loved taking walks with him and enjoying comfortable silences. He was smart and asking for his opinions on things like college applications or what to invest in made me feel taken care of. It was one of the biggest mysteries of life. Loving someone so much and not trusting or understanding them at all. It gave me hope.

"How has he been sleeping at home?" my dad asked, rocking Noah in the crook of his arm while shoveling spaghetti in his mouth with the other hand.

I smiled at them. This, right here, was the biggest reason why I was able to allow him back into my heart. My dad wasn't a great father to me and as an adult, I was still trying to figure out exactly how we would exist in each other's worlds. But he was a wonderful grandfather, and it gave us a second chance of sorts. It didn't feel like making up lost time or needing to bury past hurts, it was like a fresh start because we both loved this little guy more than life.

"It's still been tough, he was co-sleeping with his parents and suddenly there's just one of them. Claire has been doing her best to keep it together in front of him. It's almost impossible. A huge piece of their world is just missing. We saw Holden at the grocery store the other day and he wouldn't even look at him. I think it hurts too much, to see him and know that things will never be the same. What's the right way to handle this?" I asked him.

My dad gave me a sad smile. "Yeah, I'm probably not the best person to ask about that."

I laughed a little and pushed my plate away. "Thank you for getting her to eat. That has been my biggest struggle in the last few weeks. I feel like

Macy would be able to do it, maybe pretending like she didn't want to share her food."

At the mention of Macy, my dad's eyes got cloudy and his cheeks reddened. I knew no one wanted to talk about her, but I missed her too much not to.

"Anyway, he has been sleeping a little bit better. I have been trying to sleep train him to be in his own bed so that Claire's sleeping habits aren't affecting him. Then she can relax without worrying about him rolling off of her bed. One is old enough for an almost big boy bed."

He nodded. "Maybe we could go shopping for a special one. A race car bed might convince him that its better than sleeping with mom."

I leaned forward to watch Noah sleep, his small cheeks pressed against my dad's shirt and his lips looking like he was blowing kisses.

"I think it might take more than a race car."

"I didn't catch your name," I said, sitting down and crossing my legs.

I had expected the young girl to still be in the graveyard and wasn't disappointed. She sat near a willow tree, trying to pick up the leaves scattered around her headstone. I had a feeling that she was one of the girls that I had read about online. I still needed to make sure. I was really hoping there wasn't more than one case like this floating around Spokane unsolved.

"Emily."

I nodded, relieved. Her excitement over me coming back was palpable. Her image vibrated as she tried to calm herself down.

"Emily. I'm Claire."

"You are going to help me?" she asked, twisting her hands in a prayer-like gesture.

"Tell me about Kadence."

Emily lit up and I let myself relax a little bit. She loved her; it was obvious.

"She was the best person. Just the best. Inside and out. Our moms were friends when we were babies. I don't remember anything before her. I knew we would be friends forever. Do you know what that's like? She made me laugh so much, only like Kadence can."

Tears began to fill my vision. When I was sad Holden had always bought me a new book and surprised me with it. He listened to every damn thing I said and always remembered which one was on the top of my to-be-read pile. He got it right every single time. I understood having a best friend like that.

"Yeah, I do."

Emily barely seemed to hear me. "She was my best friend. And I need to find her so that I can tell her that I'm sorry."

"Sorry for what?" I asked, having a feeling that I didn't want to know the answer.

Emily wiped a tear from her chin. "We used to do everything together. Then it happened. She got a boyfriend. My mom said that we were too young, and she wouldn't tell me who it was. It changed everything. She wasn't acting like my friend anymore."

I agreed with Emily's mom. These girls were eight, which was way too young to have a boyfriend. The situation must have scared her entire family, especially if she was keeping it a secret and acting differently. My first thought was that it had to be someone older, which made the situation even worse. I tried to push my own experiences from my mind and focus on the little girl in front of me.

"What happened?" I asked softly.

Emily's eyes blazed. "He took her away from me. I told her that I was going to tell her mom that she was still talking to him and she gave my friendship ring back. I was so angry with her and said some really mean things. And I never got to say that I'm sorry."

I patted her back as best as I could as she flitted from solid back to wispy.

"I'm sure she knew."

"How do you know?"

She sat up suddenly and stared at me. The intensity gave me goosebumps.

"Do you think that he hurt us?"

My hands went cold as I came to that same obvious conclusion.

"I don't know. Did you know who it was?"

Emily shook her head. "No. Katie wouldn't tell me, and we weren't friends anymore. I found this in my hand when I woke up in that box."

She opened her hand to reveal a friendship ring.

"Why would they bury this with me?"

My mouth was a desert as I struggled to understand. Something was off. My consciousness and instincts screamed into my mind that this wasn't right. She was a little girl who seemed just as confused as me. I wanted to believe that she was just a little girl. The psychic part of my brain told me that I shouldn't let down my guard yet.

I had trusted the wrong person before, and it almost destroyed my family. Every part of me wanted to believe that a child was not capable of committing murder. A child couldn't possibly be part of this. However, maybe her child form wasn't her true form. I had ghosts trick me before. Barbara pretended to be my friend and instead tried to get me to kill my unborn child.

I bit my lip. "What exactly do you want from me?"

I didn't expect the ring to be firm to the touch and was a little startled when she was able to drop it into my palm. Emily paled and looked like she wanted to throw up.

"I just want to make things right."

"How did you die?" I asked, staring at the ring instead of her.

"I can't remember. I remember Kadence and fighting and cold. And it's all dark."

I shivered. "What do I do with this?"

Emily's tears were flowing freely now. "I want to see her again, I want to know what happened. I don't know how to get to her. I can't leave here for some reason. I thought that if you gave her the ring, buried it where she is, she would be free. And if she was still my best friend, she would be able to find me. We could both move on."

I gently touched the ring, the sunlight bounced off of it. I wished that I had the kind of gift that allowed me to gain visions from touching objects; it was something Macy was able to do sometimes. All I felt was the soft grass beneath me and the unsettling cold of the jewelry clasped in my hand.

"What if she doesn't come to find you?" I asked.

Emily wiped her face. "I thought about that too. I guess it doesn't matter anymore. I loved her and want to play with her forever. If she doesn't want to, I guess I know then. I can't leave if she is still here. If she is free and able to find heaven, I guess I can go too."

When I first received my gift, I was confronted by the ghost of a childhood friend, a boy named Rusty that I had played with and abandoned as a little girl. I was able to help him move on and say goodbye to his father. Seeing him reach his eternal light and knowing that I had a hand in it saved me that year; it helped me survive my mother's death.

Seeing the pureness in that light reminded me that death is just another journey and that I was put on this earth to make sure that spirits weren't trapped when their time here was up. I felt that Emily was genuine even if she was avoiding the truth. I understood loving someone so much that it kind of destroyed you. Friendship was intense and painful when you were young and trying to find your place in the world.

Maybe my gift would help save me again. Maybe I could save Emily and my sanity in the process.

"Do you know where she is buried?"

***

"How did he sleep?" I asked Lyn, smiling as Noah reached up for me.

Holden's mother shook her head and drained the coffee cup in front of her, laughing a little.

I settled him into my arms and took in the scent of his lavender baby shampoo. It was hard to be away from my son, but Lyn had begged me for a sleepover last night. It wasn't that I didn't trust her. It was just that not having him in my arms was even harder now that I was alone.

"He slept like a champ until about four. I got up with him for about an hour and he went back to bed for another two."

I sat across from her. "Yeah, that's been his schedule no matter what I try. Keeping him up later doesn't seem to work."

Terry shook her head. "Nope. It was a disaster."

Lyn laughed. "Babies will be babies. Do you want some coffee before you head out?"

"Yes, please," Terry answered quickly.

Lyn was a pro at white chocolate mochas, and Terry was powerless to refuse them. Lyn squeezed my shoulder before heading into the kitchen. While her husband was fighting cancer for the first and second times, Lyn had thrown herself into redoing her kitchen. She tore out the wooden counters and replaced them with hand-poured concrete countertops. She learned how to tile the floor and install a new lighting fixture. When that was done, she started collecting different kitchen appliances. Her latest obsession was her cappuccino machine, complete with a milk frother and French press.

I could understand needing the distraction and encouraged it as much as possible. Bonding over her teaching me how to use Russian cake tips and a doughnut pan would always be something I looked back and smiled on. Taste-testing with her son was a harder memory to swallow.

44

"Did you and Nana have fun?" I asked Noah, tickling his little armpit and being rewarded with a huge sleepy grin.

A creak in the hallway made me look up, and I saw a surprised Holden trying to turn before I saw him.

"I'll be right back," I said, gently handing Noah to Terry.

She followed my gaze and gave me a guarded look. "Okay."

Holden stilled when he saw me approaching him.

"Hey," I said softly.

"Hey."

"Did you stay and hang out with Noah?" I asked, hopefully.

Holden sighed. "I was here for bedtime and sat with him for a bit."

I smiled. "I'm glad."

Holden stared at his feet.

"You're not?" I asked, starting to feel overwhelmed with how closed off he was.

Things had never been like this between us before and it was still hard to not be able to make him smile and laugh. In the past, it had always been me hurting him and having to trip over myself to apologize, and Holden being gracious and teasing me before kissing it all away. Now, Holden was the one being hurtful and he didn't seem to care or want to make things better.

"You know that this is hard for me."

I bristled. "This is hard for you? I am doing this all on my own Holden."

He looked up, his face hard. "What would you have me do?"

"Just be with me," I said before I could stop myself, my voice more broken than I wanted it to be.

45

Holden's eyes got misty but were full of resolve. "I can't."

I threw my hands up. "When it did become like this between us? When did keeping your stupid secrets become more important than our family?"

Holden shook his head, his face becoming flushed in anger.

Terry appeared over my shoulder. "Why don't you come over for dinner?"

He shuffled his feet and blushed.

"It's okay Terry. I don't want him there if he isn't sure how long he can stay. I don't want to be just a tiny part of his time when he feels like he can carve out a moment. I think we deserve more than that."

Lyn came out of the kitchen holding two steaming mugs. I turned from Holden and went back into the living room. After chatting for a few moments, I looked over my shoulder and wasn't surprised to see that he was gone.

I wanted to feel better. Talking to Holden used to make everything better. Now, talking to Holden hurt more than I wanted to admit. He was my best friend and I was going through the hardest chapter in my life. All I wanted was for him to be with me, to share my torture with him and figure out what came next. I didn't understand why he was unable to be part of my life anymore. I didn't understand why he had betrayed me, how I wasn't his first choice anymore.

When Holden told me that he was leaving, I thought he meant he was upset and needed to take a walk to clear his head. We had gotten into a huge fight; something happened earlier that summer with Macy and he refused to tell me the whole story. The wedge between us became a chasm and we weren't able to cross it anymore. It was poisoning what we had; the lies were new, and this new Holden was not the man I fell in love with.

I refused to think that this meant he still wasn't in there somewhere. I just had to find him. I hated Holden for pushing Noah and me away. I had no idea you could hate someone you still loved.

***

When I was pregnant, I wondered what my son would look like, I dreamed of future holidays and the sound of his little voice. I wasn't disappointed. Noah's eyes were deep brown just like his Dad, and his little cheeks just absolutely killed me. I couldn't stop myself from kissing his nose constantly and I never felt as complete as I did when his sleeping body was wrapped around my waist, pinning me to the couch as he dreamed.

It was also so much more than just the stuff of dreams. Being a mom was terrifying. Being a mom was having to confront the worst parts of your childhood because you were afraid of making the same mistakes. Being a mom was loving this person with every fiber of your being and worrying about hurting them somehow. It was worrying about the world hurting them or them being disappointed in the cards life lent them. It was feeling like you were failing before you even began because they deserved the fucking universe.

It was feeling irresponsible for bringing them into a world that was so broken and giving them a future in a world that was dying. But also believing maybe they could be the key to saving the world.

Being a mom was knowing that they were teething and that you were absolutely powerless to make the pain go away. It was knowing that you needed to let them cry themselves to sleep and having to sit in front of a fan to try to drown it out because hearing it was a fever you felt in your very bones.

Meeting Noah was like truly understanding why I was put on this earth. Not to become a mom; I didn't like thinking that life began and ended with a domestic role. We were connected in more ways than just giving birth to him; he was important to who I was supposed to grow up to be. Noah challenged me, he helped me love myself because how could I not be powerful if I was capable of creating something as wonderful as him? Noah was my reason for keeping true to myself; a lot of days he was the reason why I woke up at all.

Being his mom was the hardest thing I would ever have to do; he was the best surprise the universe could have possibly given me. It was exhausting, emotionally and physically. Sometimes I felt like I was losing myself in whoever he needed me to be, and then I was shocked when I found myself again in his laugh. It was the best and worst of everything.

"What do you do when he cries like that?" Ash asked, looking flushed.

She had come over to watch him while I showered and somehow looked flustered after only fifteen minutes.

I smiled at her. "It's his first molars. There isn't anything you can do. He isn't a fan of teething rings but will chew on a frozen washcloth. After a nap, he will feel better and we can go to the park."

Ash watched him sleep for a moment before easing the door shut.

"Okay, back to business. What did you find?" I asked her, sitting across from her on the couch as she pulled her laptop out of her purse.

As always, Ash was my partner in this new investigation. Nothing made her happier than looking

48

up other people's dirty laundry and pretending to be a psychic too.

"You really know how to pick them. A serial killer?" she said, giving me an arched eyebrow.

I shrugged. "They pick me."

"I looked up the last name combined with Spokane keywords and murder. I found the same articles you sent to me, which were terrible by the way."

I agreed. "Right? There's no way that's accidental. Bare bones and then it just disappears from the news. I don't even remember hearing about it, and we are in the same town."

"Here is where it gets really interesting. The last name Simmon brought up another article about Stan Simmon. He was a cop for twenty years, including the time of the murder, before he was fired for drinking on the job. It was a huge scandal."

She turned the computer so that I was able to read the page.

"How is he connected to the family?"

"He is Emily's father's brother. Her uncle."

I sat back. "He is a cop and suddenly begins drinking so much that he is fired?"

Ash gave me her detective's face and I had to stop myself from giggling. "Exactly. What is he hiding? That kind of fall from the wagon is caused by extreme stress. Extreme guilt."

"Did you find his information?"

"No, but I did find the number and address for Emily's parents. They still live in town, in the same house. We can set up a meeting with them and try to get some more information."

"It's only been a few years. Do you think they would actually meet with us?" I asked her.

"It's our only choice at this point."

***

"If I try to make you wear an orange bridesmaid dress, will you disown me?" Terry asked, flipping through a bridal magazine and wiggling her eyebrows at me.

"Yes. Make someone else wear orange. I call dibs on yellow," I said, shaking my head at her.

When Terry first told me she was engaged, I could see all of the warring emotions written across her face. I could see the guilt etched across her features and could imagine what was going through her mind. How dare she move on when I lay broken? She worried that we would make it back to the days where we tiptoed around each other and fought enough to make each other cry. How much she would give up if it made my life easy.

I saw the forever look in her eyes when CJ was around and how she glowed whenever she saw his name on her phone. I knew that she deserved this happiness and that CJ was without a doubt the person who belonged to her in this world. I wanted to be part of it and clung to it like a life preserver. So, I cried and hugged her, telling her I couldn't be happier. If fighting about colors was all we fought about this year, then I could be happy.

Ever since we were little, Terry had her heart set on a fall-themed wedding. She wanted to wear a sparkling green wedding gown and wanted the bridesmaids to wear the various colors of fall. Yellow was not my color. However, it was much better than looking like a corpse in orange.

"We are thinking about forgoing the traditional lineup and just sticking with a small party. CJ's brother, Dad, and you and Noah. Maybe asking Lucy from work?"

"You have to have a flower girl at least, what about CJ's cousin? Allie?"

Terry laughed. "Allie is seventeen."

I thought back to the sixth birthday party we had attended, and my stomach clenched. Thinking about time being able to slip through your fingers in that way terrified me.

"I guess we'll have to wait for another baby to be born," I joked, then immediately wanted to throw up.

At this rate, we weren't going to have a new baby in the family for quite a while.

Terry flushed. "Or stick with nontraditional."

I buried myself in one of Terry's magazines, accepting her offer of coffee so she could escape to the kitchen.

"What was your wedding like?" Lenore asked, appearing next to me.

I took a deep breath, appreciating the comfort that engulfed me when she was around.

"Bright. We got married in an arboretum in late summer. Noah was our little ring bearer and we wrote our own vows."

Walking down the aisle, I only saw Holden. I wanted to run towards him because I couldn't wait for our forever to start. I could still feel the laugh in my throat when he started to put the ring on his own hand instead of mine, his arms around my waist as he spun me during our first dance. We had both given Noah a special present to represent our official family unit and instead of taking a honeymoon, we had gone to the zoo together. On the way home, I held hands with Holden. Noah was snoring in the back seat with sticky cotton candy cheeks. I had never felt so present and loved as I did that week.

All of a sudden, I missed him so much that I couldn't breathe. Because all of that was in the past and now, we couldn't even be in the same room with each other. It was unbearable. I leaned forward and attempted to put my head between my knees.

"I'm sorry, I didn't mean to upset you," Lenore said, rubbing my back.

"It's okay, I just miss him."

"Why?" she asked, jumping as if she startled even herself.

"What?" I said, sitting up, shocked.

Lenore blushed. "Sorry, again. I just... whenever I see you guys together, I can't imagine the way you were only a few short months ago."

I shrugged. "I wish you could have met him sooner."

The first time Lenore met Holden, we had just had the huge blowout that led to him leaving. I was a complete mess and Lenore tried to help me pick up the pieces.

"Tell me about *your* Holden, because I don't think we've met," Lenore drawled, rolling her eyes.

I laughed a little, wiping my eyes. "You are definitely seeing him at his worst."

She gave me a gentle smile.

"He was kind of unseen for a long time. We went to high school together and he was that guy who you would talk to about your boyfriend problems. I don't know if I ever really looked at him, you know? The summer my mom passed away; he was there again. Being that same sweet person I had taken for granted so long ago. He helped me through it without making me feel like it was a burden to him. I don't know if I would have made it through that year without him."

Lenore squeezed my hand. "You would have. A relationship doesn't make or break you."

I grinned. "I don't mean physically. I mean I don't know if *I* would have made it through the year. If I had to go through that alone, I would not be the person I am today. He helped me keep my heart open. Well, he forced me to keep my heart open. I rejected him over and over because I was terrified of being in love. It was impossible not to fall for him. You can't not fall in love with Holden."

She nodded.

"I've had other boyfriends. Being with Holden was like nothing I ever experienced before. This was being two whole people together instead of two people waiting for the other to define them. He wasn't afraid of my anger at the world and forced me to be honest with myself. I was able to grieve and learn to love myself again, forgive myself. I fell in love with him. He became my family."

"He really pushed you to be your best?"

I agreed. "Not just me. He saved my family and helped us glue ourselves back together. He was in Macy's corner when she needed an ally and they were hilarious together. And he and Terry were best friends, sneaking coffee way too late at night and watching crappy dramas when no one was home. It was like he was the missing piece we never knew existed. And now he's just… gone."

Chapter 3

Terry August 2017

"What do you think of this?" CJ asked, turning his phone so that I was able to see the pallet sign with a giant C and T on it.

"What is it?" I asked.

"A guest book. We leave Sharpies by it, and our guests sign it. Then we get to hang it up in our room instead of just packing a book away."

I forced a smile, already overwhelmed.

"It's nice."

CJ had been trying to convince me to watch the latest *Die Hard* for months and I was actually trying to pay attention. I wasn't a fan of action movies and I owed him. I had forced him to watch enough Disney and needed to at least try. Also, something completely out of my genre was a great distraction from the mess going on in my head.

CJ's eyebrows furrowed and he laid his phone down. "Are you mad at me?"

I blew out a breath. "No, there's a just a lot of mixed emotions for me right now. I am so excited to marry you. It's all I have ever wanted. I want our day to be perfect.

He held my hand and kissed it gently.

"But?"

"I keep finding a way to feeling insanely guilty for talking about a wedding when everyone's heart is still reeling."

CJ nodded, looking pained.

"Did I tell you that I asked Holden to be my best man?"

I shook my head, tears coming to my eyes. "When?"

54

"We were drinking some beers and barbecuing in the spring, right after they got married. I showed him the ring I had bought and told him I was planning on popping the question soon. My brother is lost in his own little world. This would make Holden and I brothers, and I wanted him to stand up there with me."

"What did he say?"

CJ's face was flushed as he struggled with the memory. "He said he would be honored. Then everything happened, and we haven't really talked since."

I nodded. "See? It's like trying to walk through quicksand and nothing is stable."

I had been planning my wedding in my head since middle school. I loved a good party and this would be the ultimate. I wanted a fall-themed wedding, a green wedding dress with jewels around the bodice and the bottom of the skirt. I wanted my bridesmaids to wear the colors of fall and to dance in the dewy grass without my shoes. I wanted karaoke and twinkly lights at the reception. I wanted to dance to old country songs with my sisters and kiss CJ under the setting sun.

It was hard to picture that being my reality. Every part of my vision was now tinged in sadness and uncertainty as my family fell apart. I didn't have both of my sisters beside me. My mom would never toast me and cry as she helped me put on my veil. It was going to be hours of unfulfilled fantasies even if it was an amazing day.

"Are you worried about who will walk you down the aisle? Did you talk to Claire about it yet?"

I laid back against his arm and snuggled in, wishing we could elope even though I would eventually regret not going through with my original vision.

"I wish it could be my sisters. I feel like they are the only ones who could truly give me away. But asking them instead of my dad would hurt Claire so much.

"What are we going to do? It feels like it's going to become more about pleasing everyone else than doing what we want."

I agreed. "At least we have the honeymoon."

CJ grinned and wrapped his other arm around me as well. "At least we will enjoy planning that."

***

"Are these really you?" I asked my dad.

I dusted off a silver frame that held a six-month photo of Noah before looking around the living room to find a place to hang it up.

He shrugged. "Claire might have mentioned that this place felt… non-descript was her wording. She said it was time I put roots down, and photos somehow helped with that."

I laughed; that sounded like Claire. She had grown up here and loved it. However, living in the house mom had created really changed her ideas of what made a home. My dad's house was sterile not because he didn't care about where he lived, decorating just wasn't how he nested. Our mom's house was a representation of who she was, warm and cozy. She wanted this place to be homey for Noah as well, for him to find warmth in both places. And I agreed, nothing about this house expressed who my dad was.

I wondered where he kept his record collection and the cheesy action figures he had collected when we were growing up.

"I get that. But a silver frame? Did you pick this out?"

He blushed. "I might have asked the sales lady for some help then was too embarrassed to tell her that it was something a woman might pick out."

I patted his shoulder and affixed the photo next to his entertainment center. "I like them. And Noah can make any frame better."

My dad looked at the photo again with renewed interest. His eyes were a little dewy when he looked at his grandson.

"That he does."

I looked to where Noah was sleeping in a bassinet next to the couch and went to sit next to it, my dad following me and absent-mindedly patting him on the back before joining me.

"So, I have some news."

That phrase sent a shudder up my spine as I remembered saying a familiar phrase the week of the accident when I tried asking him to my award dinner. He wrung his hands together, and I wondered if he was thinking about the same conversation.

"Okay."

I pulled my engagement ring out of my pocket and slid it onto my hand. "I'm engaged."

My dad's eyes widened, and his smile almost made up for that long-ago conversation that ended in tears.

"CJ?"

I laughed. "Who else?"

He leaned forward and hugged me awkwardly before looking more closely at the ring.

"Have you set a date? I can help out with money if you need it."

"I am hoping for a fall wedding. We still have a lot of details to iron out."

His cheeks blazed, and he struggled with his next question.

"Will you be asking one of your sisters to walk you down the aisle?"

I took a deep breath, fighting between anger and relief. I wanted him to want to walk me down the aisle, and his question immediately made me think that he was not interested at all. The way he struggled to be calm and not react twisted my stomach. Was he asking because he didn't want to? Or did he assume that I wouldn't want him to do it and was trying to support me anyway?

"I would love you to walk me down the aisle, Dad."

His flush disappeared as tears filled his eyes.

"I would be honored."

I relaxed, realizing that this is what I wanted all along and never believed could be a moment that happened between the two of us. Life has taught me that it can be full of second chances and choices if you let it. CJ had given me a second chance and his forgiveness had given me a chance to watch all of my dreams come true.

Maybe it was the same for my dad. It took watching his family completely fall apart, but he was finally taking accountability for his part in it. He was trying like hell to become a different person to keep it from falling through his fingers all together.

I wiped my eyes delicately and leaned forward to hug him, no awkwardness between us now.

***

After missing multiple sessions, Cheryl was beginning to get worried about Kelsi. Her suggestion of going to her school and asking her to lunch sounded like a better idea when it had just been an idea. High schoolers looked at me suspiciously while I leaned against my car outside of the cafeteria. I tried to smile and was beginning to feel like a full-on creeper.

I was thankful that it was summertime and the only kids on the campus were ones trying to make up enough credits to graduate. Finally, Kelsi came out, her head buried in a book.

"Kelsi," I called out, trying not to startle her.

She jumped anyway then narrowed her eyes.

"What are you doing here?"

I raised my hands in surrender. "You missed two sessions. If we don't talk soon, your mom is going to kill both of us."

She slowly lowered her book, seeming to consider her options. She could ignore me and endure her mom's wrath later. Or, she could just get this over with.

"Are you in the mood for Taco Bell? We could go through the drive-thru and get you back in time for your next class."

Kelsi shrugged and stomped over to the car.

We drove to the restaurant in silence. I had to coerce her into getting more than just a bean burrito. When she was sufficiently fed, I turned towards her as much as I could while stuck in the driver's seat.

"How have you been?"

"Is this the counseling part of your visit? Is that your thing? Pretend to be nice so that you can get your quotas of crazy for the week filled?"

I laughed. "I don't think buying you Taco Bell is a huge gesture. If I really wanted to butter you up, I would have at least sprung for Olive Garden."

She looked up at me, fighting a smile.

"Yeah, this is also part of the deal. I won't lie to you; you don't lie to me."

"What do you want to know?" Kelsi asked, crumpling her burrito wrapper and tossing it in the bag by her feet.

"Tell me about the party."

Kelsi's face hardened. "What do you want to know."

"What was the occasion? Someone's birthday?"

She slightly relaxed, knowing I was building up to the finale.

"Not really. Just a party. I was new at school and was trying to make friends. The girls I came with ditched me pretty quickly to play beer bong. I'm not a big drinker and didn't want to make a fool of myself."

Kelsi laughed; it sounded more like a crass bark.

"Me either. I spent more nights eating Top Ramen in my dorm than partying," I told her, smiling a little. "What happened next?"

She started to tear up and angrily swept them away. "I was alone and felt like an idiot for even going. Then... I met Guy. He was so nice to me; he had actually introduced himself during math class a couple of days ago and he started asking me about yesterday's homework. It was one of those conversations where it's just easy. Like you know them already. Do you know what I mean?"

I nodded, thinking of CJ. Considering the fact that Kelsi came home bloody and bawling, I am assuming Guy was probably not the person she thought he was.

"I'm not usually one of those girls. The kind that falls for someone in a single night. I wanted to like Guy. Having a boyfriend would have made things so much easier. It would have made making friends easier because he would have introduced me to his friends. He could take me to football games, and I would slowly find my way. So, I let myself be swept up. We ended up in a bedroom."

60

Kelsi swung her hands together, and her tears slowly stopped. I knew from experience that it wasn't because she was less upset by what came next. It was that she was forcing herself to be numb because it was the only way she could recount what happened.

"I was okay with kissing. He wanted more than that and we started to argue. But we had just met. This wasn't what I wanted. And… we didn't have sex; you can tell my mom that."

I shook my head. "I meant what I said. This is between you and me. If you didn't have sex, consensual or otherwise, you need to decide if that's something you want to share. If it's important for her to know, you can tell her. Or you can ask me to tell her."

Kelsi nodded. "Would you? I just feel like she is disappointed in me on top of everything else. And that's almost harder to swallow."

I nodded again. "Of course. I can talk to her. What else happened?"

She tried starting again and dissolved into tears. Getting this much out had exhausted her. She started crying so hard she could barely breathe, her chest hitched over and over. I shushed her and gathered her into my arms, letting her reset herself. I didn't know the whole story and that was okay. She had let me in, I knew how lonely she was, and she was allowing herself to be comforted.

This was more than progress. This marked the beginning of when she began to trust me and count me as a friend.

***

When it was easy between us, I was beyond grateful for the kind of person that CJ was. Movie nights with shared kisses, terrible 80s movies, and popcorn was a touchstone in our relationship. Then last year had changed everything.

CJ was still CJ, but Barbara tried to break down everything that made us great together so that I would go after the love of her life instead. She threatened to hurt him, she sent me visions when I was with CJ to distance me from him, she high-jacked my heart. I actually tried to break his heart during one of our movie nights. I still couldn't believe the nerve of trying to ruin one of the most sacred parts of our life together.

When I thought about last year, it was like looking through a pair of those polarizing glasses. I couldn't walk straight or see what was really in front of me. I had retained all of my memories and remembered what it felt like to have Barbara connected to my soul. Feeding on me like a diseased parasite. Once we were able to rip Barbara from our home and my heart, it was like waking up from my coma all over again.

I remembered everything and it still didn't feel real. I didn't feel connected to the person who had done those things to my family and CJ. But that didn't mean I wasn't responsible for how sick I had become. It didn't mean I didn't have a lot of making up to do.

CJ thought I wanted to just be friends and had chosen the guy from my past. He was ready to forgive me even as I destroyed our destined future together.

I finally escaped from Barbara and knew that losing him wasn't what I wanted. I had finally found my way to where I was supposed to be all along, wrapped in CJ's arms and heart. And because he was CJ, he put his pride behind him and welcomed me back in. I made it up to him over and over even though he swore he didn't need it. He knew my soul and knew that he had me back, it was enough for him.

I was still kicking myself for how close I had become to ruining the best blessing of my life. Movie nights being easy again made me count my lucky stars because I had almost lost them and him altogether.

"How do you feel about only playing songs from John Hughes movies at the reception?" I asked CJ, feeding him a piece of caramel corn.

He leaned in and kissed my cheek. "As you wish."

I laughed. "Claire would only complain a little bit. You can only hear 'Don't You Forget About Me' so many times before losing it completely."

"I think she'll let it slide on your wedding day."

I shrugged, thinking he didn't quite understand a Claire grudge against music.

"Did you get ahold of your brother to see if he is able to come into town?"

CJ exhaled loudly and set the bowl on the coffee table. "Yeah, it's going to depend on a couple things."

"Being?"

"Good behavior. He is in jail again."

I rolled my eyes. "I'm so sorry."

CJ tried to shrug. I knew better. I knew it killed him to see how his brother's life had unfolded. He and Chris had been really close growing up, and then he had turned eighteen. He made the wrong friends, made the wrong choices, and was now living a life that was so alien to us. He hadn't hit rock bottom yet, so it was impossible to try to talk to him about it. You had to want it for yourself.

I was beginning to wonder what rock bottom looked like for him. It was far from the first time he had been in jail. He had stolen money from CJ and his mom, he was fired from his job, evicted from his apartment, and had gotten caught selling drugs. What else would it take?

"Why are the babies such messes?" I asked him, thinking of Macy.

Macy had tried to pretend like she was fine when she hadn't gotten into university. She applied for community college and stayed home her freshman year. That was where the pretending had ended. She missed her girlfriend Britney so much that she was drowning in it. She came home drunk almost every weekend, skipped class, and I had seen more than one random guy sneaking out of her room at two am. I hated watching what she was doing to herself but knew that being an adult meant being accountable for your actions.

Macy being Macy meant that when it got too big, she checked out. She wanted nothing to do with forgiveness if it meant admitting that she was wrong. I was so angry at her for giving up but being angry with her hurt so much when she wasn't here to defend herself.

***

"Why is it so damn hard to pick out jewelry for men?" Lucy asked, running her hand along the glass case that held wedding bands.

"Because most men would rather stop a garbage disposal with their hand than wear jewelry?" I told her, laughing a little.

"He has never worn anything. Not even a class ring?"

I shook my head then stopped, thinking.

"When I was fifteen, we spent our first summer apart since becoming friends. My mom encouraged me to be a camp counselor so that I could put it on my college applications. I was kind of shy and extracurriculars weren't my thing."

Lucy nodded.

"I missed CJ so much. I made him one of those leather bracelets that you could burn words into. Do you remember those? I had the other camp counselor write our initials on it and the date. I thought it was corny and he would laugh at me. He ended up loving it and still wears it. I don't think I have ever seen him without it."

Lucy looked like she was thinking back to the last time we went out to dinner together.

"I thought he just really liked Nickelback."

I laughed. "No, he just really liked me."

"No, that's good. Incorporate that."

She searched the case until she spotted a thick titanium ring that had a clear center to display a weaved pattern.

"Excuse me, is this a set pattern, or do you have other options?" Lucy asked the woman working the counter.

"We can put anything you want in there. What do you have in mind?"

"A strip of leather?" I said, already feeling excited.

This was beyond perfect; this brought that untainted piece of our relationship into our married life. He was going to love it.

Claire August 2017

"Does this feel super shady to you?" Terry asked, straightening her blouse for the sixth time.

I looked up at Emily's parents' house. Both the Simmon and Morton family home was located in an upper-class gated community. The houses were really nice but so similar to the next that it kind of creeped me out. The Simmon home was bright white with green trim that was too bright to match. The grass was cut and immaculate. The flowers were struggling when compared with the homes around it. The yard was fenced and I could see the wooden clubhouse in one of the corners of the back yard. There was a gate surrounding the backyards and woods behind it.

The suburbs were such a strange place for a tragedy. Or maybe the perfect place. My idea was to pose as part of a community outreach program offering family support. I had no idea how to reach out to them and was desperate. I needed the information for their daughter. Pretending to be a journalist would get the door slammed in my face and admitting I was seeing their daughter would stall any and all progress immediately.

"No, we do care. You are a counselor. We aren't planning on using the information to exploit them or anything. However, we do need to know what happened. Emily needs to know what happened," I told her, squeezing her hand before pressing the doorbell.

Terry put on her therapist face and it was even easier than I expected to get invited in by Emily's mother, Krista. Emily was a perfect miniature of her mom. They both had the same shoulder-length brown hair; Krista's was pulled into a low pony instead of pushed back by a headband. They had the same green eyes, and I had a feeling the same smile was hidden in there somewhere.

"How have you been doing?" Terry asked, patting her hand and thanking her for the coffee she brought out.

Krista sighed and ran her hand through her bangs. "My support group keeps telling me that it will get easier as time passes. I am not there yet. I still wake up every morning, thinking that my children are coming home."

I raised my eyebrow at Terry. "Children?"

She stiffened. "I have an older son, he is nineteen now. He recently moved away to go to university. Having a completely empty nest is hard, harder now that I don't have Emily to take care of."

Terry nodded, but my skin prickled with lies of omission hanging in the air.

"May I ask what happened?" Terry said quietly.

She shrugged slightly. "We still don't know the whole story. Kadence was here for a sleepover; the girls used to love sleeping out in the clubhouse. Our community is gated, so it was safe."

When she talked about the girls, she seemed lost in memory. There was a faint smile on her lips. She had cared about Kadence as well. She was more than just her daughter's friend. She had been like another member of their family.

"They went outside to go to bed. I followed them to the door and gave them a kiss and a flashlight. The next morning... they were both gone."

"Did they ever find the person responsible?" Terry asked her.

With that, Krista came out of her trance. She looked around, craning to see the clock on the wall behind her.

"I'm sorry, my husband is going to be home soon. I need to get dinner started. I'll see you girls out."

"Maybe we could come back at another time?" I asked, shutting my notebook.

We had barely arrived. I still needed help; her daughter still needed help.

"I'm not sure," she said, wringing her hands.

"Maybe your son needs some support still? We could visit him at university to look in on him and make sure he is adjusting after everything."

Krista's eyes flashed, and I took a step back.

"I don't want him having anything else to do with this. We lost our daughter, he lost a sister. He is starting over a new chapter of his life."

"Of course," Terry held out her hand and Krista started at it for a moment before taking it.

We stood, shaking hands with her. Terry gave me a significant look, meaning she had caught something through Krista. She was pushing us out. Krista could ignore whatever it was she was afraid of and would still never be able to fool herself. Her body was screaming whatever secret her brain was trying to conceal.

When we settled into the car, she talked as she drove.

"I saw her fighting with her husband. She was blaming him for the accident and hitting him on the chest. I know it's close to the night of the deaths but couldn't pinpoint it because of her emotions. She is still very angry with him and thinks he is responsible."

"Responsible? Responsible because he shouldn't have let them sleep outside or he is the one who killed them?" I asked, my hands sweaty.

He could have been home when we came over. Is it possible that Emily's killer was still walking free and waking up in her home every morning?

"I'm not sure. She was very scatterbrained. She was hiding something and might even be suppressing information because she can't process it in her grief."

I bit on my nails and thought about the visit.

"So, we basically got no new information."

Terry stopped the car in front of our house. "No, her reactions were very telling. Something is going on with the brother. She definitely feels like he is gone as well, and it was more than just college. If she is afraid of her husband, she might have sent him away to protect him."

"That supports the killer theory."

Terry nodded. "What's next? This is definitely not enough to contact the police about."

I agreed. "Next, I bring the ring to where Kadence is buried. Emily thinks it will free her so that they can be reunited. Maybe Kadence will be able to tell us what happened that night before anyone else gets hurt."

***

I didn't know exactly what was supposed to happen. Emily thought that if I buried Kadence's ring at her gravesite that it would move her spirit on. I rolled the ring in my hand, smiling a little. It looked like something Ash would have given me in middle school. The metal was light pink, and it had half a heart on it with the word 'best' written in script. Emily had been wearing the matching ring when we met, the friend looking forlorn without its mate.

I dug a little hole with one hand and placed the ring inside before covering it with loose soil. I waited, staying quiet to try to pick up on any change in the wind or feel of the graveyard. There was nothing.

After an hour, I dusted off my jeans and headed home. Emily was going to be disappointed and I had no idea what else to do. I had never tracked down a specific spirit before and didn't know where to start. Maybe Lenore would have some ideas.

When I pulled into my driveway, I saw a little girl pacing in front of our house. Had Emily somehow found her way to me? Our warding was keeping her away, I could see it shimmering in the sun. She bounced against it in her frenzy.

"Emily?" I called out, walking towards her.

She stood and turned to me in anger. She looked nothing like Emily. Emily's hair was brown, and her green eyes were bright with determination. This little girl had the silkiest dark hair I had ever seen paired with piercing blue eyes. Eyes that were pinned on me with betrayal and disgust. This must be Kadence.

"Why would you do that?" she screamed, the dead leaves in the yard swirling in her fury.

"Do what?" I asked, trying to put my hands on her shoulders to calm her down.

"Bring that back to me, I didn't want it. That's why I gave it back."

I kneeled in front of her. "The ring? Emily thought it would bring you enough peace to move on."

Kadence's eyes narrowed and she looked like she was going to be sick. "Why would she do that?"

"What do you mean? She is your best friend. She was worried that you were trapped somewhere."

She looked defeated, as if she still couldn't believe the situation she was in.

"Emily killed me."

I sat back on my heels, looking at her more fully. Nausea crept up my throat and I saw black spots attempting to overtake my vision.

"She... killed you?"

Kadence sat in front of me, her anger gone and dissolving into tears. "Yes."

"Why?"

She shook her head, furiously. "She hated me."

I put my hands over my eyes. How had I allowed myself to be tricked? This felt like Rusty all over again. I never knew who to trust and hurt people so much. Would I ever get the hang of this? Would I ever be able to bring these spirits peace without wounding them even more?

"I am so sorry. I was just trying to help."

"Now she can find me. I hid for so long, and now she can find me whenever she wants."

As she cried, the pieces fell into place. Emily had needed me to bury the ring with Kadence to connect them once again. She wanted to use it as a siren to release herself. I had helped her do the one thing she couldn't in order to find her victim.

I looked past her to our house. After Barbara, we had cast a warding around our property to keep any spirits from coming inside. Our home needed to be a safe place for my son. But maybe it was the only place where I could keep Kadence safe.

I owed her that.

"No, she can't. You can stay here until we figure out how to get rid of her."

Kadence turned to face the house as well, her color starting to come back a little.

"Stay here?"

I nodded. "Emily can't come here. Our house is guarded against spirits who mean harm."

"Do you promise? You'll keep me safe?"

The fear in her face made her look even younger than eight. The idea of another child being able to hurt her blew my mind. I should know by now that anything was possible. What happened in the past didn't matter as much as protecting her here and now.

My family was not going to be happy about this, but it was part of our life. I did not want to go back to waking up to shadow figures in my bedroom. Yet, facing the darkness came with the territory. I hoped that I was strong enough in my gift now to be able to keep it away.

"Lenore!" I called, in and outside of myself to my spirit guide.

She appeared next to me quickly as if she had been listening all along.

"Is there any way to allow Kadence in without breaking the warding?" I asked her, seeing distrust written all over her face.

"No, there's not."

I stared at her, waiting for her to give me another alternative or idea. When she was silent, I understood that she didn't support this. Lenore knew that I had no choice; with that being said, she wasn't going to give me her consent. This had to be my choice.

"Okay, take it down long enough to allow her to come in. Can we do that?"

Lenore nodded and spoke the words that Missy had taught us. We saw the same silver bubble over the house that had held us while exorcising Barbara last year. It shimmered before disappearing altogether.

"Come in," Lenore said, taking Kadence's hand and walking her to the front door.

I watched them and then recast the warding. I hoped that nothing else had made its way in during the small lapse. As I made my way in, Lenore was laying Kadence down on the couch and gestured for me to meet her in the kitchen. I felt like a kid that came home past my curfew and trudged in to wait for her. When Lenore finally joined me, she was flushed and angrily sat across from me.

"You can't bring home strays, Claire. You know what's at stake here," she began.

I shook my head. "Lenore, you know that there are going to be times when I don't have a choice. Emily wasn't as innocent as I thought. She gave me the ring to find Kadence's soul. She killed her. How is it fair that she would be able to torture her in the afterlife as well? Especially if it's my fault."

"The only thing that is your fault is that you did this without me. You can't make these decisions on your own. Your gift is too new. You are too new at this. When you meet a spirit and need help, you come to me. That is what a spirit guide is for. We agreed to help Emily. I should have been there from the beginning. I might have been able to see her true intentions before Kadence was involved at all."

I rested my head on the table. Lenore was right, I wasn't allowing her in. Helplessness swam over me, making it hard to breathe. I just wanted to be able to do one thing right so badly.

"I'm sorry, Lenore. I didn't mean for this to become a huge mess. I just wanted to help her."

She collapsed into the chair across from me. "I'm sorry for getting angry. I care about you and see how you struggle. This place needs to be your haven, you need to keep it safe for Noah. If you allow yourself to open up your home again, it also is opening little holes in your boundaries. I can't keep you safe if you aren't working with me."

"I know, I know. What do we do now?"

She laid her hands flat on the table, examining the rings on her fingers.

"We help Kadence. That's where we are right now. I can look in the spirit world and see if I can find Emily. We can't move her on if she doesn't want to, we can exorcise her if it comes to that. On your end, find out everything you can about the case and their families. Even if Emily did kill Kadence, Emily's killer is still out there. There might be something in the case files we can use."

I nodded. "I can do that."

Lenore leaned forward and covered my hand with her own, filling me with a sense of calm and peace. She was an empath in her natural life and retained some of that gift in the afterlife. She was always able to center me when I needed it most.

"We can do it together."

***

This book was just not happening for me. The first two novels that sat in local bookstores with my name on it were written from a personal perspective. I tried to find that same balance for my third book. I couldn't do that this time. The only ghosts I had dealt with lately were Emily and Kadence, and their journeys were too new to write about. I knew that you couldn't edit a blank page. I didn't seem to have any new words left inside of me.

"Do you want to go for a walk?" I asked Noah from where he was playing on the floor next to my desk.

He reached up for me, and I slipped on his shoes before buckling him into his stroller. Getting out of the house usually helped get my creative juices flowing. It was impossible not to be distracted by just watching Noah and calmed by his simple view of the world. After everything we had been through the last year, I soaked him up as much as possible. We spent almost every afternoon taking walks in our neighborhood, me pointing out how the gardens and trees were changing with the seasons and listening to him chat with the various cats and dogs.

Before I really understood where I was going, I found myself in front of Holden's parents' house. Lyn was pulling weeds in her front flower garden and turned when she heard us approaching.

"My Noah!" she exclaimed, standing up and dusting off her hands.

After unstrapping him, she leaned forward and pecked me on the cheek.

"Come on in. I just made brownies. I had a feeling I would see you today."

We settled in the living room, and Noah fell asleep in Lyn's arms. She got comfortable in a recliner and gently wrapped him a blanket.

"What are these?" I asked, gesturing to the albums on the table.

Lyn sighed. "I had a bad night. I want to remember how things used to be. Some nights it makes it easier. You don't get to keep your loves forever. You do have to remind yourself that you loved them as much as humanly possible when they were in your arms."

I grabbed the album nearest to me and gingerly flipped through it. I recognized Holden's baby photos and his father thirty years before. Seeing so much of Holden in Noah's feature killed me. My throat tried to close, and I struggled to find my breath before shutting it and leaning back.

"This helps. I had no idea I could love another baby this much. And then I met you," Lyn said quietly, giving Noah a small kiss on the end of his little nose.

Seeing them together helped me as well. Lyn had been so much like a mother to me and was always there when I was falling apart. However, I knew that she didn't belong to me. Without Holden, I didn't know if I belonged here anymore at all.

Lyn started to doze in the chair as well and I wondered if she had gone back to sleep after getting up and looking at photo albums in the middle of the night. I smiled at them and headed into the kitchen to get a glass of water. An older woman sat at the kitchen table; my body broke out into static tingles as I froze behind her.

Seeing ghosts was never easy and they were still capable of scaring me and catching me off guard. It was even worse when I was in public and had to pretend like nothing was happening. Lyn was a lot of things. She was sweet, a ridiculously good baker, and always was always able to make Noah laugh. As great as that was, there was nothing unconventional about her. This was something she would never be able to understand. She loved me, but I could never share this with her.

I wished for the hundredth time that I could be visiting my mom. That I could ask for her advice, take photos of her and Noah, come over for dinner on the nights I couldn't pull myself together enough to make a box of mac and cheese. I wished for the past and hoped that Noah's future wasn't full of regrets and heartache.

***

"Do you think one year will go by where we don't have to research deaths or murders?" Ash asked, sitting on my bed with her laptop once again.

I shrugged. "I have a feeling not looking would begin to feel like the weird part."

She gave me a small smile. "I think I would miss it."

I called her after things hadn't gone well with Krista Simmon. If she was unwilling to talk to us, we

76

were going to get nowhere. Our conversation with her was so short I wasn't able to ask her about her brother-in-law being fired or whether or not she knew about Kadence's supposed boyfriend. It looked like it was back to googling with Ash.

I sat next to her after checking on Noah. Terry had just bought him a talking Elmo doll, and he couldn't get enough of it. As amazed as he was, he was still unsure of how he was moving on his own and sometimes started crying when he had enough of his red friend. Right now, they were playing on my childhood bedroom floor.

Six months ago, we had moved upstairs into my mother's room permanently. I was still not entirely at home here, but it was getting easier. My old bed was still downstairs and when my brain got too-loud, I slept down there. Maybe I just missed being close to my sisters.

"What exactly are we looking for?" she asked after pulling up Google.

I opened the notebook in front of me where I had taken notes with Lenore.

"We need to research deaths in the areas with similar age groups. We already know that Emily and Kadence's deaths were paved over. If there are similar deaths in the area that could mean a serial killer. Also, different keywords could bring up more information about our girls. Maybe someone out there wrote an editorial after it disappeared from the news."

Ash typed for a few moments then shook her head. "No additional murders come up. Look at this."

Spokane Tribune July 16th, 2013

Cynthia Morton has filed a civil suit against the Spokane Police Department and Simmon family after she believes they mishandled the investigation into her daughter's death. Kadence Morton was found dead on June 25th, 2013, in the woods behind the Simmon's family home. After a short investigation, the death of Kadence and the daughter of the Simmon family, the police ruled it an accident.

The civil case is set to go to court next week. The police department and the Simmon family have declined to comment on the situation.

"I just don't understand how it could have been an accident if the girls died on separate days. We live in a tight-knit community, how were their deaths hours apart and no one heard anything? What are the police hiding?" Cynthia Morton said at the press hearing.

I sat back. "Does it say what happened?"

Ash looked lost in thought. "What kind of freak accident would kill two little girls without anyone noticing?"

I shook my head. "Impossible, because it wasn't a freak accident. Cynthia thought Emily's family was responsible for sure. She had Kadence's friendship ring returned to her and Emily was buried with it. Maybe this is some kind of cover-up? No one thought Emily could possibly be a killer, so they didn't release the info. Kadence's mom refused to let it end there."

"Then how did Emily die? Someone else had to know."

Goosebumps crawled up my arms and a nauseating sense of déjà vu unfurled in my stomach. Emily was definitely sick and responsible for at least one death. That also meant that another killer was out there and seemed to be free.

"Okay, right here it says that the civil suit was dropped before it reached court."

"Why would they drop the case after all of that publicity?"

Ash shut her laptop. "Someone must have paid them off. She was going after the police department. That can't be good for public image."

I sighed. "Of course not. That's definitely more important than two little girls dying."

"What's next?" Ash asked.

"I already talked to Emily's family. She didn't mention anything about the civil suit and just was really nervous. Terry thinks that she might have sent her son away to protect him from her husband. He is my first pick for serial killer of the year."

"Next is Kadence's family?"

"I guess. This part is going to be the hardest part of all. Talking to the families is worse than the ghost stuff."

"Harder than moving the girls on?" Ash asked.

"I think so. The only way to move them on is by talking to the families still grieving their daughters' deaths. One raised a killer, and the other never got the justice they deserved."

Ash nodded. "Killers are usually close to their victims. Which means that if there is another killer out there, it could be one of their family members."

I took a deep breath. I knew that was true, all of our research supported that theory. Then I thought of Lucas and everything my family had been put through two years ago. Terry had been connected to Gina through her job. Macy and I were complete strangers to her. That didn't stop her crazy boyfriend Lucas, from kidnapping us and nearly killing us.

Emily's dad could be the killer. Or, it could be a complete stranger, just like Lucas. That didn't help us. The girls were outside. Someone had been stalking them. It was entirely possible that Emily had snapped and killed Kadence before her true predator was able to get close enough to hurt her. Ignoring signs and living in a bubble had almost ended my life once before. I wouldn't make that mistake again.

I gingerly rubbed my wrist where Lucas had buried a knife and Ash squeezed my knee. I smiled back at her and she nodded, knowing it was time to change the subject.

"How is Kadence doing?" Ash asked.

I thought back to the last week. Kadence walked around the house, unsure of herself and wasn't solid for the most part. She loved Noah and watching him play brought her a lot of joy. However, whenever I tried to talk to her about what happened her spirit started to fade in and out and the edges of her spirit were darkening.

"I think she has been in the in-between for too long. Her spirit is going dark because she is still very angry and scared."

"I can imagine."

"I'm going to talk to Terry about counseling her. I might be able to see her, but I have no idea how to reach her. She is a little girl and has already been through so much."

"Not only that, staying in the in-between too long increases her chances of experiencing the shadow figures and beginning to change herself," Ash looked equally scared of that possibility and proud of her knowledge on that subject.

"She has already been touched by so much darkness. I refuse to let it consume her."

Chapter 4

Terry September 2017

It had been a long time since I had really had "girlfriends." In high school, I tried to make friends and it was always hard. Girls were so weird about secrets. There were parts of my life and my family that I couldn't share with them. I think they could tell that I was keeping them at arm's length. Also, a lot of the time they only wanted to be friends with me so that they could get closer to CJ.

Without enough practice, I was terrible at trying to make adult friends. Over the last month, Lucy had been begging me to eat with her and the other receptionist at the center, May. Lucy and I were friends, but being introduced to new people was the worst. I could tell so much about them from our first hand shake and forgot how much I was actually told.

"This cleanse has been the worst. Did you guys have to bring the most delicious smelling lunches on the planet?" May asked, grimacing at her lemongrass and cayenne pepper water while looking longingly at my BLT.

I tried not to smile too widely at her, from patting her back earlier I had seen her devour a pan of brownies the night before. She would be very embarrassed to be outed. She had already been beating herself up about it all morning. Right now, she was probably planning on a similar episode with a sandwich that looked a lot like mine.

"Why the cleanse in the first place?" Lucy asked, digging into her orange chicken from Panda Express.

"I'm trying to get into a smaller size bikini. Brad bought me this adorable polka dot set and it's just a teeny bit too small for me. I want to wear it for him when we go to Lake Tahoe next month. So, detoxing it is."

I tried to eat nonchalantly. That was another thing she had passed onto me. Brad had bought the bikini as an "incentive" to help her get down to the weight that he thought she should be. It really hurt May's feeling. On the other hand, it had been forever since she had a boyfriend, let alone one for long enough to vacation with.

"Have you been to Lake Tahoe before?" I asked, instead.

"No. I hear it's beautiful."

I nodded. "It is. Just remember to gas up the night before when there's less chance of evaporation. Hummers are guzzlers, and it's a long way."

May stopped with the water bottle halfway to her mouth. "How did you know Brad drove a Hummer?"

I froze. I knew because when he bought the bikini, May watched him climb out of it. In her memory.

Lucy looked from me to her. "I told her. We were talking about what car she should get when she trades hers in and I told her not to go the Hummer route. You are always telling me how much money you have to put into it weekly. It's insane."

May slowly nodded, still looking at me. I'm sure she's heard the rumors about me, everyone has. She might be deciding whether or not these rumors are enough to keep us from having lunch again. No one likes feeling like they are out of the loop or not safe within their own thoughts.

"It is crazy. I would go with a smaller car for sure. Especially if you like to travel," May told me, relaxing only slightly.

When she went back to her water bottle, Lucy smiled at me. I smiled back, grateful for her save. It felt familiar, something CJ has done for me my entire life. This would take some getting used to and maybe I would never be able to be friends with people who didn't know the truth about me. With friends like Lucy, maybe I would get there.

***

CJ's mom Gem, had been like a second mother to me my entire life. Growing up with CJ, we had taken turns spending weeks at the other's house and cleaning their kitchen out of snacks. Gem was there for me when my parents divorced, bought me flowers for our ninth-grade graduation, and saved me during a very embarrassing Aunt Flo moment before an eleventh-grade presentation. Her opinion meant so much to me, which is why I was asking for her help finding a wedding venue.

It was also why her holding back hurt so much. After last year Gem had been the last to forgive me.

"What do you think about this?" I asked, gesturing to the stumps as seats in the botanical garden.

Gem slowly turned around. "I just don't see... CJ here."

I smiled. "He said to pick what I liked, and it would be what he liked."

Gem pinned me with her eyes. "I think his opinion matters, too."

I blushed, unnerved from the subtext in her words. I wished it was easy between us again.

"I think his opinion matters. He is very invested in the cake flavors and has set up at least four tastings at different bakeries. The venue was not something he cared about."

She sighed. "Okay. Outdoors it is?"

I nodded, wishing I had asked Claire instead. I wondered why I thought this would help us bridge the distance that had been created after my accident. Maybe involving Gem was the worst idea. I didn't want any more pieces of this wedding being tainted by last year and all of the pain that surrounded it.

"I imagine… flowers everywhere. Our guest carrying confetti and glitter to send us out and 80's music. I'm not planning on wearing shoes, and CJ wants to wear suspenders and a bow tie. Maybe a trellis with vines and huge lilies where he would wait."

For a moment, I am lost in thinking of him waiting for me at the end of that floral aisle, his smile and his feet already dirty from the path of soil. I catch Gem watching me and turn to look at the choices in arches.

"Ter," she says softly, touching my back.

"Yeah."

"I know that you love him."

I turned to look at her. "I do. I always have."

Gem nodded slowly. "I always believed that. And a million times I have imagined how your wedding would look. I imagined him proposing to you and becoming a grandmother to your children, because it's what he wanted more than anything. And then…"

I stared at my shoes. How many times did I have to apologize? I didn't like thinking about hurting him. It was much worse than Gem could ever really understand.

When Barbara took control of my mind, she forced visions of me physically hurting CJ into my brain. I watched her use my body to bash his head in with a skillet and slit his throat with a tape dispenser. I didn't only push him away just because I thought I was linked to a different love, I pushed him away because I wanted to keep him safe.

How could anyone but CJ really understand that? Gem had watched me grow up and still would have never understood my visions. I thought of how many times CJ asked me to use my gift on her to get information about his father. If she knew that I had done that without asking, I couldn't imagine the betrayal she would feel.

She loved me like a daughter and this was asking her to learn to love something that hurt her son this way. It would be CJ every single time, it had to be.

"Just... promise me that you will take care of his heart. Because he will not hold back. He will love you for the rest of his life. Be worthy of that. Take care of his heart, Ter."

I locked eyes with her, trying to feed to her everything that I could never put into words. How I felt the night I asked CJ to take me back at Sally's. The millions of milkshakes that went to waste while we kissed under the starlight. How it felt to share every single first with CJ and imagining all of the firsts still ahead of us. I would love him forever, forever wasn't even enough.

"I promise."

She smiled and squeezed my hand. "This garden is actually pretty perfect. I like that the flowers are already arranged. We just need to get some lilies up in here."

As she walked on and told me her ideas, I settled back into myself. Not settling back into the past because what had happened changed all of us irrevocably. Instead, I settled into the future that we would share as a new family.

***

Kelsi was ignoring me again, which I should have expected, regardless of how well our last conversation went. While I was venting about the situation to Ash and Claire, Ash suggested looking her up on social media. It might feel invasive but would give me an insight into her social status more than anything else would. It was easy to find Kelsi and her profile ended up being semi-private.

I scrolled through her page, already sick with what I was seeing. At least ten posts a day were from her classmates, calling her a slut or homewrecker. Some urged her to kill herself. Some said that she was already dead to them. How had it gotten this bad so quickly? She was a new student last year. Around the time of the party, there were a bunch of links to a video that had since been deleted.

That timeline was important. I knew it was something I couldn't push her on if I ever really wanted to learn the truth and help her.

I sat back in my chair, printing off the pages to put in her file to discuss with her mom. I had to tread carefully. Maybe this bothered me so much because Kelsi reminded me a little bit of my baby sister. Macy was so full of light and fun. It was easy to think that was the only version of her. She often pretended like she was tougher than she really was.

Macy had a wonderful time in high school for the most part. She had great friends, excelled on the dance and cheer team, and did well enough in class to pass without too many late nights. When she came out as a lesbian during her junior year, things began to change. Her relationship with her girlfriend Britney made her senior year pretty turbulent. She loved her, that much was clear. Being out came with a price and dealing with the world's opinions on that had almost broken her.

When Britney got into an out of state school, and Macy didn't, she had fallen apart. They tried to stay together even though it was already slipping away. Macy didn't do well on her own. She stayed out late every night, failed her classes, and ended up sleeping around and losing Britney altogether.

I remember trying to talk to her about it. She was embarrassed and didn't want to admit to how bad it had gotten. I would watch her face when I tried to confront her, and it was almost like I could see a door slamming in my face. And now she was gone altogether.

I didn't want to fail Kelsi the way that I had failed Macy.

***

"Do you hear that? It's like a sucking noise," Gem said, peering into her drain while CJ worked on the pipe from under the sink.

"It's a clog, mom. You can't shove leftover food down the drain. You don't have a garbage disposal. That sucking sound is last night's spaghetti trying to hang onto the pipe instead of letting the water go down."

Being back in Gem's house and the weirdness between us being gone was like coming home. I had grown up here and feeling like I was a stranger had been torture. I knew where she kept the good snacks, where the towels were, even where she kept the vacuum cleaners she only used when she had out of town guests. It was nice for this to be normal again.

"Well maybe you need to install a garbage disposal," Gem said.

She wrinkled her nose at me and stuck her tongue out at CJ. I laughed and patted his leg, a vision crawling up my arm as I sat next to him on his mother's kitchen floor.

"I just don't see how this helps you," Gem was saying, clearing plates from the kitchen table.

CJ shrugged, the closed-off look on his face didn't look like it belonged.

"What else am I supposed to do? Terry wasn't kidding. This isn't what she wants. I have to move on. And she's nice."

Gem had run into CJ while on a date. She thought it was too soon for him to be dating and thought that if he waited, I would come around. CJ didn't agree with her. He was broken and thought that dating would help him move on. If I was able to sleep around with random strangers, why shouldn't he?

I quickly moved my hand as I tried not to throw up. These moments of anger always surprised me and broke my heart. I understood. I couldn't even imagine having to hear him tell me that he was in love with someone else and that our past didn't matter. Yet, having to relive it over and over made me feel like I was never going to move on.

As we finished up, CJ suggested we get some dinner. He looked at me worriedly and grabbed my hand. I froze and tried to avoid a vision. I let out a deep exhale when all I felt was his concern.

"What's wrong?" he asked, kissing the back of my hand.

I sighed. "I got a vision from you in the kitchen."

He hesitated before continuing walking. "Was it bad?"

I shrugged and he stopped to pull me into his arms, not even having to ask from when the vision was.

"That is not us anymore, Ter. It wasn't you. It doesn't matter. We are back together and building a future together. Soon all of those memories will be so far away that it will be crowded out by all of the new happy memories we are creating. I promise."

I nodded and couldn't stop myself from thinking that I wished I didn't have to see it at all. It didn't feel like penance, it was more like torture.

"Do you ever wish I couldn't see it? That I didn't have visions?"

CJ pulled back to look at me.

"Sometimes. This gift is what connected you to Barbara and almost broke us."

I nodded, tears coming to my eyes.

"Mostly, no, I don't wish it away. If you didn't have this gift, you wouldn't be the Terry that I fell in love with. I love you and want all of you, visions and all."

I smiled, feeling the truth of his words.

"Kiss me," I said, needing his escape and his hope.

He grinned and leaned down, reminding me that this moment was more important than the ones from last year.

Claire September 2017

"How many tests did you buy when you thought you were pregnant?" Ash asked, her face pale as she perched on the edge of our bathtub.

I rubbed my hands together. "Seven. I took the first at a gas station and the rest at home."

"Why did you do it alone? I can't imagine having to look alone," Ash said, looking over at the test on the counter.

I followed her eyes, feeling like I really wasn't in my own body. I wondered if this was ever truly a happy moment for people. Ash had missed her period and happened to be on a break with Ben. It was much more likely that she would end up a single mom than for Ben to suddenly grow up. I had been afraid of ruining my relationship with Holden and being a bad mom because I was still grieving my own. Those moments flew through my mind. It wasn't the hardest memory to swallow.

It was Macy's positive pregnancy test. I remembered coming into the bathroom to brush my teeth and seeing her shove the package in the trash. A package too familiar to ignore.

"What is this?" I asked, pulling it out of her hand. When I held up the box, the test fell out. The positive sign shone up at us, too perfect to be unclear.

"Macy?" I asked again, looking up into her stunned face.

It was almost as if it wasn't hers, and she was seeing it for the first time as well.

"Are you pregnant?" I asked, the words catching in my throat.

"It's positive," she finally said, not answering my question.

A million emotions surged through my body. Mostly, just blind rage. Because she had been drinking every single day. Because there was a chance that she didn't know who the dad was. Because she was supposed to love Britney.

"How could you do this to yourself?" I asked her.

Torment played over her features. I couldn't take it back, I wasn't sure I even wanted to. I saw her future laying broken on the floor along with that test.

A timer buzzed and pulled me from the past.

"It's time," I said, starting to stand.

Ash grabbed my arm. "Wait. I'm not ready."

I sat back down and took her hands. I would not be as happy for Ash as I would be if she was really in love and wouldn't be doing it alone. I would not be that person again, reacting before I thought about the person in front of me. I would not make Ash feel like she was alone in this.

"If you are pregnant, it doesn't matter if you're ready. What do you want to do? Will you tell Ben?" I asked.

She nodded. "I would have to. I could never get an abortion. I know myself. I would raise this baby. They would be mine."

I squeezed her hand and pulled the test off the counter. It was negative. Ash collapsed into my arms.

"Oh, thank God. Thank you, God."

She cried anyway and I understood. No one wants their life to change that way. Planning a pregnancy isn't the same thing as life throwing you a curveball and finding yourself unworthy. When life does change despite what you want, you start to see hope in that new chapter. You start to see hope in who you could be as a mom. I should have seen hope in it for Macy.

***

Missy had been experimenting with scrying using objects and thought that she might get an insight from the ring that Emily had given to Kadence. It was weird burying it in front of Kadence's gravestone in the first place. Something about having to remove something and take it back was even more strange.

I knelt in front of her gravestone, wiping the dirt from her name and shining it the best I could. I still saw a small mound from the ring and gently uncovered it, but when I tried to take the ring it was frozen to the broken soil. I dug underneath it and saw that it was somehow bonded with the plot.

I clapped my hands over my ears as a thousand screams filled my head. Shadow figures crept near and I saw a small figure being pulled across the graveyard to where I was kneeling. It was Kadence, screaming and fighting her way over to me. She was on her belly, and her nails bent as she dug them into the dirt. Her eyes were wide with terror.

"What's happening?" I yelled, trying to grab onto her hands.

She shook her head. "I don't know. I was swinging in the backyard and got ripped backward. Back here."

I looked at the ring again and jumped when I saw Emily leaning over the gravestone with her elbows resting on top.

"I can't believe it worked."

"What did you do?" I asked, attempting to pull Kadence into my arms.

Kadence was staring at Emily with complete terror and seeing her have that effect on such a little girl hurt my heart. Seeing another child be capable of that made me sick.

"Shadow figures have a few tricks, and they loved showing them to me. One is bonding spirits to objects to trap them."

Her voice sounded aged beyond her years, and I shivered as I thought of an adult shadow figure feeding her this information.

Emily gestured to the ring that I had brought back to the gravestone. To where I had trapped Kadence, where Emily could torture her whenever she wanted to.

"Do you remember our sleepovers? Whispering to each other all night and making bracelets for each other?" Emily asked Kadence.

Kadence nodded, crying.

"And then you ruined everything. This is what you deserve."

I held onto Kadence's hand; she was almost solid in her fear. She thought that this was going to be her forever. Her best friend had murdered her and now would have the power to tear her spirit apart.

"Bonding a spirit?" I whispered to myself.

Emily's eyes flashed as she looked over to me.

"Shut up. This is between Kadence and me."

I ignored Emily and tried not to see the shadow figures dancing around us. I flattened Kadence's hand against my palm, my wedding ring shining up at me.

"I bind you to me, Kadence. I bind you, to keep you from harm. I unbind you from Emily, this friendship ring is no longer yours. It has no power over you."

My wedding ring began to hum and Kadence screamed. She held onto my hand as the band burned white. Emily vibrated with anger, grabbing the now worthless friendship ring and throwing it at me. Her screams were so loud that they barely registered in my ears and instead tore through my mind.

"Let's go," I whispered to Kadence, pulling her back to my car, running and hoping the shadow figures were distracted by Emily's fit.

"You can't hide from me!" Emily yelled, leaves
and dirt swirling around her. She would have been
beautiful if it wasn't for the way she was cutting her
palms bloody in her fists.

When I ushered Kadence in and reworked the spell
on the house, Terry pulled up in her car. Her eyes
were concerned, and she hurried over to me.

"Did it fail somehow?" she asked, sitting her
groceries down to help me.

"No, don't," I said, trying to explain that I was
chanting a protection and not a warding.

Terry was already unsure about sharing our house
with another ghost. I was pretty terrified to admit that
I was currently running from shadow figures because
I had bound my wedding ring to the same ghost. I had
to beg her to accept Kadence in the first place. The
only way to make sure that she was safe in the house
was to leave the warding down so that she wasn't
locked out. A protection spell was the only thing I
could think of at the moment.

"So, you bonded your soul to her?!" Terry asked,
looking behind her into the house where Ash was
watching over Noah.

"What other choice did I have?" I asked, wringing
my hands.

"Claire, you bonded her spirit to yours. How could
you? After everything that happened to me last year."

Seeing the pain on Terry's face was almost too
much, but this was different. Terry hadn't given
Barbara permission to come into her life, Barbara had
stolen Terry piece by piece.

"She's a child, Terry. This is my gift. I am the only
one who can see her, who can help her. Was I
supposed to leave her there to be tortured? Emily is
dark, she is planning on making Kadence just as dark

94

as her. Do we really need more shadow figures after us?"

"Leaving the warding down to protect her leaves Noah open to danger. It puts this gift above him."

She froze as she realized what she said. I sat on the front steps crying. She sat next to me and wrapped her arm around my shoulder.

"I didn't mean that. I'm sorry. I just have no idea how to do this and how to protect him."

"Do you think this is what I want? To worry about ghosts and murder investigations instead of which mommy and me class we are going to this week? All I want is for Noah to have a wonderful childhood free from confusion and hurt. You know that isn't the way the world works. It isn't the journey that God has us walking, this is his legacy as well."

"I know," Terry said softly, kissing my temple.

"I am not a bad mom for trying to prepare him. I refuse to hide from who we are anymore. He will be proud of me," I said, trying to convince myself as well as her.

"He will. You are a great mom. We just have to communicate about this stuff so I can help you. If we need to be chanting more often or sageing the house, I need to know. You are not in this alone."

I nodded. "I know. I just didn't want you to be disappointed in me anymore."

Terry shook her head. "It's hard to be disappointed when I am so in awe of how strong you are."

She folded me in her arms, taking care of me like she always did. It almost made me feel as strong as she said I was.

***

I was always able to feel him before I saw him, which didn't help when being around him was the farthest thing from easy these days.

"The warding is down?" Holden asked, standing in the doorway of what used to be our bedroom.

"Did Terry tell you?" I asked.

He shrugged. "Is everything okay?"

I nodded. "It will be."

I stood and leaned in the doorway with him, watching his face.

"Why are you here?" I asked him, not wanting to fight and for him to leave.

When he doesn't answer, I follow his eyes over to where Noah was asleep in his crib. Through the grates, I see his little rosebud mouth blowing imaginary bubbles.

"You can't be here when he wakes up. It's too confusing for him," I whispered.

I knew that I begged him to come back. I knew that I blamed his absence on him and him only. As much as I didn't want to admit it, I was beginning to see what Terry was talking about. Noah deserved all or nothing. I had to uphold that for him.

Holden looked down. "You know that I don't want it to be like this."

I shrugged, utterly exhausted with this back and forth. It didn't seem to matter what I wanted.

"I know. I also know that it's not okay for you to be here just when you feel like it. You are either here with me or you're not. It's not fair to him."

"Or us," Holden said softly.

I shook my head. "Nope."

"If you need me, will you call?" he asked, looking pained.

There was so much between us now. Good things. Pots and pans, senior rings, pancakes from Denny's and singing to each other in the dark. Thinking of holding his hand in the car or watching him make us dinner hurt so much I felt like it could physically kill me if I dwelled on it. Now, there was also so much else between us now that created a dark chasm that I refused to look at.

Secrets, betrayal, and abandonment. It was hard to think that this was the same guy that promised me that there was no version of me that he didn't want. It turns out there was a different version of him.

"Okay," I said, not sure if I meant it anymore.

I wanted to trust him and it didn't matter. I had to put Noah first.

***

Being able to teach Terry to meditate felt like hitting a psychic milestone. There was a time when I was so bad at it that I wondered if I was ever going to be able to control my gift. When Barbara had been posing as my spirit guide, she used these lessons to weaken me so that she was able to use my sister as her vessel. Being able to pass this new strength onto my sister made me feel like there was more to these gifts than we could ever discover.

Terry had been having trouble closing off her visions since waking up from her coma. If she was able to filter them, she would be able to focus on the ones that were important. Meditation would help her get back in control.

"Now, begin to come back," I said quietly, Lenore nodding at me proudly.

Terry let out a big breath and opened her eyes, grinning.

"That was great," I said.

Terry nodded. "I really hope it helps. Being this open is really hard at work. I can hear the visions from the waiting room and experience them all at once."

I grimace, with the kind of people she helps that must be extremely painful.

"I think it will. While we are on the subject of your job, I need to ask you for a favor."

She raised an eyebrow, curious.

"Kadence is taking this whole situation really badly, obviously. She is terrified and it is creating a lot of anger. Her spirit is beginning to darken, which is dangerous for everyone."

Terry nodded. "Like Len?"

I thought of him turning into a shadow figure and using his abilities to pin me down while trying to assault me. He thought that we would be able to have some kind of relationship and refused to take no for an answer. I tried to think about it as little as possible; it was still something I was working through.

Yesterday I was cooking dinner, and Kadence was practicing manipulating objects; this time her goal was to grab a spatula off the table. When she couldn't master it, she screamed, and the utensils fell everywhere, hitting me in the back. Her aura was tinged with an angry navy blue, and Lenore had to help me calm her down.

"Exactly. I was hoping you could counsel her. Talking to someone will not only help her let go of what happened so that she can move on when it's time, it also might give us some insight into what happened that night. Right now, she isn't open to discussing it."

Terry looked at me thoughtfully, I could tell that she was touched that I asked her to help at all. Being able to work through our gifts together has been one of her biggest dreams for most of her life.

"Absolutely. I'll put together a file and start tomorrow if she agrees. Did you and Ash learn anything new?"

"Just the civil suit and that it was settled out of court. I did finally track down Kadence's parents address and think that another visit is in order. I think they will be a lot more open to discussing the case."

Terry agreed. "They were silenced once before. We might be the only people who are still willing to hear their story and get Kadence the justice that she deserves."

Chapter 5
Terry October 2017

"I feel like it should worry us that it's still so warm outside when it's supposed to be fall," CJ said, turning Noah around so that he was facing the picnic table at Sally's.

I smiled. "But then going for ice cream would make way less sense."

Noah leaned forward, clapping and cooing. He reached for the caramel toffee ice cream cone in front of him and smashed it into his face. I laughed and kissed the top of his head.

I have been lactose intolerant since I was in elementary school, which didn't keep ice cream from still being a solid food group for me. It was the first thing CJ ever bought me, it was what we bonded over, it was Noah's current favorite food. How could I deprive myself?

"How many do you want?" CJ asked me.

I raised an eyebrow. "I really should stick to one if I want to be able to function for the rest of the day."

He laughed. "No, children. How many kids do you want?"

I sighed, loving these conversations. It was different from when we were friends and he was just listening to my thoughts on a hypothetical situation. This was our future. This was him asking for my insight into the rest of our life together.

"At least two? I can really picture being a boy mom. I feel like being a mom to a daughter would be harder when I still miss my mom so much."

CJ leaned back, his eyes a little misty. "Our little girl, though. Can you imagine? Dark like Noah. Freckles like nobody's business."

I smiled at Noah, wiping his little cheek and my heart swelling. I couldn't wait to be a mom. Being his aunt and loving him had shown everyone in our family that life truly went on. He kept us going through all the parts that seemed so dark that we might die from the bitterness. He made us excited to wake up the next day. He was everything to me.

I wanted this for myself, a baby to love somehow even more than the little boy right in front of me.

It was also hard not to see how these changes and these miracles would change our life for the worst. Holden and Claire moving in with Noah made sense at the time. Claire was still working on her second book and royalty checks weren't exactly reliable. Holden had a good job but was buying the house his parents were living in. Being able to take care of Noah during his first days was a blessing in so many ways.

Yet, us continuing to live together after CJ and I were married didn't quite make sense. Our home wasn't big enough for two full families. The part of our life where we had to say goodbye to each other to exist on our own was coming up.

I was ready to walk around without pants on and to be able to make out with CJ on the kitchen floor of our future home. I wanted to be able to make our own traditions without asking someone else's opinion. Picking out a new home that was just ours and was completely fresh for making our new lives. I was ready to be an adult in ways that had terrified me when I was in my 20's and newly graduated from college.

I was excited and terrified all at the same time. I wasn't sure I was ready to say goodbye to my sister, even to move down the street. I wasn't sure if I was ready to say goodbye to Noah and only see him on the weekend. I wasn't sure if I was ready to say goodbye to the walls that had tracked my height and seen every single one of my Christmases. I wasn't sure they were ready either.

***

"This isn't quite an engagement gift. I was waiting for something big to happen in your life to give this to you," Missy said, wringing her hands together in a very uncharacteristic way.

I was suspicious when she called me and wanted to go to lunch instead of coming over or inviting me over to her house. Missy had always been like family and going out to lunch was very formal. I don't think we had ever bothered with it before, instead choosing one of our kitchens and cooking together. I assumed whatever she wanted to talk to me about wasn't supposed to include Claire.

"What is it?" I asked nervously.

When she pulled the journal out of her purse, I recognized it before she told me who it belonged to.

"I took this when Marlo died. She started it after divorcing your father and once told me it was where she wrote what she could never tell you girls out loud. I didn't think you were ready for it while you were still healing and grieving."

"I'm still grieving," I told her before I could stop myself.

For some reason, I was afraid of what her journal could hold.

What couldn't she say to me in person? Was it regret about becoming a mother? Was it regret about her divorce with my father? We were more than just mother and daughter; we were best friends. There wasn't much that was off-limits between us. I couldn't help feeling a little betrayed by her secrets.

Missy gave me a sad half-smile. "No, you're not still grieving. And that's okay. Missing her is different from drowning in pain."

I patted her hand, knowing she was speaking from experience.

"Why did you want to wait until something big happened in my life?" I asked her.

She sat up straighter as if she wasn't sure I would agree with her.

"Before you and CJ became engaged, what your mom wrote might have scared you from it altogether. She believed that her gift came with a cost. Did she ever talk to you about that?"

I nodded slowly, remembering a conversation I had with Claire while astral projecting from my coma.

"My mom believed that having a psychic gift to come with some kind of loss as a way of balancing the universe. She thought that her 'sacrifice' for her gift was losing my dad."

Missy patted the book. "Honestly. I don't know if that's true. I think your dad might be one of those people who needed to grow up in more ways than one before he could truly love someone enough to accept them one hundred percent the way that they are. I am so happy that he is finally finding his way. The idea that Marlo loved him in a way he was incapable of returning at the time wouldn't really make her feel better, would it?"

I looked at her hand over the journal. "No, that wouldn't help. It might be easier to blame it on some kind of supernatural balancing system."

"Exactly. So, please read her words with that in mind. There might be something out there that decides these things, who gets to be happy and who has to carry burdens in order to keep their gift strong.

I don't know everything. And neither did she. Don't believe her words as the gospel just because you love her and miss her. Read them because you love her and it's honoring her, but don't walk her life journey just for the sake of remembrance."

I hugged her and we said goodbye. I didn't wait to get home before cracking the journal open, finding a place in the middle.

What if I had given it up? This gift has caused so much suffering. Why is it fair that I have to be the one to hold their hands as they die? Why would I be given a gift like this in the first place? A gift that told me when someone was going to die, and I am not supposed to change it? Why give me the future if it's only the parts leading to an ending?

Is there a way to give them up? I think there is. I don't think they can be extinguished altogether. Even souls are energy and have to move on from their shell when their heart stops beating. I think there's a way to transfer it to a different person.

If I hadn't had so much pride and had been able to do that, would Jess have loved me back enough to make this marriage work? Would our girls have had a better childhood if they didn't have to worry about being different? Would my relationship with Claire be different...

I shut the journal carefully, wiping the tears from my face. It made sense that mom had her doubts. She was human, after all. Still, something about her seeing her doubt like this, her anguish, made it feel like everything I believed was true was built on a house of cards.

I wanted CJ more than anything in the world. I wanted my gift to be able to make a difference in the world and be worth all of the trouble that it brought.

Would I be allowed to keep both? Did I really want both anymore?

***

Kelsi had been amped up since she walked through the door. Every comment I made was met with sarcasm and I couldn't help feeling like I had pissed her off somehow.

"Okay," I said, shutting my folder. "What's wrong with you today?"

She scoffed before meeting my eyes and finding them serious.

"I know your secret. My mom kept hinting that you were a 'special counselor'."

I raised my eyebrow at Kelsi. "Special how? My credentials are up on the wall behind me."

Kelsi snorted again. "I googled you. One of your patients is on death row?"

I nodded woodenly. I never knew what my future patients would think of my history with Gina. Would they feel like they couldn't trust me because I testified against her? Would they think I would turn them in if they also fantasized about killing the man that tortured them? Would they not take me seriously?

"How does that make me special?"

She leaned in. "Its more than just the news story. There's a Reddit board of abuse survivors. Women who have come to you and seen what you can really do. Gina didn't confess to you, did she? You were able to see it without her telling you. One girl claimed that you knew details about her abuse that she had never told anyone."

I broke out in a sweat as I processed that. I wondered if the board was a support board where my patients came together to see how my gift could help or if they thought I was a monster as well.

105

"Does it matter?" I asked in a small voice, completely caught off guard.

Kelsi leaned back, seeming surprised that I didn't try to deny it.

"Can you always do it?"

I shook my head. "No, and I don't go looking for it. It usually comes to me on its own. It does help the people that I work with. If they are unable to admit what happened, I can't truly help them heal."

"How does it work?" she asked.

Kelsi looked at her hands, unsure if she was asking because she believed me or wanted to know how deep my crazy went.

"I don't force the… visions. I just get them sometimes if I touch someone. It's always a memory from their past. And I won't touch you if you don't want me to. I won't look into you like that if I can help it."

"You told on her?" Kelsi asked, tears filling her eyes.

Realizing she was talking about Gina, I leaned closer to her.

"Gina was not like my other patients. Yes, she was beaten by her boyfriend, and for a long time, I thought she was the victim. Then, she completely snapped and used my family and me as an alibi. She killed her elderly mother, who was in a nursing home so that she didn't have to pay for her care anymore. After that, she killed her boyfriend. He had broken into her home and planned on killing her. She had just committed her own murder and was able to kill him first. It doesn't make either death okay. I told because Gina wouldn't have stopped killing people. She was too far gone."

Kelsi processed that and slowly nodded. "What if you see darkness in someone new? A new patient?

Can you tell if there's intent behind it or if they are just broken and sad?"

"Of course. Being upset and wanting to hurt whoever hurt you is completely natural. The difference is deciding to take your pain out on someone who can't fight back."

Catherine fighting for her life ran through my mind, and I had to swallow back tears.

"What do you see inside of me?" Kelsi asked.

I held her hand. "Are you afraid of me finding whatever darkness you are talking about?"

Kelsi began crying lightly. "I'm just so angry all the time."

I took a deep breath, trying to prepare myself for whatever came from her. There were no visions from Kelsi right now, only a bright light that was dirty from having to crawl back to herself.

"There is no darkness, Kelsi. Whatever happened to you wasn't fair. It didn't change who you are on the inside. All I feel and see is strength and light."

Kelsi leaned into me, letting me wrap my arms around her. Kelsi knew, the big black secret I had been trying to run from. I was so terrified of this moment, a patient finding out and being afraid of me. Kelsi challenged me, but Kelsi never hesitated.

***

"And this is Ariel. Do you see her red hair?" I whispered to Noah as he snuggled into my belly.

CJ was passed out next to us as I continued Noah's Disney education.

"Wed," Noah whispered back, loving the quiet game.

"Red, yes. Just like Aunt Terry. She was my favorite princess when I was little like Noah."

"Aunnie," Noah said, nodding and turning back to the screen.

CJ thought that Noah was too young to remember any of these movies. I still found it important to my duty as his aunt. When I was growing up, I remembered there being two kinds of kids. One group grew up with parents that wanted to treat them like little adults so that their own life didn't change. They watched movies with ratings that should have clued them into a problem, played by themselves, and their ability to be creative deserted them so early on.

Then there were Disney kids. When my parents divorced, I made it my mission to make sure that my sisters were able to stay kids. It was way too easy to decide that you were old enough not to need that kind of comfort and that was bullshit. We watched Disney every afternoon, played pirates out in our playhouse, and it took us years to finally put our Barbies away. It didn't feel like avoiding reality or being immature. It was survival, keeping ourselves cocooned in our little world as long as possible because anything was possible in that world.

I wanted that for Noah so badly. I wanted to hear the stories he made up while walking to school. I wanted to make him a space helmet and go to Mars with him in the backyard. I wanted him to savor his childhood because it was a time in everyone's life that they looked back on for a good reason.

Life was hard enough; everyone deserved a little pixie dust.

"Explain how this works one last time?" I asked Lenore, holding up a bundle of sage and waving it around the perimeter of the house.

"Well, officially asking Kadence to stay here until you can move her on means that ghosts have to be allowed in as well. We can do everything possible to make sure the ghosts welcome here are not connected to shadow figures in any way. We ask that no ghosts that have ill will towards your family be allowed near your home. It does need some maintenance though. The protection spell will need to be strengthened at least weekly," Lenore said, looking at Missy for confirmation.

Missy agreed. "You are taking a risk, for sure. But I agree with you. It needs to be done."

I took a deep breath, thankful for her support.

"Terry was so upset. She thinks it's still possible to hide Noah from all of this."

Missy gave me a small smile. "Terry grew up loving her gift. After everything, she has to find her own way back to peace with it."

"I understand that. This isn't just about us. I refuse to hide from my family anymore. Noah has to grow up with this like it's normal because that's the only way to make sure he knows how to protect himself. What if he met a ghost without knowing what it was and accidentally allowed more shadows into the house? I might not be able to protect him from that."

Lenore nodded. "You're right. He needs to be taught."

"It's his legacy too," I told them.

"No males have ever been given a gift before, right?" Missy asked.

Lenore shook her head. "Not in this family. It must be something in Carla's genes. That doesn't mean it's not possible. Other males have gifts, it just depends on the bloodline."

"I don't know if I even want that," I laughed.

I tried to imagine what kind of gift would be given to my beautiful Noah. Ours all seemed tied into our personality and all Noah was interested in these days was chewing on his toys and stealing French fries off my plate.

"You might not have a choice, sweetheart," Lenore said softly.

I agreed with her, hoping I got some kind of cosmic warning if that was the case. If a male had never had a gift in our family before, it might be completely different from ours. Parenting was hard enough without worrying about a sudden psychic gift instead of puberty.

**

Terry kept warning me that I had to be wary of Kadence and I tried. Kadence made it so hard. She was a beautiful little girl and her smile was contagious. Noah loved watching her dance around the room and making up songs. It wasn't hard to see how much he was going to miss her entertainment when she had moved on.

"Do you want more babies?" Kadence asked me, lying next to Noah.

He had fallen asleep on my bed, and she curled around him.

I turned from where I was working on my computer. I thought back to taking that pregnancy test in a gas station, how scared I was and how I had wished the situation away. I was convinced that I didn't know how to be a mom and would ruin his life. Now, I couldn't imagine my life without my son. It felt like every decision, ever good and bad thing, had led up to him belonging to me.

"I don't know. Right now, I am just loving him and learning how to be his mom."

She looked at him sadly. "My mommy was pregnant. We were waiting to find out if it was a baby sister or a baby brother."

I sat on the other side of Noah. "What were you hoping for?"

Kadence gave me a silly smile. "A boy. I wanted to play with him and not have to share my dolls."

I laughed a little. "I had a hard time sharing with my sisters too."

Kadence's eyes began filling with tears. "Mommy probably had her baby. And now I'm not there. She probably loves the baby more than me."

I took her hand, shaking my head. "Of course not, Kadence. Your mommy loves you and always will. Having a new baby doesn't replace the first one you held in your heart."

"My mommy used to say that someday she would be my baby's grandma. Isn't that crazy? Not now. Now I don't get to grow up. Or go to middle school with Clara from down the street who wears lipstick. I don't get to drive a car or get married."

"Maybe that's what heaven is, getting to do all of the things that were so magical to you while you were here. Doing all of the things you never got a chance to do."

Kadence's tears slowed a little as she processed that. "I thought I found some magic here."

"Really?"

She sat up and turned towards me, her eyes burning with intensity.

"Emily and I had a clubhouse with a little mailbox. I started finding letters in it. From an imaginary friend, I thought. I used to think about them being a little fairy or something. Isn't that magical?"

I nodded. "That is. Did you find out who was leaving the letters?"

The light in Kadence's eyes burned out. "Yes. And it wasn't as magical as I thought. I found out that magic doesn't really exist at all."

I bit my lip. Kadence had been tiptoeing around the fact that she had been receiving attention from someone that wasn't appropriate. As much as I wanted nothing to do with something like that while I was still healing from my own experience, I thought that maybe I would be the only one who could truly understand what she was going through.

That didn't mean that having the conversation would be easy for either of us. Being confronted with the truth of what happened to her could be the only thing that drove her way altogether.

"Kadence, when I was little, I thought I found magic, too," I started, feeling sick and nervous.

"Really?" she wiped her face so that she could see me better.

"I didn't have a lot of friends, and it made me really lonely. One day I met a boy at the lake. I was the only one who could see him, which made him special."

"Wow," she said, her tears slowing.

"Wow is right. I thought he was the best. And he was older. I felt really special when we were together, and he really listened to me and cared about what I had to say. Do you know what I mean? Sometimes grown-ups don't really listen to you."

She nodded earnestly. "Right. Someone listening is nice."

I took a deep breath. "Then… he wasn't very nice anymore. He wanted to play these new games that were a secret because he was doing things he shouldn't have."

Kadence stilled. I knew this was hard for her, I was sick myself. That kind of terror that was surging through my body was exactly why I had to keep going.

"I didn't like the new games we were playing and at the same time I didn't want to get him into trouble. I didn't want to get in trouble if I told. Do you know what that's like?"

She stared at me as if she was unsure of how to respond. I had wanted her to confide in me, but all I seemed to do was terrify her.

"Playing games like that are for dirty girls," she whispered.

My mouth dropped open. I expected denial and maybe anger. Her shutting down and being able to make me feel gross for even mentioning it blew me away. I blushed and shut my mouth.

"Did you tell your mom?" Kadence asked.

I shook my head. "No. And that meant the bad kid was still able to hurt other kids."

Kadence shrugged. "At least it wasn't happening to you anymore."

I had no idea what to say. The way her life had turned out wasn't okay. When she was alive, she was victimized and died horribly. Now, she was being stalked by the same child that killed her and blamed her for the abuse. Some stories ended without the happy ending we think we are promised.

She laid back down, turning from me and pretending she was asleep. Her shoulders still shook with the force of her tears. I laid down and wrapped an arm around her and Noah.

I wished I could tell her that I could take her ending away and that she got to grow up after all. It wasn't fair that she was trapped in everything she would never get to do and experience. I hoped heaven was close for her and made up for what she had lost.

Seeing her torment reminded me of my last conversation with Holden, and tears filled my eyes as well. Maybe this was our life on earth. A long list of all the memories we would never get to make.

I would never get to watch Noah snuggle with Macy, or to have her stealing bites of his six-month-old cake. I would never get to French braid her hair again after a school dance or catch her eating chili fries in the middle of the night after Zumba class.

And it wasn't just my sister. I would never get to grow old with the love of my life. I wasn't going to get to do any of the things I had always taken for granted. Picking out plates that we would use on Thanksgiving, planning our anniversary vacation, or just being able to kiss a bad night away in his arms. It was all gone, and I would never get it back.

I never wanted Noah to feel this way. To look back on his life and see regrets instead of hope. How could I protect him from that when I couldn't even protect myself?

***

"Someone was coming into Emily's yard to leave letters? That means someone had been watching the girls for a long time," Lenore said, giving me a look that could only be described as disdain.

"I know, it creeped me out too. However, that kind of narrows things down for us. It had to be someone who lived close or even lived in Emily's house. This supports it being her Dad."

Lenore shivered. "Ya know, when I was young, a case like this wouldn't have ended this way."

"What do you mean? Police were better?"

"No, dear. When I was a topless dancer, I remember one of the other girls finding out that her boyfriend was messing with her daughter. She was heartbroken, of course."

I nodded, still having to suppress a smile from having her mention her stripper days so casually.

"One afternoon, he disappeared."

My mouth dropped open. "She killed him?"

Lenore shook her head, smiling a little. "No. She did have two older brothers and the police had the good sense to leave it alone. Sometimes families take care of business themselves."

I thought of Emily's family. "I think that might have been the problem. Emily hurt Kadence and someone took care of it. This wasn't justice. This was murder."

***

Halloween was one those holidays that seemed so hard a couple years ago when Terry and I were far away from each other. It was her favorite holiday, yet, after she woke up from her coma everything changed. She was warring with another life trying to crowd out her own memories. We were walking on eggshells around each other and trying to forgive a million past mistakes. I made her popcorn balls using our mom's recipe, and we watched movies together. We reconnected and I wished it had lasted. Instead, we had to come up against each other over and over again before trusting each other again.

Last year was Noah's first Halloween. He was only five months old, and breastfeeding was still a challenge. Terry and CJ went out for their first Halloween as a couple and the only thing I have to remember that night is a Polaroid she left on the coffee table. Holden, Noah, and I were passed out on the couch. Noah was bundled up in his candy corn costume and I was wearing a pirate patch. We never made it trick or treating. The three of us woke up the next morning refreshed, it was the first time Noah slept through the night.

I was so afraid that so much heartbreak this summer would take Terry and me back to those dark days after the accident. That holidays would be strained with so much left unsaid between us. Having her back made celebrating a million times easier. We weren't tiptoeing around each other and trying to simply exist in the same space, we were both on a mission to make it the best day possible for Noah. Loving him made us love each other more.

In the afternoon, we made popcorn balls, watched Halloweentown with Noah, and I helped her do her makeup for her Ariel costume. She and CJ were going to a party with Lucy from the office, and she couldn't wait to get back into her epic costume tradition. I took a million photos of them before they left, partly because I wanted to be able to tease CJ about his open-chested shirt later on.

After saying goodbye to them, I slipped my wiggly one-year-old into his Scooby-Doo costume. Lyn had found it for him after making him try on fifteen other costumes. Whenever he saw it, he ran away as if he was sure I was going to force him into another fashion show.

"Let's go get some candy," I told him, strapping him into his stroller and straightening his dog hat.

He looked at me suspiciously before beginning to play with his orange pumpkin bucket.

The air was frigid and clean, my favorite kind of night. The leaves crunched under the stroller wheels and kids ran up and down the street. Nights like this made me feel grateful to live where I did. Spokane could be a scary place, especially downtown. I was grateful that we lived on the edge of the city in an older suburb. To me, Spokane had looked like this growing up. Families out with their kids and enjoying the natural beauty of our city. I took Noah to three houses before he started fading.

"Has he stolen anything out of that pumpkin head?" Holden asked, startling me.

I shook my head at him. "What are you doing here?"

He looked embarrassed. "I knew Terry had plans. I wondered if you wanted some company."

I looked down at Noah, who was beginning to fall asleep as we headed back to our house.

"Okay."

As we walked, I soaked up the feeling of having him next to me.

"What was your favorite costume growing up? Your mom made Noah try on almost every costume in Target."

Holden laughed. "She was upset that her hands are giving her so much trouble and that she wasn't able to sew it herself."

I smiled.

"My favorite costume was a Cowardly Lion one she made when I was in first grade. I got teased for it and it was okay. She was so proud of it. It really was great. It's in the attic somewhere still. What about you?"

My mom really tried on a sewing machine, but my favorite costumes were usually ones I picked when I was trying to be rebellious.

"I wore a huge egg shirt one year and Ash dressed as a devil. It cracked my mom up."

Holden grinned at that. As we walked in silence, we came to one last house. I picked up Noah and he gave Holden a huge gummy grin. Holden leaned

117

down and kissed him wordlessly, giving me another image to break my heart.

"Trick or treat," I said cheerfully to the preteen manning the bowl full of Reeses. Noah stuck his pudgy little hand in the bowl and came back with three. The preteen looked like he was going to argue and Noah pinned him with a huge grin. Instead of saying anything, the young man just smiled back.

When we turned the corner next to our house, Holden slipped his hand inside of mine.

"Thank you for letting me join you."

"Thank you for wanting to. I know it's not easy."

He looked down to where Noah had fallen asleep in his stroller with his little cheek pressed against his bucket. He snored into the opening, the space making it echo.

"I know you try to understand how hard it is," Holden said, before squeezing my hand one last time.

***

The idea of dredging this up for Kadence's family was much harder than talking to Emily's family. Terry assured me that we had no other choice and that she could do this. I was still sick to my stomach. Under the same guise, we had been welcomed into their home by Kadence's mom, Cynthia.

"It's been four years, why are they assigning us community outreach now?" she asked, handing us both cups of tea.

Kadence's father, Richmond, sat next to her on the couch. He squeezed her knee as if to calm her. She leaned into him and closed her eyes for a moment. I had expected Kadence to look like her mom and was surprised by her blonde hair and green eyes. After meeting Richmond, I was able to see where Kadence got her silky black hair and blue eyes. I thought of how hard it must be to look that much like a child you had lost and had to fight back oncoming tears.

"Well, families get a lot of support after the initial tragedy and then it tapers off. Our center just makes sure that your needs are still being met. Time passing doesn't mean that what happened is no longer important," Terry said, genuinely.

She might not be operating under any order, however, she really did care and want to help these families.

Cynthia nodded. "Thank you for that."

Terry took a deep breath. "I'm going to be honest with you. I don't want to bring up any unneeded stress for your family, I need to ask a few questions. There isn't a lot in your file. In order to help, I need more information."

Richmond looked at his wife with a confused expression. "What do you mean?"

"Well, I see that your daughter was murdered and that it was ruled an accident. You filed a civil suit against the Simmon family, and it was dropped."

"Yes," Cynthia said tightly, obviously still upset.

"I understand that the killer was never found. I need more information so I can try to help you," Terry said carefully, holding each of their eyes.

Cynthia's cheeks flushed then began to glow as understanding set in.

"What do you want to know," Richmond asked.

"What do you think happened? It seems like the investigation was never completed," I said, grabbing a pen from my purse and a notebook.

"That's right. That bastard Darryl's brother was on the force and made sure only minimal efforts were made. Basically, Kadence was found dead on the Simmon property, in the woods behind their backyard. Emily was found in the playhouse where the girls were supposed to be having a sleepover. Their times of death were two hours apart. That somehow didn't send any red flags up for them."

"What about the causes of death?" Terry asked.

Richmond nodded. "That was another thing we could never figure out. Kadence was bludgeoned to death with a heavy object, it was horrific. Emily's neck was simply broken. Why would she die second if she wasn't the person they were after? Kadence's death being so much worse makes me think that she was the only target and Emily just happened to be there."

It was clear that they had thought about this every day for the last four years. My stomach flip-flopped so much that I thought I was going to pass out. They knew that the Simmon family was connected. It was the only thing that made sense. Yet, they had no idea that Emily wasn't in the way, she was one of the killers. It wasn't the time to tell them but holding it back didn't seem okay either.

"Is there anything else you could tell us that might help our... program better serve you?" I said, trying to breathe through my nausea.

Cynthia shook her head. "That's all the police released to us. We were given Kadence's friendship ring. I gave it back to the Simmon family. We used to be friends, I actually met Krista in a mommy and me group. That's how our girls became friends. After the 'accident' I saw their true colors. I didn't want anything from them."

"Things started to get strained before that night," Richmond said, looking uncomfortable.

"Strained how?" I asked.

Cynthia shared a look with her husband. "Emily and Kadence spent a lot of time together. They took turns spending the night at the other's house. I cared about Emily like a daughter. Then, one-night Kadence called us to come get her in the middle of the night while she was at the Simmon. She was bawling and said that she and Emily had a fight."

"Did she say what about?" Terry asked.

Richmond shook his head. "No, just that she didn't want to be friends with her anymore. For the next couple of weeks, she was really jumpy and had accidents. She was quick to potty train, so we were really worried."

"We took her to a counselor, who said that she was experiencing normal adolescent stress. It just didn't make sense. Just as quickly as it began, she went back to being our happy girl. A few months went by, and Emily asked her over for a sleepover. Kadence wasn't sure, I encouraged her to go…" Cynthia made a choking noise and covered her mouth.

Richmond rubbed her back. "Kadence didn't have very many other friends. She was lonely. We just really hoped that they could make up. The same night we invited the Simmon over for a dinner party so that we could all try to reconnect."

I tried to hide my surprise and had to look down to conceal it. All of the parents were at a dinner party? If all of them were together, how could Emily's father be responsible? Why did Krista blame her husband? Terry's face was flushed as well, and I wrote down all of my questions to discuss it with her later. I tried to focus on the conversation happening around me as I processed the shock.

"After the accident, what was their response to you?" Terry asked, patting Cynthia's knee and giving her a break.

Cynthia shook her head and pulled herself together as best that she could.

"They lawyered up immediately and refused to talk to us. It was like we had never been friends."

"What about the civil suit?" Terry asked.

"We wanted to take them to court. At one of the first meetings with our lawyer the judge decided that we lacked evidence. So, we dropped it before we spent Jaime's college fund only to be left empty-handed," Richmond said.

"Jaime?" I asked softly.

Cynthia smiled. "Our daughter. I was pregnant when Kadence passed away."

She had a baby girl. I wondered if that would be harder for Kadence to hear.

"Do you have any idea who might be responsible? There was some talk about it being a predator in the area," Terry said, trying to look confident.

This was something we had gotten straight from the girls. Neither parent had mentioned the letters or attention so far, we weren't sure if they knew.

Cynthia drained of all color, and Richmond looked at her nervously.

"Where did you hear that?" Richmond asked.

Terry reached over to pat her hand. "It was a theory for the police. There was so little evidence that they assumed it was someone in the area. In these types of cases, the victims are sometimes targeted beforehand."

Cynthia shook her head, vehemently. It didn't seem like she disagreed with that theory. She was unable to consider that if it meant that a predator was still out there. Terry gave me a warning glance, telling me to leave it for now. If Cynthia never got an answer, talking about that idea might hurt more than help.

After a few more questions, it was time for Jaime's swim lesson. We said our goodbyes by the front door.

"Jaime!" Cynthia called upstairs, holding a swimsuit from the dryer.

As Jaime walked down the stairs, I felt like the carpet was suddenly moving underneath me. It was as if Kadence had been reincarnated and instead of napping with Noah at home, was in front of me, four years old again. Her black hair swung as she bounced down the stairs, and her blue eyes sparkled in the natural light coming from the open front door. When she looked at me and smiled was trapped by her grins charisma.

"She looks like Kadence," Richmond said, seeing my reaction and smiling a little bit.

"Yes, very much so," I said, trying to get ahold of myself.

We saw ourselves out and sat in Terry's car, organizing the notes we took.

"I think that went very well," Terry said.

"Do you really think we will be able to help them?" I asked, thinking of the hope she lent them.

"I really do. This whole thing is fishy. The police officer who might have covered it up isn't even on the force anymore. If we go to the cops with enough evidence, they might want to put it to rest to save face."

I nodded as the family came out and headed to their van. A plastic playhouse sat in the front yard and Jaime skipped over to it, checking the mailbox affixed to the front. Every hair on my body stood on end as I absorbed the disappointed look on her face when she found it empty.

Chapter 6

Terry November 2017

"Ahhh!" Noah screamed happily while splashing in the tub.

I laughed and tried to lean away from him while still washing the suds from his wispy blonde hair.

He smiled up at me as the water ran down his face. Noah was always impossibly adorable. However, something about his red cheeks in the tub and bedhead made him over the top cute. I kissed his little nose then turned to Claire.

She was smiling at him but her eyes looked far away. She was struggling to stay in the moment. As always, seeing her like this made me feel impossibly helpless. I knew that it would kill Mom to see how broken she had become. Being a single mom was hard. Claire was having a hard time shaking her pain in order to be present.

I thought she had been doing better, focusing on Kadence was a great distraction. I didn't expect that to change everything. We still had bad days, and they were always harder than the one before. Claire would be back to her old self for just long enough to knock me off my feet when she fell apart again. I tried not to be devastated each time but it was impossible.

"Hey, you okay?" I asked, wanting to probe and knowing she would shut down if she thought I was asking about more than just today.

Claire came back into herself. "Yeah, sorry. Just tired. I had an idea for my book last night and couldn't sleep until I wrote it down. When I got out of bed, all I did was stare at my laptop."

I patted her hand. "You'll get back into the swing of things."

She shrugged. "Yeah."

124

Aside from the sounds of Noah playing in the bubbles, the silence stretched between us. I continued looking at my sister as she zoned out again. The rings under her eyes were deep and she looked like she had aged five years. Her skin was sallow, and even her hair was becoming brittle. It was as if her body was becoming as fragile as her heart.

"Is it more than just last night? How well have you been sleeping overall?" I asked.

Claire sighed and sat next to the tub.

"Not great. I can fall asleep. Staying asleep is impossible. My brain is too busy."

I nodded. "Have you taken anything for it?"

She shook her head. "I had some sleeping pills from the car accident, they didn't last very long. It didn't have any refills."

"You should make a doctor's appointment. You can't keep just running on steam."

Claire nodded like she was listening but she was drifting away again.

"Maybe he can refer you to someone who could prescribe something more than just sleeping pills."

That got her attention, and she looked at me carefully.

"Like an antidepressant?"

She didn't sound upset, just thoughtful, so I agreed.

"If you need it. The last two years have been crazy. It makes sense that your brain would need a break. Asking for help isn't weakness. You have to take care of yourself. Some kind of counseling and prescription might help take some of it off your plate."

Claire was looking off into space for so long I thought she didn't hear me and was about to repeat myself until she told me she would think about it. That wasn't the answer I wanted, but it was a start.

"How is it going with Kelsi?" Claire asked, trying to turn towards me while still looking at her son.

I smiled. "There has been some progress. She is still having trouble trusting me. I think it's because she thinks I will ask more of her once I have her confidence. This isn't about me, though. What happened to her was awful, Kelsi has to want to speak up for herself. If she even decides to at all."

Claire shook her head. "Filming yourself beating someone. Was high school this cruel when we were kids?"

"I don't think so. People find more interesting ways to hurt each other every day."

And sometimes we do a good enough job of hurting ourselves.

***

At the beginning of each counseling session, I had Kelsi circle a face on a dry erase sheet that correlated with her mood that day. Today she picked three. Shy, passionate, and depressed. I had a feeling she was making fun of it, so I just put it in her file and asked her what she wanted to talk about.

"Have you ever noticed how in high school you don't really belong to yourself?" she started off, looking tired.

"How do you mean?" I asked.

"Who you are is completely dependent on which group you are trying to fit into. If you want to be in the play, you have to act like you are dramatic and into black and white movies. If you are into sports, you aren't allowed to be smart. I just don't understand how we know that people are made of more than one thing, but in high school, that reality is just suspended."

"Are you thinking of one person specifically?"

Kelsi gave me a cynical half-smile. "Every person at my school?"

"Okay, tell me about one situation."

"Okay. I am supposed to be this big slut now. You know Guy? The boy I told you about from the party?"

I gestured for her to go on.

"Well, I didn't know it because I was new, he had just broken up with his girlfriend that same day. And his girlfriend is this beautiful chick at school who is really popular. When I went into that bedroom with him, a bunch of rumors got started. Which I get because I had just met him. Which isn't fair because I had no idea that he had a kind of girlfriend. Everyone at that party did."

"People talk about it now?"

She laughed. "Oh, man. That was my first week and my first impression. Now I get propositioned all the time by gross guys who assume I just sleep around. And girls are mean to me because they think I am a boyfriend stealer. That's not me. Not at all. I was shy at my old school and have never even had a boyfriend. It doesn't matter. Because that's who I am now."

She had been trying to put on a brave face and it was starting to crack.

"I have no friends. It's like everyone is afraid of talking to me because this whole thing might rub off on them. They don't want to be a pariah too."

"What about Guy? Did anyone say anything to him?" I asked.

Kelsi shook her head, tears starting to escape her eyes.

"No, of course not. He started talking to me, knowing exactly what would happen. He and Shannon got back together. Shannon has been making

127

my life a living hell. Every day I am paying for that mistake, and they are just… untouchable."

As she lifted her arm to brush away her tears, I caught sight of a line of little cuts across her forearm. By habit, she pulled her sweater sleeve back down. Now wasn't the right time to bring it up. Because those lines didn't tell me anything she hadn't just told me in words. She was drowning at school and didn't belong to anyone because she had been labeled before she was given a chance.

She was feeling just as helpless as I was in this moment trying to lie to her and say it would be okay. I must have stared for a second too long because she looked down at her arms and blushed.

"I don't do it anymore. It made my whole crazy girl image worse," she told me.

"Did you think it would help?" I asked, honestly.

I could see the cuts and knew that she had tried to commit suicide. The idea of that didn't fit the Kelsi I had come to know. I wouldn't have believed it if her mom hadn't told me about her history.

Kelsi nodded. "It's supposed to, right? Feeling physical pain somehow made the pain inside of you smaller?"

"That's what I hear. It's also connected to eating disorders and control."

"That makes sense."

"Why did you stop? My mom told me that you tried to end your life, and that's why she looked me up in the first place."

Kelsi froze. I rarely pushed her, and this was way deeper than we had gone so far.

"I stopped because it didn't work. I didn't feel numb, I was disgusted. And that night… I just wanted to escape from it all."

She looked like she was made of stone, and her face didn't match the words coming out of her mouth. She seemed so removed from her actions.

"How did you feel when you woke up?" I asked her.

Kelsi smiled at me, picking up on my choice of words.

"Relieved."

I smiled back. Wanting to escape and wanting to die were worlds away from each other. Kelsi didn't want to run away anymore. I think she was getting ready to fight.

***

Once again, I was completely astounded by how many chili fries fit inside of CJ's body.

"Babe," I laughed as he dug into his fourth carton.

He wiggled his eyebrows at me. "This might look like stuffing my face. It's actually part of my master plan to seduce you."

I handed him a napkin. "Then I recommend wiping your chin. I'm not into sharing food."

He wiped his face and leaned in, kissing me on the cheek.

"So, we got some college brochures in the mail the other day addressed to you. Were you thinking of going back to school?" I asked him.

When I first went off to school, I wanted more than anything to share the experience with my best friend. He wasn't so sure. High school had been really hard for CJ. He just wanted a break and went to work and that year off turned into almost ten. Imagining CJ at college wasn't impossible, it was strange to have them arrive at our house and know nothing about it. I felt uncomfortable bringing them up, as if he was hiding them for some sinister reason.

CJ blushed. "I might be looking into it."

"Why didn't you tell me?" I asked, not used to having to ask.

"I didn't not tell you. I just wasn't sure. It's weird even thinking about being back at school and I didn't know if now was the right time."

"Because of the wedding?"

"Because we just found our way back to each other. Everything is changing. I didn't know if I should change one extra thing on purpose."

I studied him, finding his nervousness adorable and new. Was he worried about disappointing me? Of me worrying that our new life together wasn't enough?

"Talk to me," I said, holding his hand and kissing the back of it.

"I'm thinking of going into the social worker program through Spokane Community College. It's a two-year degree. And it won't make a lot of money. I would make more at the hardware store and not have crazy hours."

I smiled at him. He was worried about making enough money to support me. I wanted that to feel nice but all it did was break my heart a little bit.

"I think you would be an amazing social worker. And if it's your dream and makes you happy than I don't care what you would be making. I'm in, babe."

He grinned and kissed me.

"Social work?" I asked, going back to my lunch.

CJ shrugged. "Seeing everything you have gone through the last few years have been pretty incredible. I want to help with the other end of someone's journey, after they have had the courage to ask for help. You inspire me."

Tears unexpectedly came to my eyes. "I inspire you?"

"Why does that surprise you?" he asked, looking bewildered and kissing me again.

Moments like this made me so damn grateful for our life journey and where we were right now. I was CJ's first kiss; we went through the hardest parts of our childhood together. We stayed close as our lives went separate ways, and he had always been my home and safe haven. Getting to watch him grow up had been amazing. Getting to watch him become the man he was always meant to be gave me goosebumps.

***

I had imagined wedding dress shopping a million times since middle school. Today didn't look anything like any of my fantasies, but Lucy and Claire were trying their best to make it as memorable as possible.

"What about a mermaid?" Lucy asked, taking out a tapered style and holding it up to my body.

I laughed. "I am under five feet. I will not look like a mermaid. I will look like a stout goblin."

She laughed and put it back. "Okay. What about trying to match the dress to the venue?"

Claire's eyes sparkled, and I smiled. The wedding had been providing some much-needed distraction for her. On one of the nights she hadn't been able to sleep, she had put together a binder for me with inspiration and timelines for everything from the rehearsal to the sendoff.

"It's this gorgeous botanical garden. Wicker arches, weeping willows, flower gardens based on moods, natural lighting. I have a photo."

As Claire showed Lucy the photos she had taken at the venue, I wandered around the room, thinking of the flowers and being barefoot. Kissing CJ into

131

forever. It made me feel like I was made of champagne.

"Sticking with the venue feel is a good idea," Claire said, joining me.

After an hour of trying on dresses with completely the wrong cut, Claire found a green satin gown towards the cosplay area of the boutique. As soon as it flowed over the top of my arms and settled onto my waist, I knew it was perfect.

The top was a fitted corset in emerald green with a gold leaf pattern. It was off the shoulder and had flowy quarter sleeves. The skirt was a layered green satin that looked luscious and heavy. Instead, was light and assured me that I would be able to dance all night.

When I made my way out to where the mirrors were, Lacy and Claire both clapped their hands over their mouths.

"Is that bad?" I asked, laughing.

Claire was tearing up, making me dangerously close to crying.

"You look like a Viking princess," Lucy said, coming over to check the skirt out.

"How do you feel?" Claire asked, glowing.

I wiped my face. "Like I have been looking for this dress forever. I feel beautiful."

"It's perfect. CJ is going to love it."

I looked at myself in the mirror, feeling like a supermodel. I imagined a delicate baby's breath headband across my forehead and a green jewel in the middle. No veil and carrying a huge bouquet of flowers.

After getting measurements done, I was light with happiness. As we were leaving, we passed the bridesmaid dresses. Neither girl even looked at them and I appreciated that. Yet, I yearned to be able to spend another hour having them try on dresses and laughing about a bachelorette party.

We hadn't even decided on a wedding party yet because things were still so unsettled. I knew what colors I wanted. I had dreamed of their bouquets and shoes.

Claire in yellow with roses and flowers braided into her now shoulder-length hair. She would walk Noah down the aisle or pull him in a little wagon. Lucy in yellow with her bright blonde hair shining with shocks of ribbons throughout. Macy wearing red and being the only one with enough guts to pick a dress that had a thigh-high slit, getting multiple numbers at the reception.

Doing any of it without Macy made me feel like I was living in some kind of sick twilight zone. I could have everything I had ever wanted, it just couldn't include her. I didn't want to do this without her but couldn't stop living my life because she wasn't by my side anymore. There were going to be a lot of moments like this ahead of me, it didn't make this moment any easier to swallow.

Claire November 2017

Seeing Terry worry about me like this doesn't help me feel any better, so I am trying to save face for her. Last year she told me that cleaning her room after getting out of her coma helped her feel closer to who she was now. At first, that didn't make any sense to me. I knew that she was different and I wanted to blame it on Barbara's influence. Now I couldn't deny that it was true. Tragedy changed you, it molded you into whoever you needed to be to make it through the next chapter of your life.

Terry losing Mom shook her entire world. She didn't have her confidante anymore; she woke up seeing that I was taking care of Macy and second-guessed her role in our life. She was tempted with a past life that allowed her to escape. She had almost missed her chance at a life with CJ.

Even after Barbara was exorcised from our life, she was different. She was Terry. She was also a completely new person.

She was mushy and told CJ she loved him once an hour. It was almost as if she remembered being Barbara so much that she had to keep reminding herself that she was free and with the person she was always meant to be with. We didn't fight anymore. Losing Mom had taught both of us how important family was and how much we truly needed each other. Terry had finally finished growing up into who she was meant to be.

As I sat on my floor with two boxes and a trash bag, I wondered what in here could give me clues into who I was supposed to be now.

It was hard not to hate the things that reminded me of who I was when I was 16. The way our paths diverged had changed me as well. I didn't feel like I was special and persecuted against anymore. I was embarrassed by how far I had pushed myself away. I was disgusted by how much time I had wasted. At the time, nothing could have been worse than my family unit falling apart. Now, losing my sister and Holden seemed to be the tragedy that defined me.

What was worth keeping? What was important to this next chapter of my life? I was sleeping in the room that had been my mother's along with Noah, but my true room would always be the one that was downstairs with my sisters.

I ran my hand along my bookshelves, taking out a yearbook. This is what I would always keep to remind me of my best friend. In the front cover, she had dedicated an entire page to writing out the lyrics of a Lil Wayne song she loved. Ash was never worried about us drifting apart and told me that she didn't need to write me something epic that encapsulated our friendship because it was still something in progress, a story still being written. Our high school years wouldn't be as important as the years still ahead of us.

Next to the yearbooks sat a stack of recipes I had taken from the kitchen to scan onto my computer. Food has always been something that Terry and I bonded over. In elementary school, she would bring me a root beer when I was sad and make biscuits and gravy for my birthday mornings. Last year she reluctantly taught me to cook and I made our mom's popcorn balls for her to break through the walls she had been trying to build. After Noah was born, we spent a straight month going through moms cookbooks and making them into a scrapbook, remaking our favorite recipes together and cementing the new relationship we shared.

Under the recipes, I had saved one of the crystals from the night that we exorcised Barbara from the house. It was one of the most terrifying and healing nights of my life. Not only did Terry and Macy finally trust me, with their gifts of all things, my mom came back to us and we got to meet our grandma Carla's spirit. As our power surged through each of us, I experienced the extent of my mom's gift.

I never told my sisters this, but I saw into each of them. I felt them, their soul. I saw my mom's memories of us growing up and when she looked at me. How deep her love for us was curled around me like smoke. I never wanted to forget it. At that moment, she taught me so much about motherhood. We could drift apart from each other and some days we wouldn't like each other. At the same time, we would always love each other more than anything else in the entire world.

Next to my bookshelf I had a small dresser with a CD clock radio that I used all throughout high school. Sitting next to it was a stack of CDs. No one used CDs anymore. That didn't keep Holden from making me three mixes when we started dating. I put one in, letting the music wash over me. He told me that he made mixes about how he felt about me while he pined for me in school and this was the best way he could share it with me. It was coming full circle for him. He had a way of connecting songs that told a story, our story. I remembered listening to it and feeling like I was seeing him in a new way, falling for him all over again. We danced to metalcore until we simply fell into bed.

All of that was hard, impossible to let go of. However, the ribbons next to the CD's were the only thing in the room that tore me apart. When Macy was in elementary school, we were best friends. We took turns sleeping in each other's rooms, she followed me around at recess, and we made poor makeover choices on the weekend. When I turned nine, she had just spent all of her allowance on a new Barbie and felt terrible about not being able to buy me a gift. Outside she found a bright blue ribbon in our grass and thought it was a sign. She brought it inside and told me it was beautiful and reminded her of me. Every year she brought me another ribbon as a nod to that first gift.

When I moved out, our friendship slowly broke apart, and I had no idea how to bridge the distance. She began buying me gifts, and that somehow hurt more than anything. I thought she had not only forgotten that first ribbon but all of the other memories that were tied to it. When our mom died, we moved back in together. I tried like hell to make up for everything that had gone wrong. And Macy being Macy, she had forgiven me.

We found our way back to each other the way that only sisters can. We shared so many memories with each other and while we were jointly being allowed to remember them together, we let ourselves rewrite our future. We didn't have Barbies to bond over anymore, so we made a new path for ourselves. We found our way with crappy Lifetime movies, Taco Bell in the middle of the night, and sleeping together on nights when the nightmares became too much for one person alone.

For my first birthday after having Noah, she slipped a black ribbon with cherries into my card. It was the best one yet. And it would probably be the last ribbon I ever received.

***

Noah's walking was precarious at best, but he was a pro at crawling. I smiled and watched him chase a grasshopper across the grass. Kadence walked next to him, keeping an eye on his every move.

"He's okay, Kadence," I laughed.

She gave me a skeptical eye. "I'll just stay close. Grasshoppers can be scary."

I nodded at her and brushed the dirt off of my hands so that I could take the bag of yard debris to the curb. As I walked past our peeling clubhouse, I saw something sticking out of our mailbox. Macy and I used to keep books in it to read during sticky summer days. I smiled, wondering what book had gotten left out here.

I put the trash bag down and walked over to the mailbox. Confused, I pulled out a pile of papers. There were loose pages from a Tale of Two Cities, a scrap piece of paper that looked like it fell out of a textbook of Macy's, and a cream envelope with Kadence's name scrawled across the front. When Kadence saw it, she froze and somehow lost all color.

"Kadence?" I rushed to her and tried to gather her in my arms.

She was so upset she kept oscillating between solid and smoke.

"He found me. She found me..." she muttered, grabbing handfuls of her hair.

I shook her a little so that she would come back to me. "Explain to me what is happening so that I can help you."

"You can't! You can't! I told, and it didn't matter," she said, crying and shaking her head furiously.

I squeezed her hands as well as I could. "Come back to me, Kadence."

She stopped hyperventilating long enough to look me in the eyes. As soon as I had her attention, I pulled her into a hug and stroked her hair.

138

"You are safe with me, please just tell me what is going on."

Kadence nodded, taking a shaky deep breath.

"It's the letters. Emily had a playhouse in her backyard, and we started getting letters in it. Both of us at first."

I agreed, remembering the way she had started crying and talking about not believing in magic anymore.

"Both of you at first?" I asked.

"Yeah. They had glitter on the pages. I thought they were from fairies even though Emily said that was stupid. They asked about our favorite things. Ice cream, toys, TV show. It was fun. Like those quizzes in a magazine, my mom sometimes read to me."

I kept stroking her hair as she went on, her spirit getting stronger as she fell into her memories.

"Then Emily's letters were short, and mine were still long. She told me that the fairies liked me better and it made her sad. When the letters started asking me to do things, I hid them from her."

"Why? What were they asking you to do?" I asked, getting more uneasy.

"To wear my yellow dress because it was their favorite. To braid my hair into pigtails so they could see my face better. To ask my mom if I could have a sleepover with Emily."

My brain processed that in overdrive, spinning when it wasn't able to scratch the itch fully because Kadence leaned forward and had started opening the letter.

"Maybe we shouldn't," I started.

She already had it out and was reading it with shaky hands.

I miss you, oh yes, I do.
But you will never leave me here,

139

Because I have a piece of you.

She looked up at me in confusion. "This is different than the other letters. What does it mean?"

"I don't know sweetie," I said, putting it back in the envelope. "Let's bring Noah inside for some lunch. I can put on Mickey Mouse Club House on for you guys."

When the kids were settled in front of the TV, I called Terry upstairs and showed her the letter.

"In your professional opinion, what the hell does this mean? Do you think that the ring isn't what's holding her? Maybe Emily has something else that is keeping her tethered?"

Terry nodded. "Yeah, that would make sense. That's not what has me the most worried."

I arched an eyebrow at her, and she almost laughed.

"Okay, my therapist's brain is obviously not on the same page as a medium brain. There is some obvious abuse going on here. She started receiving letters asking her to dress a certain way so that they could see her. Asking to spend the night at Emily's? That's either someone living in Emily's house or a neighbor that wanted to know her whereabouts so that they could take her."

Unease climbed up my spine and settled into the pit of my stomach.

"Emily killed her. Is it possible she left the letters?"

"And some for herself as well? She was upset when her letters became shorter. She was never the object of the obsession. These were written by a pedophile. This is classic grooming behavior."

"If they weren't after Emily and Kadence was killed before they could take her, what does that mean for us?"

140

Terry let out a deep breath. "No one is going to want us looking into a child murder or accidental death that is supposedly closed. Especially if the person who was leaving letters like this is still walking around free. People like this don't stop, they just find new victims."

"I think it's time for Kadence's first counseling session."

***

Terry usually would talk to her patients alone. In this case, I needed to be with Kadence in order to project her presence.

"Claire showed me the letter she found in the clubhouse," Terry began, smoothing it on her lap.

Kadence nodded, looking terrified.

I squeezed her hand and smiled.

"You're not in trouble, sweetie."

She took a deep breath. "They made Emily so mad."

"Why? Because her letters were shorter?"

"Because they stopped. When she found out I was still getting letters, she cried. She told me it was her clubhouse and it wasn't fair that the fairies only liked me."

Terry smiled. "Do you still think they were from fairies?"

Kadence's face went white, and she shuddered. "No."

When she didn't elaborate, Terry moved on. I shrugged. Her not talking was better than the completely blank face I got whenever I tried to bring it up to her.

"I want you to think about that last sleepover with Emily. Did you want to go? You two had been fighting a lot."

141

She shook her head. "No. My mom didn't understand and wanted me to make up with her. She said friends were important. She invited Emily's parents over for a dinner party, they were next doors to us. She said if something went wrong to come back home. I hated it there."

"Why?"

"I didn't like to go to the bathroom alone."

Kadence started to shiver, signaling the end of the session. If we pushed her too hard, she would resist talking in the future. As she went to lay down, I shut the door to Terry's room and sat across from her.

"The dinner party. We keep coming back to this. Emily's Dad couldn't possibly be the killer."

"What about the bathroom comment? She didn't like to go alone. I doubt it was because the house was haunted."

"No, she was definitely attacked in the house or around it. If the person responsible was staking out the neighborhood, it's possible that he was someone who worked maintenance and had access to the houses. Maybe he was there while she was sleeping over? Fixing a sink when she came in to use the bathroom?"

"What do we do?" I asked, shivering.

Terry sighed. "Right now, we just give her space and make ourselves available. Until we know who the other killer is, we can't make assumptions. As soon as we move, whoever it is will get a jump start on making sure we never find them. For now, everyone is still a suspect."

***

Organizing mom's recipes on the counter might not make creating a Thanksgiving dinner any easier, but it did make me feel like she was closer on a holiday that was hard to celebrate.

"Are we doing mac and cheese and mashed potatoes even though it will only be Ash and us?" Terry asked.

I gave her an overly shocked grimace. "Which do you propose we cut?"

She laughed. "You're right. Go big or go home."

"I wish Dad could have come."

Terry nodded. She was actually the one to invite him, which meant a lot to me. However, he was going to Florida to visit his parents. It had been years since he last visited, so it was really important to him.

Holden came up from downstairs. I had begged him to come, and he had agreed to come after Terry came to him on her own to ask him over as well. I could accept him not living here, having to accept him missing a holiday with Noah was still impossible.

"He's out like a light. I think we have at least an hour," he told me, sitting at the table and beginning to fold the pile of napkins from the dryer.

"Noah's first real Thanksgiving," Terry lamented, wiping her tears a little.

Last year Noah was just a baby and cried throughout dinner. He wasn't able to try real food yet, was horrified by everything we offered him. This would be the first time he actually enjoyed his meal and could look forward to the pecan pie Terry made.

"No, no. We are not getting started with the tears yet. The day has barely started," I told her.

"Yeah, Terry, keep it together."

A voice from behind us made both of us jump. I spun to see Macy standing in the kitchen doorway, looking terrified. It couldn't be real, she couldn't be real. I hadn't been sleeping enough. This was a hallucination. My mind struggled with what I was seeing. I wanted to close my eyes and go back to a year ago, I wanted to go to an alternate universe

143

where we were all celebrating Thanksgiving together and it was normal and okay. Because if she was here then everything was wrong. My bubble was popping and I couldn't do anything to hold onto the mist. Here she was, beautiful with a pregnancy bump.

"Macy," Terry rushed to her and pulled her into a huge hug.

Mac kept her eyes on me, watching me as my shock turned to rage.

"Why is it okay for you to come back now? Did the holidays make you lonely? Make you feel guilty? Why do you deserve to come back now after how long you stayed away?" I asked, throwing the dish towel I was holding onto the counter.

Macy flinched as if I slapped her. "No..."

"No? You didn't feel guilty? For leaving us to clean up your messes, yet again."

Macy's face flushed. "I didn't want to leave. You told me to leave."

Terry tried to stand between us. "I think we all need to take a deep breath."

I pushed Terry away. "I told you I needed space. I didn't ask you to change your number and leave the city. This isn't about me, it's about the fact that you fucked your life up and wanted to blame someone else."

Macy was crying and wrapped her arms around herself. "My life is fucked up? Look at you, Claire. It's been almost seven months. And he is still here? How selfish can you be?!"

Holden looked down, blushing.

I shook my head. "Stop."

"Claire, he's dead! This isn't fair to you or to Noah. Or to Holden. You need to let go and get your life together."

The room started to spin under my feet, and I rushed towards Macy. I lifted my hand, wanting to slap her, wanting to force her to leave again because I couldn't handle what she was trying to say. Macy couldn't be here, because if she was here, then Holden was really gone. If Macy was here, then I had to exist in a world where the love of my life had been murdered. Macy grabbed my hand, pulling me into a hug instead. I struggled and screamed.

"Don't touch me, you bitch! Don't touch me!"

She gripped me tighter, crying into my shoulder. She didn't let go as I fought her.

"He's dead Claire. I am so sorry, he's dead," she repeated.

"No, please, no."

Memories flooded my consciousness, almost blotting out what was really in front of me. Answering the phone and being told to come down to the hospital, thinking that Macy and Holden had been in some kind of accident. As soon as I saw Macy sitting on that bed crying into her knees, I knew. It still didn't keep me from being unable to accept it when the doctor told me that Holden was gone.

I simply sat on the tile and focused on breathing, floating away and out of my body. He couldn't be gone. Because it took us this long to find each other. Because it took me this long to let myself love him, and I did. I loved him so much that it made it hard to sleep at night, I didn't want to waste a minute of the time we had together. He couldn't be gone because Noah was here, and he still needed a Dad. I needed us to raise our son together.

He couldn't be gone because he was a part of me, and I didn't know how to live with this big of a hole in my heart.

"I am so sorry, I'm sorry," Macy sobbed, her legs giving out.

I pulled back to look at her, wanting to hate her for leaving me when I need her the most. Seeing her gutted over what happened was what I wanted when I first found out. Now all I wanted was for her to hold me.

"You left, I needed you. He was gone and I didn't understand *why*. I wanted to die."

She nodded, wiping her face, unsuccessfully. "I couldn't tell you; I didn't want you to hate me."

I gripped her hands, still caught between throttling her and wanting to kiss her cheeks.

"Please don't leave again," I begged her, collapsing into her lap.

Macy took a deep breath and hugged me tight. "I'm here now."

Terry sank to her knees next to us, enfolding us in her arms.

For the last seven months, I wanted to live in the past because the present was too physically painful. When I thought about that day at the hospital, I couldn't function. It was fake, like I was watching a movie about someone else's life. With Macy here, it was too real. I was going to have to face it.

"I can't do this," I whispered, looking at Holden over Terry's shoulder.

Macy turned my face so that I was looking at her instead. "You don't have to do this alone; I promise."

When I turned back again, Holden was gone.

Chapter 7

<u>Terry December 2017</u>

Kelsi wrung her hands. "I'm a little nervous."

I nodded. "We don't have to do it this way. We can just talk it out."

Kelsi shook her head; she had been dead set on allowing me to see what happened to her because putting it into words was too difficult. At the same time, allowing me to touch her and try to force a vision was obviously scary for someone who had no idea that it was possible a few months ago.

"Do I just hold your hand?" she asked.

"Sure. I can also share it with you so that you can see exactly how much you are sharing and explain it if you need to."

That seemed to help, and she extended her hand to me. I gently held it, smiling at her.

"Thank you for trusting me."

Kelsi gave me a nervous grimace that might have been a smile and closed her eyes, going back to that night.

"I'm saying no. Do you understand no?"

Kelsi and a boy -Guy- were sitting on a bed in a dim room. The room looked like it belonged to another teenage boy. Kelsi was wearing a T-shirt and a pair of jeans. Not an outfit that a girl looking to steal someone's boyfriend would wear. That was important to her, that she had dressed like herself and wasn't caught in that position trying to dress like a slut.

"I understand the word no, I just don't think you mean it. Why did you ask to be alone? You're not dumb, what do you think that meant?" Guy asked, his face not so attractive when twisted into that kind of sneer.

Kelsi stared at him. He gently caressed her cheek, and she tried to pull away.

"I didn't ask you to be alone. I said the party was loud and you told me that you knew somewhere we could talk."

Guy stared back and then slowly understood that she had really no idea what that could mean. This was her first party, after all.

"I'm sorry, you're right. We can just kiss."

Kelsi nodded and had allowed him to kiss her again. The door slammed open, and three teenage girls strode in, leaving the door ajar. The light from the hallway spilled in and hurt Kelsi's eyes with its abruptness.

Guy leaned back, and Kelsi had bolted to her feet.

"Shannon," Guy stated, rolling his eyes at her.

"What the fuck is this? We break up for two minutes, and you are already hooking up with the new girl?"

Shannon was leggy with light copper hair and perfect skin. She was beautiful. No one would ever accuse her of being kind.

"No, we weren't hooking up," Kelsi tried to say.

Shannon just ignored her and strode around the room.

"How could you do this to me?" Shannon asked Guy, trying to look hurt and only being able to pull off furious.

"What can I say, she came onto me," Guy said, looking at Kelsi.

As everyone in the room looked at Kelsi, her face burned.

"No, I was sitting alone, and he came to talk to me."

"And he just... forced his tongue down your throat after throwing you over his shoulder and bringing

148

you to a room. All alone?" one of Shannon's friends asked.

"No."

Kelsi's mouth opened and shut like a fish. She was completely at a loss. This was the opposite of what she wanted. She wanted friends, a boy, to introduce her to his group and make her part of it. She just wanted to stop feeling so lonely. As everyone stared in, she wished she had stayed alone.

"You know, we have a way of dealing with new girls who try to slut it up with our boyfriends. It usually solves the problem," Shannon says, glancing at Guy, who was trying to suppress an arrogant smile.

It's clear he loves what is happening. Being fought over is a turn on for him. Foreplay for a relationship based on hurting each other.

"I'm sorry," Kelsi said, trying to push past Shannon's friends to leave.

One of them pushed her back into the center of the room. Shannon laughed and slowly took off her sheer cardigan and tossed it onto the bed next to Guy. The friend who had pushed Kelsi took out her cellphone and started filming.

"Yeah, it's not going to be as easy as I'm sorry."

She strode over to Kelsi and slapped her across the face. In shock, Kelsi slapped her back. It was the only thing about the night she wouldn't regret. Shannon punched her this time, right under her eye. Kelsi had never been in a fight before, and the shock that lit up her brain was incredible. She tried running again and was grabbed by the friend who was not filming. She jerked Kelsi's hands behind her back and held her in place.

In her panic, Kelsi struggled so much that she only succeeded in exhausting herself. By the seventh *punch, she stopped struggling and instead attempted to just float out of her body. Shannon went feral. She screamed the word slut at her over and over as she punched, kicked, and scratched Kelsi until she was bleeding and barely conscious. The door had been left open, and people from the party cheered her on, high fiving her and giving her a drink when she tired out.*

Kelsi was left on the floor. Guy and Shannon left hand in hand.

Kelsi didn't know how long she laid there before getting the courage to stand up. Her eyes were smudged with blood, and her clothes were ripped. She couldn't go through that party and risk running into Shannon again. She climbed through the window despite the spasms in her ribs and made it back to her car. She drove herself home, begging her body not to shut down while she was still behind the wheel. She tumbled through her front door.

As Kelsi pulled her hand back, I saw that she was crying again.

I wiped the sweat from my brow. My body wasn't used to receiving visions that physical anymore. I was nauseous and sore from experiencing that along with Kelsi.

"Are you disgusted?" Kelsi asked, avoiding my eyes.

"By you?" I asked, confused.

"Yes! I just stood there, allowing myself to be beaten. I couldn't even go to school because everyone had seen how weak I was. Everyone else thought that if Shannon could do it, so could they."

"Kelsi, what's disgusting is that people could think that putting someone through that was the night's entertainment. You did the only thing that you could really do at that moment."

"Give up?"

"No, Kelsi. Survive. You survived."

I kneeled in front of her, ignoring professional protocol and just needing her to hear me. I pulled her chin up so that we were looking at each other.

"You did not deserve that. That was a game to them, and it wasn't even about you. As for everyone else, teens can fall into a mob mentality that is more like self-preservation. If you are the one it is happening to, they are somehow safe from it. It's not okay, and you don't have to take it."

"What do I do?" Kelsi asked, looking even more terrified.

"Right now, all you need to do is come to Starbucks with me for a cheese Danish and caramel macchiato. We can figure out the rest later. We accomplished a lot today."

Kelsi gave me a smile, wiping her face.

"Can we make that a cranberry bliss bar?" she asked.

I laughed a little. "Of course."

The road ahead of us wouldn't be easy. If the entire school had participated in the bullying, then it was unlikely that things would get better on their own. The videos had been deleted, that could have just been smart thinking on Shannon's part. What happened could have put Shannon in jail, and also incriminated everyone who had watched and filmed it.

This would be a huge fight and Kelsi would need to be in it 100% if it was going to happen. I didn't even know if she would be up for it or just want to change schools. Either way, telling me what happened made my job easier. Now I could fight for her.

***

This was just a room at one of her friends' houses, not our home. I understood that it was also what Macy needed at this moment. Macy had tried to bring touches of herself to the room that I had to smile at. A lip-gloss collection on top of the dresser, a bright bedspread with watercolor roses, and rows of shoes lined up against one wall.

"So, what's the plan?" I asked, at a loss and needing to be close to my baby sister again.

I wanted to know everything. What exactly happened between her and Holden to make her leave. When did she find out she was pregnant? Whose baby is it? What about Britney? Is she keeping the baby? What the hell is she going to do?

These were questions I had wanted to ask for months. When Macy first disappeared, I was frantic. I thought that she had been kidnapped. I had called the cops daily to get updates. Finally, they recommended that at 18 she could make her own decisions. She was allowed to fall off the face of the earth if she wanted to.

I remember feeling desperate when our mom passed away. I remember hating the feel of my own skin and grief that was suffocating. If I had felt somehow responsible for that death, I don't know if I could have lived with myself. I was furious and terrified with Macy for leaving with so much left unsaid. At the same time, I knew that if I didn't give her space, she would never get the courage to come back.

Macy shrugged. "Claire hates me right now, which I get. I can stay here until the baby comes. Stacey has been great. I just got a job at Roasted and Toasted, so I will be able to pay rent."

I sat on her bed next to her. "I'm not Dad, Mac. I wasn't asking if you needed money."

She raised an eyebrow, and I laughed a little bit.
"Okay. I might still try to give you money."

Macy looked at her shoes and slightly swollen ankles. "What do you want to know?"

A million questions flooded my mind. Only one had the courage to creep up my throat. I worried it was the one that would send her running again.

"Why did you leave?" my voice broke a little.

She nodded, knowing this was coming. After that night in the hospital, Macy had come home. Claire and Macy had gotten into a huge fight and Claire screamed at her to leave. She had just found out that her husband had been killed. I knew she shouldn't have said it but understood.

Macy, she couldn't handle it. She couldn't handle the questions and guilt. The next morning, she left. There was no note and she changed her phone number after we filled up the voice mailbox. She just disappeared, and we had no way of finding her. I was terrified that she was dead somewhere.

"Has Holden told you guys anything?" she asked.

I shook my head. "No. He refused. He said it was your secret and he couldn't do that to you. He and Claire aren't together anymore. I mean, obviously, because he died. She hasn't let that stop her though and tried to move on like it never happened. In this afterlife, it has just been fighting and trying to find out how everything fell apart."

"And it's my fault," Macy said softly.

I put my arm around her. "The secret was obviously really important to you."

Mac rubbed a hand over her belly and looked up at me.

"Can I show you?"

My vision from Kelsi had been intense and this might tear me apart. It didn't matter, I had to take the

153

in she was giving me. If she is responsible for Holden's death, she has been carrying around a lot of guilt for the last seven months. When we got to the hospital, the cops told us that he was found in a parking plaza and that didn't give us any insight.

"Of course," I told her, extending my hand.

Mac held on and tightly closed her eyes, already crying.

I never thought I would be here. Making these choices and kissing these guys… and more. It was just a sad decision I made while missing Britney. I never thought that I could get pregnant. I never thought I would be dumb enough to get knocked up during a one-night stand while cheating on my girlfriend.

I never thought that I would be planning on having an abortion.

"What's next?" Holden asked, squeezing my hand.

I looked at him, knowing my fear was written all over my face. I felt like I was dragged out to the middle of the ocean on a damaged kayak and told to make it back to shore. I was slowly sinking and had no idea if it was better to give in or swim. I wanted to do this all alone and never tell anyone, but the nurse said that I had to have someone drive me home. I had to prove that I had support.

I couldn't tell my sisters. They would be so disappointed in me, and I couldn't face that.

Holden was the most forgiving and understanding person I had ever met. He loved me like a sister and promised to keep my secret even from Claire. He promised to keep me safe.

"Lunch?" I said, attempting to make a joke.

He gave me a sad smile. "How about re-enrolling in college? I support your choice. I think you know that you need to make it count. If you do this, make it worth it. You know?"

154

I nodded, looking at our clasped hands. He was right. I needed to make this a choice that led to a better life and not just a way to escape from a choice I made at two am. I needed to go back to school, I needed to make it up to Britney, I needed to become a better person.

When I decided to get an abortion, I thought it was the only choice that I had. I couldn't imagine being a parent and was ashamed of what led to this moment. Yet, the more I thought about it, the more disgusted I became with myself.

I needed to become a better person. Couldn't I do that as a mom? Was a baby something to hide? A decision to forget? I thought about Noah and couldn't breathe. What if this baby was meant to be his cousin? What if I was meant to be their mom? What if this baby was important to saving me and forcing me to become someone new?

"Macy Shaw?" a nurse stated, standing in front of an open door that led to exam rooms. That led to the end of this life and solidified this choice.

I turned to Holden, bawling and scared.

I was sure. "Get me out of here, please."

He smiled like he knew I would make this choice. He believed in me and knew I could do this.

Holden pulled me up, and we walked through the front door together. The sunlight was dazzling, and I couldn't see for a moment. We had to park far away, and I followed him to the car in a daze.

"How could you do THAT after ruining my life?" I heard from the car next to ours.

I turned to see Simon, his face red and blotchy. My stomach dropped to my feet. At the end of senior year, we had gotten him expelled for sexual harassment and assault after he forced my best friend to give him oral sex. I heard he had lost his scholarship to college and hadn't thought of him in months.

"Simon," Holden said, coming to stand next to me.

"You made everyone believe that you weren't a slut. That you didn't want what I did to you. That Shayla didn't. And now, here you are, coming out of an abortion clinic with your sister's boyfriend. What the fuck?" he slurred, and drool was shooting out of his mouth with each word.

"What are you doing here?" I asked, beginning to shake.

The emotion from running out of the abortion clinic was still coursing through my body. It took a minute to realize that Simon thought that I was with Holden because he was the father of my child. I wondered how Claire would feel about that and was almost overtaken with nausea. I wanted to be done with this day and forget it ever happened.

Simon looked like he wanted to forget his whole life.

"You ruined my life, Macy," he said, pulling a knife out of his pocket and staring at it like he was unsure of how it got into his hand.

"Whoa, let's take things down a notch," Holden said, his face pale and terrified.

"No, let's bring things up a notch. You ruined my life," Simon jumped at me, trying to bury the knife into my abdomen, sure to kill the new life I had just fallen in love with.

Holden jumped between us, pushing him backward. A huge gush of breath left Holden, and I saw that the knife had disappeared.

"Holden?" I gasped, pulling him towards me.

When he fell back into me, I saw that instead of my abdomen, it was buried in his side.

156

"Holden!" I screamed, going to grab the knife before realizing I needed to keep it there to hold his blood inside.

Simon watched with his mouth hanging open and his eyes jumping around spastically. He bolted his feet and left us in the parking lot, my bare knees burning on the pavement and becoming sticky with blood leaking around the knife.

"Someone help!" I screamed, begging Holden to hold onto his consciousness.

As Macy eased her hand out of mine, my chest shook with sobs.

"What happened to Simon? The cops never said anything to us. They told us it might have been a mugging. Claire was so broken that she just left it as it was," I said, trying to take deep breaths.

"He killed himself when he got home. I saw it in the paper the next day, in the same paper reporting Holden's 'accident'. There was no case because he didn't confess. What could the cops do? It was over," Macy said, her face almost unrecognizable in her grief.

"Why did you leave? Claire would have understood," I said, rubbing her back.

"She wouldn't have understood me keeping the pregnancy from her? She found the pregnancy test, and I lied and said it was Kate's. She didn't believe it, it didn't matter. She would have understood me making an appointment for an abortion and involving Holden? Simon was there to hurt me, Holden tried to protect me. He died because of me," Macy said, her entire body shaking with her grief.

I squeezed her, letting her exhaust herself. I wanted to tell her that Claire would have understood. I really didn't know. I think she would have gotten to the point where she understood Mac becoming pregnant. She would have been forced to understand her fear and the abortion clinic.

But Holden, he was her entire world. He was the love of her life and the father of her child. She would have loved that he was protecting her sister. Yet, what was worth her having to lose him?

It was the ultimate question, would she rather that Macy was alone that day if it meant her sister was dead instead of her husband?

***

"That might be too much, little man," I told Noah as he smeared yet another tablespoon of bright green frosting on his sugar cookie.

Grief seemed to make us want to smash as much holiday fun into one weekend as possible. Over the last two days, we had picked out a Christmas tree and shared cocoa with Noah, watched the Grinch four times, rearranged our glass ornaments a thousand times, and just finished making cookies. Claire still had a few presents to grab, so I shooed her out the door with Ash and cleaned up with my two favorite guys.

"How many of these are we letting him eat?" CJ asked, looking at the plate still within Noah's reach.

Noah gave him a suspicious glance then went back to stuffing his face.

"As many as he wants. It's almost Christmas," I said, turning slightly from where I was washing the dishes.

"It's also almost bedtime. Come here big guy," CJ scooped Noah out of his chair and took him over to the empty side of the sink.

I watched him wash their hands together, and Noah tried to eat the frosting as it was being wiped off his face. I laughed, loving seeing them together.

"Say goodnight, auntie," CJ told me, leaning towards us.

"Goodnight, my love," I kissed Noah on the cheek, and was frightened by a vision.

This was my first vision from a child this young.

It's dark and warm and comforting. Everything was muffled and cramped. I realize with a shock that this was Noah's view from Claire's womb. He hears her voice and knows instinctively that she belongs to him. She is talking to someone else, Holden. When Noah hears Holden's voice, his heartbeat picks up, and he moves in excitement. He knows his dad's voice right from the beginning, he knows who he belongs to.

I pulled back, and CJ gave me a startled look. I shook my head and watched him take Noah through the living room to put him to bed.

Noah was so young when Holden passed away, it would have almost been a blessing if he had been able to forget him before he had a chance to miss him. I guess that's not really possible. He might not always have that specific memory. Instead, he will hear his voice in his dreams and always feel like something is missing. Something will always be missing.

I dried my hands and waited for CJ at the little table in our kitchen.

"Hey, what was that?" CJ asked gently.

"A vision, from Noah. It was hearing Holden's voice."

CJ's face crinkled. "Wow."

"I know."

He reached over and held my hand. "Are you okay?"

I shrugged, suddenly remembering a conversation I had with Claire while in my coma. While in that in-between place, it had suddenly been really clear. Our gifts were special, they were divine in many ways. Normal people didn't gain something divine without a cost. My mom had agreed.

Were these costs real? Missy didn't seem to think so. We seemed cursed all the same. Mom lost my dad and was told that what made her special also made her a bad mom, that she was exposing her family to evil forces. Macy pushed away Britney and ran away from her sisters. We weren't out of the woods yet. Did seeing auras make love harder to hold onto? And Claire was being forced to walk through her life without her soul mate.

Was there a way to give these gifts up? If we were able to give them away would we suddenly be gifted normal lives?

When I thought about the possibility of losing CJ and the life I had planned for us, it made me want to give it all up. I loved my gift and connection to my mom, but she was gone, and I loved CJ more than anything in the world. This was supposed to be my future. Could I have that while still being trapped in the past through my visions?

***

Macy had been going to the obstetrician throughout her entire pregnancy. At the same time, being able to go with her myself made me feel so much better. I wasn't sure what she had planned, and the idea of her being a mom scared me.

At the same time, I couldn't deny the flutter in my heart when I saw that little figure on the grainy screen. This new soul was part of our family, part of our journey.

"Are you ready to go back to your friend's house? Or do you want to grab some food?" I asked Macy, watching her buckle herself in over her growing belly.

"I won't say no to food. I have been really into dumplings lately."

"Dumplings it is," I said, pulling out of the doctor's office parking lot.

As we drove the comfortable silence dragged on, and I regretted needing to end it. However, I couldn't keep myself from the questions still weighing heavily on my mind.

"Can I ask who the dad is? You don't have to tell me. It's just weird not knowing."

Macy looked at her hands, knowing this conversation would be coming.

"No, it's okay. His name is Alex."

"Alex," the name foreign in my mouth. "How did you meet?"

"How I met everyone last year. At a party. I had just dropped out and was feeling sad. I drank too much and we… were together. Just one time. He's a really nice guy. Just young. We are both so young. He worked at a gas station and was getting a general AA before he dropped out."

I nodded. "Did you tell him?"

Macy sighed. "I did. He told me we would figure it out. Which scared the shit out of me. I wasn't sure I wanted to figure it out. I told him that I was getting an abortion and just wanted him to know. After everything happened, I never called him back."

I stared at her in shock. "He doesn't know you are having the baby?"

She shook her head, crying and overwhelmed.

"Mac, it's his child too."

"I know. I don't know if I am keeping the baby. I still love Britney. How can I raise a child with someone else? I don't want this baby to feel unwanted or know that the way they were created was a mistake. I don't know if I am ready for all of this."

As we pulled into our favorite Chinese food restaurant, I turned to her.

"Did you tell Britney?"

"No! How could she understand this?"

I held her hands. "So, you love her enough to give up a baby for her, but you don't think she loves you enough to know and still love you? That's not real love, Mac."

"I know," she covered her face and dissolved. "What do I do, Ter?"

I sat back, completely shocked by every part of how she spent the last year.

"First things first, you have to tell Alex. I think it will really help. If you decide to give the baby up, you will need him to sign the paperwork. And you will have his support. And… if you decide to keep the baby, you need to decide how involved you want him to be."

She started to calm down, relieved to have a plan. "You're right."

"And as for Britney. You need to be honest with her. Let her be upset, let her process it. If she still wants to try, you try. It's unconventional, not impossible. And if she can't understand, you are not meant to be with her. No matter how much that hurts."

Macy steadied her breath and stared at me intently.

"And as for you. You need to decide what you want to do regardless of any relationship. This is your baby. You can't rely on someone else to take care of them or you. If you don't want this 100%, then don't do it."

A part of me was convinced that Macy wasn't ready for this. Another part of me saw hope in that spark of passion that went through her face when I told her that she needed to decide if she was ready.

God didn't always give you a situation you were ready for. In fact, he often trusted your abilities far beyond what you feel like you are capable of. Growing means hurting a little bit. It means having to pull yourself out of the dirt and believe in yourself.

Being pregnant wasn't hitting rock bottom for Macy. She wanted to be a mom someday. But not being defined by a relationship and needing to be okay with being alone would be the scariest thing she has ever done. It would mean loving herself as she truly was more than whoever she tried to be while in a couple.

It would mean giving up every single thing she believed about herself in order to become something even better. I would support her and didn't think I was going to have to push hard. Macy had always been a late bloomer, this was her season, she was ready to grow.

***

"That brings the guest list to fifty," CJ said, going over the guest list one last time before we ordered invitations.

I looked over his shoulder, noticing that he only had a handful of his family coming.

"There isn't anyone else you want to invite?"

He shook his head. "No. Like who?"

"Maybe your dad?" I said, offhandedly, looking at the paper samples again.

"What?"

"Your dad. I know Gem won't be crazy about the idea, but you only get married once. It's up to you."

As I turned towards him, two things hit me. One, CJ was furious with me. Two, when he first asked me to ask his mom about his dad back in ninth grade, I had lied to him.

"What the hell are you talking about?" he asked.

163

My mouth dropped open. "CJ…"

"You asked my mom, and you told me that you didn't get anything. You told me that you didn't know."

"I know. I completely forgot. I was trying to protect you."

"You forgot that you lied to me?" his face was red.

The pain on his face felt as physical as a knife twisting into my stomach.

"I didn't lie to hurt. I was trying to protect you."

"What else have you lied about?" he asked.

"Nothing!"

"How am I supposed to trust you?"

I followed him out of the kitchen, trying to hold his hand. He shook me off and grabbed his coat off the couch.

"Where are you going?"

"For a walk. Please, don't follow me."

As the door slammed, I sank to the ground. CJ and I never fought. When we did, it was Barbara coursing through my veins. This time it was all me. This time it was my fault, this time my gift was coming between us again.

***

I didn't expect CJ to come back that night. Yet, a few hours later, he was climbing into bed next to me. I sat up and turned on the lamp next to our bed. His eyes were raw, but he looked calm.

"Are you okay? Where did you go?"

A terrible insecure voice in my head had been screaming all night that he had gone back to the bar. That he had found solace in another girl, the way he did when I broke his heart last year.

"I went to my mom's house."

I watched him undress and cover himself up. He looked utterly exhausted.

164

"What happened?"

"I asked her and told her I needed the truth. So, she told me. She gave me his name and the ball is in my court now."

I clasped my hands and watched the knuckles turn white. I needed something to focus on. I could feel the tension still rolling off of him.

"What are you going to do?"

CJ sat up and covered my clasped hands with his. "Nothing. He knows about me and never wanted anything to do with me. That's the answer I needed. I understand why you two kept it from me, I do. Please never do it again. The truth doesn't have to be happy to be what I need."

I nodded. "I am so sorry."

"I know."

"Do you feel like you can't trust me now?" I asked, beginning to cry a little.

CJ shook his head. "No. I do need you to be completely honest with me. You have a jump on me, it's the reality of our life together. I need honesty from you, even if it's hard."

I agreed, and we tried to go to sleep. Even after CJ fell asleep, I heard the unsaid words floating around the room. I had a jump on him. I knew things that he didn't. I saw things he couldn't. This was a part of me that he would never understand. There was nothing but pain in the past for the two of us. It was enough to make me wish my gift away altogether.

Being in Lyn's home, it was easy to imagine the Christmases that Holden grew up with. A perfect Martha Stewart tree that she spent a month planning out and smaller ones in the dining room that the kids were allowed to redecorate all season long. Cookies always baking and free for the taking, with or without frosting and sprinkles. Permanent background music from classic artists and illustrated Bibles on the coffee table. It felt like the holidays here, even with grief so thick we could use it as blankets.

"Is your dad spending the holidays with you?" Lyn asked, helping Noah pick up his various toys before feeding him a snack.

"I'm not sure. He spent Thanksgiving with his parents in Florida. His mom isn't doing well, and he wants to make sure he is there as much as possible."

"That's tough. Even if you do want him home with you, it makes sense why he feels the need to be there. I'm glad his parents have been welcoming despite how long he was away."

I tried not to snort. "Grandma isn't the most welcoming person I know. I think it's still important to him to feel like he tried."

She nodded.

"What about you, guys? We are all set for dinner and presents on Christmas Day. What do you guys have planned for Christmas Eve?"

The year we found out we were expecting, Holden and I had celebrated Christmas by making love in front of our Christmas tree. The early months of my pregnancy had been so filled with drama that it was a rare moment where we chose to just be together without having to figure everything else out.

Creaking from behind me caused me to turn. Matthew was coming in from their bedroom, where he had been taking a nap. Holden's dad looked so much like him that my stomach clenched despite me telling my body it wasn't the same person.

"Pap!" Noah yelped, holding his hands out to him.

He leaned down gingerly and swung Noah into his arms. I watched them nuzzle and a mixture of devastation and awe swept over me.

"We usually spend Christmas Eve at home and then go to church for the candlelight service. Have you ever been? It's really beautiful and they sing a lot of Christmas carols," Lyn told me.

She patted my hand, not missing the fact that I always came over when Matthew was at work.

"I went with my dad when I was a kid."

Matthew looked at me and gave me a quick smile before going back to Noah. My hands were already getting clammy. The room was smaller, and the air slowly leaked out.

Lyn was endless love and comfort for me, Matthew was a different story. Just looking at him brought last summer back with vivid blackness. He had just been re-diagnosed with cancer and it looked like it was going to be the end. Holden had moved back home part-time to help him through chemo and we cheered him up with the baby as much as possible.

Then Holden died. Somehow Matthew's body went into remission. He felt like it should have been him that died. It didn't make sense that Holden was gone when he had gotten not a first or second chance, but a third. His confusion and misery were so close to my own that it was difficult even being in the same room.

Watching him with Noah should have helped, but the same question was on our minds. Why does he get to snuggle my son when his Dad isn't able to anymore? Why does he get to live when Holden had to die? We were both begging the same forces to change their mind and take one for the other.

***

Kadence was eight, which meant that she didn't need naps anymore. In fact, she was a ghost, which meant she didn't need to sleep at all anymore. Still, her brain was still so used to being a living person that she followed the motions just the same. Noah on the other hand, was protesting naps in a big way.

"Come on little man, mama needs to rest too," I whispered to him, rocking in my mom's favorite chair.

"My mom told me he was having trouble sleeping," Holden said from the doorway, making me jump.

Just seeing him made my body want to relax with comfort and prickle with electricity at the same time.

"Him and the rest of the world, it seems."

We stared at each other, and from his face, I knew he could tell that I wasn't allowing him to project to Noah. I hated this the most. Not being able to allow my son to see his father because it would mean more heartbreak for him.

"I'm able to dream. I didn't think that was possible," Holden said, sitting in the chair next to me.

"What do you dream about?" I ask.

Holden stared forward, thinking for a moment.

"About what if. We shop for Christmas presents after getting Starbucks and try to go ice skating. Then, I am so terrible that we leave early. On Christmas Eve I rub flour on my shoes, so it looks like Santa has walked around the living room. I can't fall asleep because I am just as excited for Noah to open his gifts."

168

My eyes fill with tears, and I nod. "I dream about that, too."

Holden looked over at me, exactly the same in our sickness. He reaches over. His hand goes right through Noah's little pajamed leg, and a gasp of strangled grief escapes him.

"You have no idea how much it hurts to not be able to hold him. I never knew you could love and hurt this much at once," he told me, his voice a picture of devastation.

I sobbed and put Noah in his crib. I walked over to Holden and took a deep breath, allowing him to become more solid through the intertwined loss of forevers. I took his hand and led him over to the crib. Together we put our joined hands on Noah's back as he slept.

Holden caressed his spine and folded into himself. It looked like he had to physically hold in his pain.

"These are his favorite pajamas," I told him.

He held onto that like a piece of expensive chocolate. "Tell me more."

Still holding his hand, I led him over to the bed that we had shared. We laid next to each other, breaking our grasp and facing each other.

"He's so curious. Way braver than me. When he is trucking around the yard chasing bugs, I am so scared he is going to hurt himself. He is so sure of himself. He wants to taste and try everything. He is going to be walking any day now."

"Taste? What is he trying to eat?" Holden asked, laughing softly.

"Everything. Dirt, grass, weeds, and whatever bug he can track down. I am so glad we don't have pets because I don't think he would steer away from a cat box at this point."

"Oh no," he said, smiling softly.

"He loves baths and tries to blow the bubbles off his hands and into the air. His favorite food right now is cherry tomatoes and broccoli, I think because they are cold, and his little molars will be coming in soon."

"Poor guy. That must hurt."

I nodded. "It's tough. I never realized how much teething affects their bodies. It's like he has a cold, and I feel so helpless."

As the night deepened and became colder, I covered up with a blanket. My voice became hoarse from telling him everything I had wanted to tell him for the last eight months. It was like seeing my best friend from college for the first time in ten years and trying to fit an entire lifetime into just twelve hours. My eyes became heavier and heavier, and the harder I fought it, the faster I fell.

I thought I felt him kiss my forehead and knew he stayed with me as long as he could. When I woke up, I was alone again. He was gone again.

***

"It's the perfect shade of green. Thank you," Terry said, looking at herself in her rearview cellphone camera to see the emerald necklace that was her Christmas present from CJ.

He smiled at her like he had this image in mind when he bought it, not how she looked wearing the necklace, but the way her lips curled up when she thought she was beautiful.

"It's just right. You have a good eye," I told CJ as he continued to beam at her.

Noah crawled over to Terry and pulled himself into her lap so that he could examine it more fully. And taste it of course.

"Noah approves," Terry laughed.

CJ leaned over and tweaked Noah's armpit, making him laugh.

"How about a present of your own, little man?" CJ asked, grabbing yet another wrapped package from under the tree.

"CJ! What are you doing? That's present number seven from just you," I laughed, shaking my head.

"What? This is my right and duty as an uncle," CJ said, feigning offense.

Noah crawled towards him and settled himself onto CJ's thigh, trying his best to rip the paper off the package on his own.

As Noah squealed over another stuffed puppy, I wondered what Holden would have wanted to get his son. For his first Christmas he had only been six months, and he was way more interested in crinkling the wrapping paper than any of the gifts he received. In a lot of ways this was his first real Christmas, and his dad was missing it. I had to keep trying to stay in this moment because Noah deserved it. And we had a wonderful holiday so far, it was impossible not to enjoy yourself around this precious little human.

Even though I wasn't able to make myself say it out loud, I couldn't help wondering what this year would have looked like if last year had never happened. Macy was coming over later on for a super awkward dinner instead of sitting right next to me, spoiling Noah as well. Holden was cold in the ground instead of kissing me on the cheek as he contentedly watched our family. Our life was still so perfect that it felt unfair when I really thought about all that I had lost.

I wanted so badly to go back to our wedding weekend. After the ceremony, Holden and I reserved one night in a local hotel before taking Noah to the zoo the next day. However, by ten pm, we had given up on being away from our son. I took a shower, packed my dress up carefully, and we picked up a pizza on our way home. We kissed our son goodnight as he snoozed in his crib and sat on the bed, eating slices of pineapple and olives.

"Favorite song?" Holden whispered.

I closed my eyes, shuffling through so many moments vying to be number one.

"The one with my sisters. The father-daughter one was formal, I knew it would be. Dancing with them, it was the true moment that I was given away. Macy cried and I kissed Terry on the forehead. We sang our song and... it felt like the end of a chapter."

He smiled at me. "In a bad way?"

"In the best way. Because they are still going to be here. They gave me their blessing to grow on my own for the first time. It's pretty huge."

Holden leaned back, looking around the room.

"So... this is our wedding night."

I laughed. "Yeah, I guess so. Are you disappointed in how we are spending it?"

He shook his head, giving me eyes that I had become accustomed to. A look that still made my heart flutter.

"Not disappointed in the slightest. I do have to admit that when I think about having you for the first time as my wife, I don't imagine it happening in the room that was your mom's."

"No?" I agreed, curious to see where he was headed with this.

"No," Holden stood quietly and held out his hand.

I took it, shut the door quietly behind me and followed him downstairs. He eased the door to my high school room open.

I stood in the middle of the room, wrapped in memories of being a teenager, fighting the insecurities of those years. Wrapped in memories of when Holden came back into my life and stole my heart and soul.

"I imagine it here. Where you came back to me. Where we found each other."

This wasn't even close to our first time, and I thought that would make tonight less special somehow. It was different. This wasn't just us coming together just because we were in the mood or because we had an argument and wanted to pave over to a better night. This was because we had taken a huge step together and were still a little bit scared. This was him as the man who would take care of me for the rest of my life, me as a wife who had no idea how to make him happy but would do it with my last breath.

This was the real beginning of us.

"Hey, you okay?" Terry asked, ripping me from my memories.

I looked at her, confused before realizing my cheeks were wet. I hurriedly wiped my face and focused on what was happening in the room in front of me. CJ had turned on the Grinch for the thousandth time, Noah's favorite, and they had fallen asleep in the armchair together. My heart melted and ached at the same time.

"Sorry, I just went somewhere for a second."

Terry swung an arm around my neck and put her forehead against mine.

"It will get easier. I have to believe that."

I nodded. I had to believe it too. Because living with this much heartache and pain didn't seem possible for long.

***

"How is counseling going?" Lenore asked, adjusting on the frozen bench we were sitting on.

173

The park was freezing as there was still snow on the ground, but Noah had begged to go to the park all week.

"It's going well. Kadence is finally beginning to trust Terry, and little details come out at each session. She's a kid. She still feels so much guilt over what happened."

Lenore patted my hand. "I meant your counseling."

I glared at her. Terry had been bugging me to talk to someone all year. It took Macy coming back to get me to agree. I had missed her so much. All I wanted the last eight months was to have my family back. However, whenever I saw her, all I could feel was betrayal for her leaving me after what she did.

I didn't want to feel this way. My broken heart wasn't leaving room for anything else.

"I have my first appointment next week."

"Good."

"Do you really think it will help?" I asked her.

"How could it not?"

I looked back over to where Noah was playing and stiffened. A battered man was dragging himself over the snow towards the jungle gym. His legs were twisted behind him, and he groaned as if his ribs were not where they were supposed to be anymore. I smelled burned rubber, a car accident. I couldn't tell how long ago. Blood made a gory trail from the parking lot over to where Noah was investigating the wood chips buried under the crunchy snow.

"There are things I will never be able to tell my counselor. As much as they want to help, they will have no idea how to separate the ghosts from my everyday life. They won't be able to teach me how to keep blood off my picnic blanket or ignore someone reliving their death outside of my bedroom door."

174

I stood up, not making eye contact with the spirit in their death state.

"Come on, little one, it's time for lunch," I picked up my son and turned my back on the park.

Lenore gave me a sad smile from the bench. "Do you really want to turn off that part of your life?"

I understood her sadness. Leaving this part of who I was meant saying goodbye to her. Wanting just one day with my family wasn't the same thing as wanting to say goodbye to it altogether.

***

I was capable of researching on my own, it just never felt right without my best friend. Ash didn't have any psychic gits, but she was my partner in this in so many ways. She was addicted to crime TV shows and novels and always asked the questions I would never think of. Also, my being able to project meant she had a new friend in Lenore, which still blew her mind.

"Did you actually Google on your own?" Ash asked, feigning shock.

I rolled my eyes. "I do know how to use the computer. I happen to be a writer."

Ash glanced at the blank notebooks sitting next to a trash can full of doodles and gave me a fake hard look.

"Could have fooled me."

I elbowed her and sat next to Lenore.

"Okay, so I am sure you did research of your own. This is what I found. Emily Simmon and Kadence Morton both died last year in June. Kadence was found in the woods by the cops. Emily was found in the clubhouse by her mother, she was the one who called the police. The causes of death were never disclosed to the public, it did come out that the times of death were hours apart."

Lenore raised her eyebrow. "Did we know that her mother is one who called the cops?"

"No, we found out that they were at a dinner party when the kids were supposed to be having their sleepover. And Terry saw Emily's parents fighting in a vision, the wife clearly blamed the husband for the accident and sent her son away. That's weird, right? She found her daughter dead and didn't try to find Kadence?"

"Super weird. And she didn't call her parents? They didn't find out that anything was wrong until the police contacted them. I can imagine that Emily's parents could say that they were in shock and not acting like themselves," Ash said, writing in her notebook.

"Do you buy that?" Lenore asked.

"Not for one second. Kadence told me that Emily killed her. So, someone else is involved."

Ash rubbed her arms before pulling her printed off research out of her purse. "I tracked down the notes from the civil suit. I know that Kadence's mom told us that they had to drop the case because of a lack of evidence. Which is confusing because the evidence feels really important. The only evidence they had against the family were letters that were supposed to have come from the mailbox in Emily's clubhouse. There were hundreds all addressed to Kadence."

"She was being groomed by an adult for sure. Every time she talks about those letters, she cries. If they found out that Emily killed Kadence, they might have cared about Kadence enough to kill Emily in revenge. Who would have that kind of access to both of them?"

I shrugged, feeling very underprepared for this kind of investigation.

"Why would the police just stop the investigation? If we can see that it was weird and that there are loose ends, the public must have as well."

"For sure. There were a ton of editorials in the local papers asking for justice for Kadence. Every time the idea of a murderous pedophile was brought up, it was buried. It was like the cops and newspapers were so afraid of a sweep of panic in the city that they ignored it altogether. No one else was killed in the same way, so they probably wrote it off as a mistake and moved on," Ash said, her face red with indignation.

"Where do we go from here?"

Lenore sifted through the papers. "Kadence's parents already tried to get justice. We might be able to contact them again and ask them some questions under the guise of trying to reopen the case through the Freedom Project."

I shifted uncomfortably. "Lying to grieving parents? That doesn't sound fair after everything they have gone through. They are going to want results after waiting all this time."

"Why does it have to be a lie? You have something that the cops couldn't have ignored, you have access to Kadence. You are the only one that can help her tell the true story and give her family peace."

"That might mean telling them the whole truth, that I can see Kadence. Them thinking I am just trying to benefit from what happened to them might hurt them even more."

Lenore patted my hand. "I don't think anything can hurt more than burying your child and thinking the entire world has forgotten and moved on without them."

Ash gasped. "Guys. The information about Stan Simmon bugged me, so I have been trying to find more information. I tweaked my search keywords and just found this."

She turned the computer so that we could see an obituary. Stan Simmon had killed himself after being fired from the force. I sat back with my hand over my mouth, but Lenore was smiling.

"Lenore?" Ash said, looking slightly horrified.

Lenore shook her head. "No, this is good. This means that we can find him."

Chapter 8

Terry January 2018

It felt like I was starting over with Kelsi. Last session, she allowed me to share a vision with her. It was such a huge step, and I was hopeful about the future of her journey. However, she had been distant all day and refused to look me in the eye. What had happened between then and now to make her regret opening up to me?

I shut my folder and turned to her fully. "Okay. What's going on?"

Kelsi blushed. "What do you mean?"

"You know what I mean. You are tiptoeing around me like you did when we first met. What's going on? Did something else happen?"

Kelsi shook her head. "No, it's not about me."

My stomach dropped. "It's about me?"

She wrung her hands. "When I first came here, it was because my mom kept telling me that you were special. I thought she knew. I was amped up after our last session that I told her everything that happened."

"What happened?" I asked quietly, my stomach now rolling and contracting painfully.

"She freaked out. She said that she thought that you just got feelings about people. That you had a gift with kids. Whatever that means. Like you could tell if they were lying or not. She started saying it must be a scam, benefiting off people who are desperate."

I swallowed, my throat scratched like it was full of asphalt. "And what do you think?"

Kelsi shrugged. "I told her that she was wrong. I was part of that vision, and it was real. You saw it, every single part of right down to how I was feeling about it. You can't fake that."

"But?"

179

"She was so scared that I wanted to keep coming. I did some research after going to bed that night."

I closed my eyes, imagining whatever opinions are online about post-cognition or just psychic gifts in general.

"A lot of it just sounded like bullshit. People wanting to have what you have. Some of it… said that having visions wasn't natural. Obviously, it's not run of the mill. These sites said it was ungodly, evil somehow."

"Did it feel evil to you? I help people who have been destroyed find the strength to face their monsters," I told her, becoming upset.

This was my true birthright. Always having to defend the supernatural so that I was validated as a person.

"It didn't feel evil. Still, I'm a little scared of it."

I nodded. "Do you want to be set up with another counselor?"

Kelsi shook her head, looking at me empathetically. "No. I just need to figure out how I feel about how we are doing this."

"Okay."

The silence stretched out in front of us. We still had twenty minutes left of our session, there was nothing to talk about if she wasn't sure if she trusted me or was terrified of what I was.

***

"This is weird," Claire said, moving herself to a better vantage point in front of her laptop screen.

I balanced the laptop on my bed and maximized my window so that I was able to see Macy and Claire on the voice call equally.

"Weird?" I asked.

"I'm literally upstairs. Why am I on this call?"

"Because you and Macy refuse to be in the same room. It's all of us or nothing," I told them.

Claire looked down but Macy stared straight into the camera, seeming to lock eyes with us. She had become so bold since coming back and a part of me had to bite back a smile.

"What's up? Why the family meeting?" Macy asked, breaking the silence.

I took a deep breath. I had told them separately about Kelsi and her mom finding out about my gift. I hadn't been able to stop thinking about it for the last week. This could have lasting repercussions for my entire career.

"Okay. This might feel unconnected. I swear this isn't just cold feet," I started.

Both of them sensed the wedding was in danger and straightened up.

"When CJ and I got back together, he really wanted to forgive me and just move on. And that's what I wanted. My gift made us so messy in the first place."

Macy's eyes softened. "No, Ter. Barbara made your life messy. That wasn't you. She preyed on you."

"If I hadn't been psychic, I wouldn't have trusted those memories in the first place. It's not normal to wake up with someone else in your head. I decided that it was normal for me. I treated him like crap because I thought I was special somehow. And it almost ruined my relationship with him."

"He took you back. You were able to move on," Claire said, peeking over her shoulder where Noah was playing in his crib.

"He did. Not without costs, though. When we first got together, his emotions were so strong that he kept projecting everything he had been going through

181

since I woke up from my coma. His anger at my rejection, how sad he was, and even sleeping with other women to feel better. I had to... feel him be with other women."

My stomach clenched at the memory. It was CJ at his worst. Using other women and letting them use him to seek a place where I wasn't on his mind even for a few minutes. How he hated himself afterward. How much he wished he hated me.

Both of my sister's faces were pale and Macy looked like she wanted to hug me.

"That's awful," she said finally.

"It was."

"That's not the point of this meeting, is it? Are you calling off the wedding because you feel like you don't want to see him being hurt anymore?" Claire asked, her eyebrows drawing together.

I shook my head. "No. I don't want to call off the wedding. I am just afraid that I won't be able to fully belong to CJ if I also belong to this world."

Saying it out loud terrified me. I have always been the biggest champion of our gifts and everything that came with it. Lately, all it had brought my family was worry and suffering. I didn't think it was because of our gifts, they weren't evil, that much I was sure of. Yet, they did make our lives more complicated.

"What are you saying?" Macy asked.

"I am saying that I want to find a way to will my gift away. I am saying that I want to be normal when I marry CJ. I don't want to bring this part of my life into this new chapter."

The shocked silence was almost tangible. Macy's mouth simply dropped open and Claire looked like she was swinging between being validated and furious with me. She took the longest to come around to her gift and I knew she would be the one who this upset the most.

"Claire, I know. And I'm sorry."

She nodded, trying really hard not to explode.

"You told me that I was hiding from my gift for so long. That we were meant for this and that it was worth all of the sacrifices. That it was worth being able to help people using our birthright. If you are simply tired of it, it's really hard to swallow how hard you were on me for most of my life."

I nodded. "I know. And I am so sorry. I understand what you were feeling. We didn't really have a choice. You had to accept your gift before it tore you apart."

"You don't have to accept yours anymore? You get to reject yours?" she asked, her cheeks red.

"No, that's not what I am saying. What if we did have a choice now? You wouldn't have to deal with ghosts anymore. We would just be normal. Noah could have a normal life," I said, knowing that bringing Noah up was so far over the line that I was losing perspective.

I was just so desperate to rest after everything I had been through in the last three years.

"I can't. I could never just turn this part of myself off. Knowing that spirits like Kadence would lose their advocate, their way to the light. Noah doesn't need normal. He needs love and a parent that believes in themselves. I might have been late to the game, it doesn't matter. This is who I am."

"I'm with Claire," Macy said.

"Thank you," Claire said, forgetting that they were currently not speaking to each other.

"Not only is this who we are, this is our last connection to the legacy that mom left for us. Would she be okay with you just giving yours away?" Macy asked.

I looked at my hands. "I can't live my life for Mom."

Macy's eyes filled with tears. "I get that. On the other hand, what if you have this gift for a reason? You would be willing to give up whatever that was?"

"If it meant that I get to keep CJ forever and choose my path, then yes."

I was sure about this choice. I didn't even know if it was possible at this point. Still, I was sure. I was sure that the peace I felt about being normal meant this was the right path for me.

"Okay," Macy said, the matter settled.

"Okay. I am not going to try to change your mind. But this will be something you do on your own. I don't support this, and I think you will regret it," Claire said, wiping tears off her cheeks.

I expected as much. It that didn't change the fact that I couldn't pursue it until they knew how I was feeling. This didn't feel like it would affect just me. This choice could send a ripple effect through our entire family. I didn't know how this worked. If I willed my gift away, it could be a package deal and steal theirs from them as well. I could be risking our entire legacy.

I had to make that choice for them because I couldn't live like this anymore. My mom believed in the costs of our gifts and proof of them kept cropping up over and over.

I had lost CJ once before because of the supernatural. I didn't want any part of it in our future. I didn't want to have to keep relieving fights with my new husband when he was feeling down, I didn't want to have to relive the ways I let my kids down in their memories, I didn't want the darkest parts of peoples past anymore.

I wanted to just be Terry, no bells and whistles. I wanted a chance to get to choose who I would be as a new wife.

***

"Hey, are you up for a walk-in appointment today?" Lucy asked, poking her head into my office just as I am taking a bite of my salmon wrap.

"New or existing patient?" I asked with my mouth full.

"It's Kelsi."

I swallowed quickly and put my food back in my lunch box. "Please send her in."

Lucy nodded and went back out to the reception area. A few seconds later a very nervous looking Kelsi came in. The cuffs of her long sleeve shirt were wrinkled as if she had had been twisting them in her sweaty palms.

"Hi, Kelsi. It's good to see you," I told her honestly.

Our last session was so stilted. I was half-convinced that she was scared of me and was going to make some excuse to stop seeing me as a patient. I was so relieved to see her in person, even if it was to say goodbye. This was so much better than her trying to spin some story for whatever receptionist she reached.

"It's good to see you too," she said, sitting across from me.

"You're scared?" I asked, seeing how her hands were shaking.

She looked up at me openly. "Not of you. I thought a lot about the whole situation. You are right, you are helping me. When I let you see what happened, I didn't feel anything but comforted because your light is so bright. I trust you."

I let out a loud breath, making Kelsi giggle a little bit.

"You're still nervous?"

Kelsi nodded. "Because I am ready. To see everything and take the next step. I am ready to move on with my life."

"What do you mean to see everything? Did you remember something new?"

Kelsi held out a hand. I smiled and gently took it.

Kelsi had been trying to float out of her body as the punches landed over and over. She knew bones weren't extremely easy to break, she was sure they were cracking every single time the rings on Shannon's fingers made contact with her ribs. It was becoming harder to breathe and her attacker wasn't losing any steam.

She looked up through the blood clumping her eyelashes together and her head rolled around. She wished someone would stand up for her, a partygoer telling Shannon she had enough. Instead, everyone just cheered around her like the mob from the Lottery. It was harder to watch them watching her be beaten down, so she stared straight ahead.

As her eyes focused, she saw Guy still sitting on the bed, his own cell phone out and pointed in her direction. He was smirking at her and filming. Her stomach rolled in tight circles. He had brought her into the room on purpose, he knew what Shannon would do. He had set her up.

As Kelsi let go of my hand, I swam back up to my own surface and consciousness.

"Don't you see? This changes everything," Kelsi said, rubbing her hands together unconsciously.

I sat back, still spinning from the vision.

"What do you mean? Guy obviously knew, what does him filming it change? The videos were taken down."

Kelsi shook her head. "The video that Shannon's friend uploaded is the one that went viral. Guy might still have his. It's like he was collecting them, for him and Shannon. It's disgusting."

I nodded. "You're right. There's a very good chance he still has it. How do we find cause to have his phone searched? Didn't the school question him?"

"They did. He blamed it all on Shannon. She admitted to 'fighting' me and was suspended. She blamed it on drinking too much, and the principal made her apologize to me. When she was suspended, she and her friend reuploaded the video that night. They started a Facebook page telling me to kill myself. The school was done by then. If they did this to me, I can't be the first one. They had it all worked out. No one at the party was surprised or tried to step in. She's done it before, and they didn't want to be in her warpath."

I stilled as her words sunk in. "There are other victims."

Kelsi sat back, exhausted. "If we find them and band together, we can stop them. We can all get justice."

My eyes teared up a little bit. This strong girl in front of me was so far from the terrified waif that first came into my office angry and mad at the world. She was ready for justice and wanted to help others even if it meant being brave all by herself.

Guy and Shannon had no idea what was coming for them.

***

Our alarm was something that was second nature to me now, Macy seemed to have forgotten how fickle the new system was. The front door swung open, and the beeping brought me up from my bedroom.

She was by the front door, punching in random numbers and cursing under her breath.

"Mac, stop! Too many wrong answers alert the cops," I told her, gently pushing her hand away and showing her the new code.

"I'm sorry. I panicked," she said.

She was sweaty like she had run all the way here and her little belly was heaving.

"Do you need some water?" I asked, trying not to stare at her.

Macy nodded. "Yeah. I'll get it."

I followed her into the kitchen and watched her drink two full glasses before settling herself in at the kitchen table.

"Better?"

"Yes, sorry for the craziness. I just had a thought, and I had to come straight here."

I slid into a chair across from her. "A thought about what?"

Macy took a deep breath. "Not just a thought. A revelation. My roommate was talking about how a girl from her college just gave a baby away for adoption. About how nice the open adoption was, she was able to live her life but still see her child every once in a while, and be in their life."

I nodded, my stomach sinking slightly.

"And it just hit me. I don't want that."

"You want a… closed adoption?" I asked weakly.

"No, Ter. I want my baby. I think about them growing quietly inside of me and think about only being able to see them a few times a year, and I can't breathe. I have never loved anyone as much as I love them. I want to be their mom, full time, every single day for the rest of my life."

My mouth dropped open, and I stared at her. She began nodding like I had argued with her.

"I know, I know. It's going to be hard. So much harder than I can even imagine or try to prepare for. I am ready to grow up. I want this. I re-enrolled for a small business program at the community college and will be getting financial aid. I also talked to Roasted and Toasted about my new situation, I was super honest about being pregnant and needing at least six weeks off. I have…"

I stopped her by wrapping her in my arms. "You're not doing this alone. Don't get me wrong, I am so proud of you for stepping up. You're not by yourself, you don't have to do this all on your own."

She leaned back so that she could look at me. "No, Ter. You don't get it. Being alone is all I have ever been afraid of. But when I think about needing to be alone to do this, it's worth it. It's so fucking worth it."

I wiped the tears off her cheek, ignoring my own.

"You're going to be a mom?"

She smiled back at me. "I'm going to be a mom."

I hugged her until she pushed me gently away.

"I love you, and I know this is huge. However, I might have speed-walked here and am starving."

"Okay, okay. What do you want me to make you?"

"I got it," she said, making herself at home and finding a deep skillet.

I watched her, cooking a meal all on her own in this house for the very first time. I knew that our family had a lot of healing and growing up to do. I also knew that we would make it. Our broken pieces might not make the same picture that they once did, it didn't mean it wouldn't be an incredible picture.

"Bon Appetit," she said, setting a plate of fried potatoes with cottage cheese on top in front of me.

My eyes widened. What kind of weird pregnancy crap was this? This was our celebration dinner?

Macy dug into it with such pleasure on her face all I could do was laugh. I took a bite and grinned at her.

"Bon Appetit," I answered.

***

Lunch with Lucy was becoming one of my favorite parts of the week. When I thought about holding her at arm's length for so long, I was ashamed. She was great and would have accepted me from the moment we met. It made me regret all of those lunches that I spent alone in my office when we could have been laughing together this whole time.

"I think you'll come around. Keep this, just in case," Lucy said, sliding her travel brochure for Thunder Down Under into my purse.

I laughed. "Luc, I have so much more on my mind than a bachelorette party right now."

She smiled, looking a little sad.

"How is it going with Kelsi? She's been coming in three times a week."

"She's actually doing great. Still, the law isn't on her side right now. We have a lot of work to do."

"What do you mean?"

"Well, the only evidence we have right now is the possibility of Guy still being in possession of the video of Shannon beating Kelsi. We talked with a lawyer, and it turns out that filming someone without their permission isn't illegal."

"What? How is that possible? Even if that video is showing someone hurting someone else?" Lucy said, her fork frozen in front of her mouth.

"I know, I was shocked too. I guess in Washington, the law applies more to child pornography situations. The law hasn't caught up with this new trend yet."

"So, what are her options?"

"She can file a civil suit against Guy and Shannon. I am not sure if it's going to be for personal damages yet or if we have the cause for assault yet. Also, this is going to be a lot more personal. A bigger case would include the school. More victims are more likely to come forward if we have more of a security net behind us. This could come down to just Kelsi against the two of them."

Lucy shook her head. "Do you think she's ready for that?"

I shrugged but had to smile. "I hope so. She's stronger than she knows."

Claire January 2018

I have never been this nervous for another person to read one of my books. I guess it made sense because this is unlike anything I have ever attempted before. Ash sat in one of the sunroom wicker chairs, her legs draped over one of the arms while she read the manuscript.

After a few minutes, she smiled. "It's a children's book about Noah?"

I nodded. "Is it terrible? I never considered adolescent literature before. I write horror, it might be received strangely. Maybe I'll choose a pen name if it's good enough to print?"

Ash sat it on the wicker table in front of us. "It's good enough. His dreams let him travel to magical places that help him change the future. That's amazing. He is going to love it."

I deflated with the weight of my relief. "Oh, thank god. I loved writing it so much. My books have been so hard to get out recently. Writing horror is so hard when it feels like I have been living a scary movie. When I started this, I was terrified because it was so easy to write it might be crap."

"No, I promise. It's great. I can't believe you have had this inside of you all this time. Maybe this is what you are supposed to be writing."

I raised an eyebrow at her. "Are you saying my novel isn't great right now?"

She laughed. "You know it's not. I get that it's a case that is touchy and hard to write about. You need to decide whether or not you are writing from Kadence's perspective or writing a true-crime drama. You keep changing your point of view, and it's giving me whiplash."

I smiled, leave it to Ash to always give me her thoughts without trying to sugar coat them. It was exactly why I loved her so much and why she was always the first person to read my books in progress.

"I know, I know. I'll figure it out."

"In the meantime, what are you thinking for illustrations?" Ash asked.

I picked up the manuscript. "I'm picturing something with watercolor and a lot of glitter and magic. Maybe my agent will commission someone?"

She leaned forward, grinning.

"Or, you could take a chance on your best friend."

"What?" I said, giggling a little bit.

Ash had loved art growing up and had actually gotten a degree in fine art. She was usually interested more in the human form and realism. She painted and sculpted for the most part. It was hard to find jobs using her degree in a small city, so she was currently working with a marketing firm.

"I read this, and I can see the pictures in my head already. Delicate watercolor with pen outlines that are slightly sketching. Bright colors and pastel backgrounds with glitter and holographic edges that sparkle when you turn the page."

My arms broke out in goosebumps. It was everything I could have hoped for.

"That would be pretty much perfect. Could you take some time off from work? It would be a big project once it's in production."

She yelped and threw herself into my arms.

"Can you imagine? Publishing a book together? It's the dream."

I laughed and hugged her back.

To celebrate, we woke Noah up from his nap ten minutes early and walked down to Sally's for ice cream. Sally's was pretty iconic for us. Its where we always celebrated. Terry and CJ began our tradition simply because it was the only ice cream place that was within walking distance to our house. However, we quickly found out that it was a town favorite because it was the best.

It was a drive-up stand with no inside seating and instead you had your pick of three picnic tables. If they were full there was a park across the street. They offered everything from tacos to ice cream sundaes. Hands down, the best thing on the menu was the caramel shake. It was the taste of everything good thing that had ever happened to me. I celebrated A's with them, becoming engaged, and I ate them with olives when I was pregnant. I wanted Noah to share a love of ice cream with me because it was the taste of my childhood.

"Is there anything better than Sally's caramel shake? I'm 99% sure there is cocaine in the ice cream base."

I took a huge bite of my mint chocolate chip sundae and smiled at Noah seeming to wrestle with his kid's ice cream cone. Sally's ice cream was so rich that it melted pretty quickly. He licked his wrist where it was dripping instead of the actual cone.

"God, I hope not. Noah's barely old enough for ice cream, I was going to wait a few years before introducing him to coke."

Ash laughed.

"What else is new with you? I feel like we haven't hung out in forever," I told Ash.

"I know. I just finished a big project at work, so I am back to a more laid-back schedule. It was a very boring ad campaign for laundry detergent. I am looking forward to something more creative. Nothing else is really going on. I do have some kind of non-news."

Ash looked nervous, so I immediately know it's about Ben. I really want to support her and be the person she can talk about this relationship too, at the same time, it's so hard to know when they are serious again when they break up every three months. He has put her through so much and has never been my favorite person.

But she is my best friend and loves him.

"I think Ben might be planning to propose to me."

"What?" I asked, almost dropping my ice cream.

Ben's idea of commitment usually revolves around planning where to go to dinner that weekend.

"I know! It's crazy. Things have been so easy between us lately. And the other night his tablet was charging, and he kept getting notifications from a jeweler."

"Do you want him to propose?" I asked, unsure of how to react.

Ash blushed. "Of course. All I have ever wanted was for him to grow up and be the man I know he can be. We have been together for so long; I don't want it to have been a waste."

I want to feel hope in her excitement and paste a smile on my face, asking her questions about her dream fictional wedding. She wanted all of this without giving him her heart. I know that she didn't even tell him about her pregnancy scare a couple of months ago.

How can you plan a life with someone you can't trust with your fear? How can he make her happy if he can't comfort her? How can she trust him with her entire future if she doesn't trust him when it counts?

***

Lenore had located Stan, and where he was hanging out made sense; he had never left the police station. Getting into an empty conference room was

195

as easy as telling a detective that I had wanted to ask some questions about a closed case for a book I was writing. I didn't think the young man was looking forward to having to tell me to go away, so we didn't have to worry about him coming in immediately. I also knew that our time was limited when dealing with spirit communication.

"How does he know that we are waiting for him?" I whispered to Lenore.

I was projecting her tentatively. I had come into the station alone and didn't want to scare whoever came in next. Before she could answer me, the door swung open, and a man in his fifties swaggered into the room without looking at us.

"How can I help you?" he said, finally making eye contact with me.

Without having to be told I know that this is Stan. The resemblance between him and Emily is unmistakable.

"My name is Claire Shaw. I had some questions about a closed case for a book I am writing," I said, giving him the same line.

He nodded. "I don't know how much I can help you out. What case were you interested in?"

"The murders of Emily Simmon and Kadence Morton. I understand that Emily was your niece."

Color came into his cheeks, and it was clear that he was trying to control his reaction.

"She was. And what happened was a terrible tragedy. What can I do for you?"

"Who do you think killed them?" I asked, trying to seem innocent.

"We believe that it was a drifter that has since moved on. There wasn't enough evidence to keep the case open."

"And you are satisfied with that? You have been on the force for a long time. You aren't able to figure who killed your only niece?"

He slapped his hands on the table, startling me. I had to remind myself that he was already dead. He couldn't hurt me.

"That's enough, miss. The case is closed. It was a terrible accident. Enough people have died over this already."

My mouth dropped open as he processed his error. Stan slowly held up his hands and turned them slightly.

"How…"

He looked up and stared hard at Lenore. She gave him a firm nod.

"How?" Stan asked in a strangled voice.

"Your own gun," she said as gently as possible.

Stan started to shake his head, fading with each shake. He finally closed his eyes, and we were alone in the room again.

I turned to Lenore. "It was definitely a cover-up. He knows who it was. Which means it could not have been a drifter or a stranger. The girls knew this person. Stan knew this person, well enough to risk his entire career to cover up for them."

Lenore agreed. "I think it's time to talk to meet Emily's father."

***

It has been a long time since I was afraid of this house. When I first moved back in, we were living with so many shadow figures that locking up at night felt like being in a Wes Craven scene. Since our protection warding had been cast, it was pleasantly… normal.

I locked the front door and glanced out of the windows looking out into our neighborhood. It was normal. Everything that Terry wanted.

A figure standing in the window across the street from us caught my eye just as I was about to let the curtain fall back. From the way she flickered in and out, I knew she was a spirit. From the way she held her hands against her bleeding stomach, I knew she was stuck in her death state. She locked eyes with me and pressed her bloody hands against the glass, mouthing words I couldn't hear this far way.

When I first got my gift, I thought I needed to help every single spirit that I came into contact with. Working with Lenore taught me that not all spirits are ready to move on. Some are simply fragments of souls and are not intelligent enough to even understand that they are still here. Seeing people in pain and reliving their death is horrible, I have to let the right spirits in so that I can keep myself safe. It was easy for shadow figures to pretend to be spirits in order to gain your trust.

I shuddered and shut the curtains. I was not about to invite a spirit that broken into our home.

As I headed into the room I shared with Noah, I thought more about what Terry had proposed to us. I couldn't believe she wanted to let go of the gift that had been the most important thing to her for most of her life. I understood that she had been through hell, I also knew that CJ loved her just the way she was.

Maybe this wasn't just about CJ. Maybe she loved herself less when she was hurt because of the gift she fought so hard to protect. Maybe she wasn't the same person she was before the accident.

Would it really be better to be normal? I had thought I was normal for most of my life and I could attest to the fact that you didn't feel more 'found' just because you weren't psychic. The world and the universe could still flip you off just because.

If she thought her cost was someday losing CJ, then I had to disagree. Holden was gone and it had nothing to do with our gifts. I would have lost Holden even if I never saw a ghost. This gift made it easier to hold onto him rather than not having the choice to say goodbye.

***

"Are you sure this is… safe?" Kadence asked, her hands fluttering around her sides like butterflies.

Kadence had been with us for months now and had all but refused to talk about why she was there and what we needed to do to move her on. Counseling was helping a little bit, yet, she resisted Terry's questions altogether once that night came up.

Emily had been hanging around more often and I had a feeling she was building up to something. I needed to know what happened to her, something about her murder was keeping her here and allowing Emily to still stay attached to her.

"Kade, sweetheart. You are already a spirit. It's as safe as it possibly can be. It will be scary. I am not going to try to lie to you about that. Reliving that night will be very hard. But, you will not be alone."

She held out a hand to me and took a deep breath. I took it and nodded to Terry and Lenore, who were sitting in a circle with us. I was used to doing this with Macy and didn't want to keep pushing her away. It was more than just my reservations though, she needed to focus on her pregnancy right now.

And I was still having a hard time being the same room as her.

"Okay, I am going to project the vision as gently as possible. I am warning you though, you will feel it as if it's one of your visions. Try to focus on Kadence

199

and not react on your own, it might break the connection," I told Terry, trying to prepare her.

Terry nodded and held my other hand. Before anyone could change their mind, I dove into that night.

"I thought we were friends again. Why are you still angry at me?" Kadence asked, already wanting to cry.

Emily had stormed out of the clubhouse and into the woods behind her house.

"You lied! Did you know that he could go to jail? I would never see him again and it would be all your fault."

"It wasn't a lie! You got the letters too. Why would I lie? I don't want to hurt him or you. I don't want him to hurt me either."

Emily turned to her now, her eyes flashing.

"He would never. You are nothing. Why would he want you?"

Kadence was freely crying now. "I don't know. I'm just a kid."

Emily's anger flickered for just a moment and it looked like she was weighing her options. It only lasted a moment because she had made up her mind.

"I loved you, Kadence. I just can't let you ruin my family."

Emily pushed her best friend into the crumbling leaves. Kadence's mouth dropped open in shock and she stared up at her. She thought about running, but it was too late. Emily jumped onto her chest and began hitting her. Kadence's survival instincts kicked in, and she used her hips to try to throw Emily off. Emily screamed and grabbed onto her hair, pulling out a chunk.

Kadence screamed in agony and closed her eyes. How could this be her best friend? How could her friend be doing this?

"I'm sorry," Emily said, her voice sounding flat and dead.

She picked up a huge rock. She picked it out from the riverbed the day before and carried it over for this exact purpose. She held it over her head and then brought it down with all the force and fury she could manage. And Kadence thought no more.

Kadence pulled her hand out from mine and launched herself into my lap, bawling. I rubbed her back and fought back my own bile. This wasn't the first murder I had post-witnessed. But seeing a child do that to another child was more than I could handle. I was nauseated and sick in my heart.

Everything this poor little girl had to go through. Lenore and Terry were pale. Terry panted to keep from throwing up.

"You did good, you were so brave," I told Kadence, kissing the top of her head.

"Did you see anything that will help?" she asked, her eyes red and still hopeful.

I nodded. After putting her down for a nap with Noah, I rejoined Terry and Lenore in the living room.

"What did you see?" Terry asked, looking nervous to be asking.

"Her hair. I read the police reports, they are public now that the case is closed. That detail was kept out of the reports. Why? It would have been clear that something happened, she would have had a huge bloody bald spot. Her head… I can see them being able to say she tripped and fractured her head that way. How do you explain away a missing chunk of hair?"

Terry nodded. "They kept it out on purpose."

"Why? Who were they protecting?"

"And where is the hair? The ring was one thing, this is technically a body part. If this is hidden somewhere it might be what is keeping Kadence here. Someone else could have hidden Emily's trophy in an attempt to protect her."

"Or protect themselves. Emily was killed that night too."

I took a deep breath. "I think the next step is talking to Kadence's parents. Emily's mother is refusing my calls. We have a detail only they would know. It might be enough to convince them that I have contact with her."

Terry agreed, and Lenore looked at me sadly.

"That poor little girl. Is she ready to talk to her parents?"

I shook my head. "Not even close. I know how she died, she still isn't fully sharing what happened between her and Emily to bring them to that night. There is something she's ashamed about and won't tell me yet. I don't know if her parents know yet. Getting her justice means bringing all the secrets up, even ones that might hurt Kadence."

"It's what we have to do though if someone was able to victimize Kadence and then kill Emily, there's a good chance he has found a new favorite. He might have a new victim in mind."

"Let's hope he's still shopping and hasn't decided to pull the trigger yet," I tell them.

***

"What are you reading?" Lenore asked, pushing the door open gently.

I was sprawled out on the bed and Noah was asleep next to me, curled into my side. I smiled at her and patted the bed next to us.

"Some Danielle Steele of my mom's. I kept a bunch of her books. Our tastes were definitely not the same, but it makes me feel close to her."

Lenore smiled. "I loved Danielle Steele. My daughter and I used to read them together."

"Were you close?" I asked.

I loved Lenore's stories. I always expected some demure grandmotherly perspective, instead I usually received tales about the time she and her husband put plastic down while moving and slid around on the floor with lubricant.

"We tried to be. My daughter was very headstrong. Some children you are able to help mold, she was just her own person. She made her own choices, good and bad. It was hard. We were not always friends. Yet, we loved each other fiercely."

I patted her hand. "Love is weird like that."

She nodded. "It is. And it was alright because she gave me three beautiful granddaughters."

"Did you get to spend a lot of time with them?"

"Sometimes entire summers. My daughter worked a lot, and I was happy to help out. They were my world. The youngest was silly and had the biggest heart, my middle grandchild was my soul reincarnate, and we could talk about everything under the sun, and the oldest was the most giving person I have ever had the blessing to know."

I loved the look on her face when she talked about her girls, it gave me an insight into who she was when she walked the earth. I could trust her, and she knew the right thing to do because she had loved so very hard and had been loved in return.

The universe could be broken, and it never felt like you were always given all the time you needed to finish what you started in this world. However, God always put the pieces back together in the exact pattern they were supposed to be in from the beginning. People could say that they couldn't see his plan, but spirit guides were something he got perfectly right.

***

Footsteps pounding the stairs is never a good thing. As they approached my door, I stood up, expecting the worst. Noah somehow fell outside while playing with Terry and cracked his skull. We needed to rush to the emergency room. Terry pushed the door open, out of breath.

"We need to go to the hospital."

I pulled Noah from her arms, frantically searching his body for blood. He looked up at me and laughed.

"Why? What happened?"

She looked at the terror on my face and shook her head. Terry was obviously freaking out, but it had nothing to do with her nephew.

"No, Noah is fine. Macy called me. Something is wrong. They are inducing her right now."

Chapter 9
Terry February 2018

Macy was about six weeks away from her due date, giving this baby a February birthday by just one day. Macy had asked me to be in the room and was horrified when they told her they didn't have to wait for me. They needed to start the surgery immediately. I was desperate to be with her and comfort her, it didn't matter. The doctor was resolute in his decision. Instead of holding her hand, Claire and I were camped out in the waiting room. Claire was pacing and giving me a headache.

A young man with a grown-out buzz cut and a brand new five o clock shadow kept looking over at us. After the fifth aggressive glance, I stared back at him.

"Are you Terry?" he asked timidly.

I nodded, the pieces falling into place. Claire looked over at him, and reluctantly sat back down.

"Alex?" I asked.

He nodded, looking like he was going to throw up.

"Why don't you come sit with us," I said, moving my purse from the chair next to me.

He sat next to me and I could see that he was shaking from the tips of his ears down to his feet. His sneakers danced under his chair. Macy had finally gotten ahold of Alex last week. I didn't know the exact details of the conversation. He must have been very humble or very naive to forgive her so quickly. We were supposed to go out to lunch on Friday so that he could meet us for the first time.

"I'm guessing that this is your first time impregnating someone," Claire said, staring at him.

He laughed, shocking, and impressing me.

"Yes, ma'am."

She suppressed a smile.

"Well, good."

"Alex Parker?" a young doctor said, pulling off a crepe surgical cap.

Alex nodded, half standing.

"Macy is ready for visitors."

He smiled, looking horrified and elated. Then he looked at us.

"These are her sisters. They can go in first."

I squeezed his hand. "Thank you."

He looked so fresh-faced and this had obviously rocked his world, but he did seem to know Macy already. He had every right to be the first person in the room but knew that this would be exactly what she wanted. I pulled Claire to her feet and followed the doctor through a set of double doors to the patient rooms.

"The surgery went well."

"What happened?" I asked, still so scared and confused.

"Her placenta stopped providing oxygen to the baby. We had to do a C section when her body didn't respond to the Pitocin. We had a limited window and needed to get the baby out as soon as possible. She did great. They are both great."

She pushed open a door and gestured for us to go inside.

Macy looked impossibly small, holding an impossible small bundle in her arms. There were dark circles under her eyes, but her smile was brilliant.

"I had a baby," she whispered to me.

I smiled. "I see that."

I sat on the edge of her bed, looking into the small face of her child. My baby sisters' baby.

"Her name is Carla."

Goosebumps broke out over my arms. We hadn't even found out what the sex of Macy's child was yet. She wasn't sure she wanted to know and kept changing her mind. My mind was reeling, and I was unsteady on my feet. Not just a little girl, but a Shaw girl. Carla, after our grandmother. My mom would have loved that. What a legacy this girl had in front of her. It was perfect and jinxing all rolled into one.

I brushed her small golden eyelashes and marveled at her small, rosebud mouth.

"Macy is going to need a lot of help in the next six weeks. She is not only learning to be a mom; she is recovering from major abdominal surgery. Will she have support after leaving the hospital?" the doctor asked, picking up a file and handing it to me.

"Of course. She will be coming home," Claire said from behind me.

Macy looked up, shocked.

It had been an awful couple of months of them walking on eggshells and blaming each other. As I watched, I was enveloped in what was passing between them. Holden had loved Claire; he had also loved Macy. He hadn't died because of her. He had died for her. There was a difference.

Holden would have hated for them to fall apart because he was there for his sister. He loved our family, he was part of our family. He would have died for each and every one of us, and we would have done the same for him. It was disrespectful to his memory to treat his sacrifice as a slight. Claire finally understood.

This is where we were supposed to be. We didn't have to understand God's plan or agree with it. We had to take the bitterness with the blessings, and this little girl was a blessing in the biggest way. If Holden hadn't protected Macy, neither one of them would be here right now.

"We will take care of her. We will take care of each other," Claire said, breaking down and making her way over to the bed.

She wrapped Macy into her arms as best as she could, one arm under her new niece. I hugged the three of them, and we cried ourselves out, forgiving and find our way back to each other. I'm sorry turned to I love yous and promises to make the future different, stronger than we were before.

Sometimes we had to fall apart to learn how much we really needed each other in the first place. I didn't know where Alex was going to fit into our lives or how hard the road ahead would be for Macy. The only thing I did know was that no matter what came next, we wouldn't be facing it alone.

When we finally parted Macy wiped her face and smiled down at her daughter, who was struggling to open her eyes.

"Baby Carla, meet your aunts Terry and Claire. This is your family."

***

I wish I could be celebrating with Macy right now. However, she had to stay in the hospital for at least three days, and baby Carla was to be a patient in the NICU until her weight satisfied the pediatrician.

Claire and I were anxious to have her home. Our little sister felt the complete opposite. I think Macy appreciated the short safety net while she healed. Having your meals brought to you after having your stomach cut open was a definite perk. Regardless, as soon as I told Lucy the news, she insisted we go out and celebrate me becoming an aunt again.

Having friends had been a strange experience for the most part. It really felt like God sent her to me right when I needed her the most. Someone who wasn't a part of our family accepting me so fully was irreplaceable. I finally understood why Claire needed Ash so badly. My sisters and I needed each other, but we also needed at least one person who didn't live this craziness every single day.

"To Macy, and to Carla," Lucy said, clinking her Sex on the Beach with my vodka cranberry.

"To new chapters," I finished, taking a small sip and smiling.

"Where is she going to stay? Is her room big enough for her and a baby?" Lucy asked.

I shook my head. "No, her bedroom is the smallest downstairs. I have the largest aside from my mother's room so I will be switching with her. Claire offered and I said no. I know that she still sleeps in there and it's the only place that she can write. I don't think she needs to say goodbye to it yet."

"You're taking the smallest room? Are you planning on moving out? I thought that staying there was the plan. When I first met you, you were adamant about raising your kids in the home you grew up in."

I shrugged, her words hitting me strongly. It had been the plan for as long as I could remember. I had always dreamed of bringing my children to that house and raising my family there. Yet, so much had changed. I had changed.

She was right, the room was way too small for us. In truth, my childhood bedroom had been too small for us. I loved sharing my space and seeing the mishmash of our tastes so close together. At the same time, it was time I admitted that things had changed for me. I kept catching myself thinking of what part of Spokane was would raise our family in and wanting to ask him what color he would paint his dream kitchen. Our lives were becoming so much bigger than just one bedroom could hold, and the house I grew up in didn't belong to just us.

"I don't know. I'm going to be married. I love my sisters and always sort of pictured us staying together forever. I get that's not reality though. Being with CJ has shown me that spreading your wings and making your own way doesn't have to be wrong and scary. I think I resisted so long because I always knew that my sisters would be able to and I didn't want to be left behind. It doesn't feel like that now. It feels exciting. I think of getting a tiny apartment with CJ, and I can't stop smiling."

She grinned at me, she had met CJ recently and was already falling for him the way my sisters had. He had a way of being self-deprecating and also making everyone in the room feel like the most important person in the conversation. He really listened to what you were saying and remembered it.

"And Macy and Claire wouldn't mind staying together?"

"I don't think Macy will stay forever. After everything she has been through, I think that someday having her own place will be really important to her. It took her a long time to grow up, and she knows that she needs to force herself to keep growing. I kind of think this is where Claire will stay forever. She is the only one who might be able to make that house her own while still somehow keeping it our home forever."

The door of the restaurant was pushed open, and our waitress went to greet the newcomers. I froze as I recognized one of the two women coming in. It was Christina, CJ's ex-girlfriend.

Last year I had come back to myself and found that CJ was trying to move on without me. I followed him one night, wanting to talk to him in private away from his friends. He ended up being on a date. I watched him talk to her the way he had talked to me, watched him kiss her goodnight. This was her.

For months after we got back together, I kept catching visions of him being with her and feeling all of that newness that he craved while still drowning in guilt because she wasn't me. It didn't make having to see them make love any easier, it was what I felt like I deserved at that point because I had put him through so much.

Eventually, he forgave himself, forgave me, we moved on, and the visions stopped. I didn't have to keep seeing them to remember them. Some things will be burned in my mind forever. I couldn't be upset with him for the choices he made while we weren't together, it was still hard to have to imagine it over and over.

"What's wrong?" Lucy asked, turning and looking at the women.

My mouth dropped open; I had no idea where to start.

She watched compassion play across my face and held her hand out to me.

"If you can't tell me, show me," she said simply.

I looked at her with tears in my eyes. I nodded and took her hand, giving her the experience and accidentally slipping in so much more. I loved CJ so much that it physically hurt. It was so scary because I had experienced what it was like to lose him. If it hurt the first time, how much more would it hurt if it happened after we had loved like this?

He was always going to have a complicated life because he loved me. Sometimes it made me feel like he deserved better. Deserved someone like Christina.

Lucy took her hand back, bringing me back to reality.

"No more. It happened. You lost yourself. It happens after a big tragedy. Yes, your situation might have been a little unorthodox."

"I was possessed. I slapped him, told him he didn't matter to me and slept with someone who tried to kill me."

"Yeah, I know. Unorthodox."

I laughed, and she smiled. Mission accomplished.

"He forgave you because he couldn't live without you. He wanted to forgive you because he understood what no one else could have. It wasn't you. You fought like hell to make it back to him. His love woke you up from your coma, and it called you back home last year. He has always been your beacon of light."

I smiled at her. "That doesn't make it easier."

"Screw easy. Easy is boring. You guys are meant to be together. Anyone can see it, you guys are disgusting. Maybe it had to be really hard so that what you have could become unbreakable."

I looked down at my hands, forcing myself to really feel her words and forgive myself for the millionth time. I wanted so badly for it to be true, for us to be unbreakable.

"To new chapters," Lucy said, echoing my earlier sentiment.

I brought my eyes back up to her and saw the challenge in her eyes. I took a deep breath, smiled, and clinked our glasses together.

***

CJ and I always had a tradition on Valentine's Day. In elementary school, we would sit in my room and eat all of the candy from our class parties and read our Valentines out loud. In Middle and High school, we were always single and would pick up a pizza on the way home from school and watch Princess Bride with some brownie batter ice cream.

CJ always joked that it was the singles club; it was secretly a date I looked forward to.

If CJ was single and I was single it was kind of like we were each other's Valentines. And then, there came the very first year that we were actually a couple, actually belonged to each other on this holiday. We spent the entire day in bed.

We wouldn't be spending this year wrapped up in each other, but it was the day Macy came home from the hospital, so it would be memorable anyways.

"Oh, its… different," Macy said, holding Carla in her carrier and looking around the living room.

I laughed and looked around. After Macy came back, Claire kind of had a mental breakdown. I caught her painting the downstairs in the middle of the night a weird lime green color that she found in the garage. Through her tears, she told me that she thought I would be okay with it because green was my favorite. I was able to get her to stop painting, but we had yet to cover up the wall massacre. I almost forgot that it was there.

"We can pick a new color together," I told her, squeezing her shoulder and leading her downstairs.

As I pushed open the door to my old bedroom, I expected Macy to be surprised by the new bed, the crib she picked out with her best friend Kate, and the new carpeting. I had spent the three days that she was in the hospital turning this into a nursery worthy of baby Carla. Light pink walls with a glittery gold border splitting the wall in half. Stuffed animals and photos of her family. I couldn't wait to show her. Instead, we were both surprised by the number of faces smiling back at us.

"Surprise!" CJ said in a whisper-yell, looking apologetic and excited.

Claire was here with Noah. She was also projecting our mother and Holden to welcome Macy home.

"Mom," Macy breathed, rushing forward.

She seemed happy, so I tried to let it go for the moment.

"Let me see," my mom said, tears in her eyes.

Macy carefully put the carrier on the bed and coaxed her sleeping baby out of it.

"Carla," my mom said, running her fingers along with her already curly hairline.

"Beautiful," Holden says from behind her.

Macy closed her eyes while Holden wrapped both of them in his arms, whispering to Mac. I didn't hear it all, but I did hear worth it wrapped up in his tearful words. Mac nodded and laid her head on his shoulder, accepting that her child was here because he was not. Loving him for what he did for her.

Claire looked on, looking happy, and content. To an outsider, this would be a healing reunion, the beginning of a new chapter. But I was watching the way that Noah stared at his dad and grandma in confusion. I was watching the way he wanted his dad to snuggle him in the same way and be able to hold him the way his mother did.

There was so much love here, and I wanted my mom. I wanted to go dress shopping with her and talk about cake flavors for my wedding with her. I wanted to see her sitting in the front row when I said my vows. I wanted my brother to stand next to my future husband. I wanted just one more peppermint mocha with the person who had become such a good friend.

I looked at my nephew. I saw the sadness brewing in his heart and mine completely broke. There was so much love here mixed with so much sadness. We couldn't keep doing this. We had to move on.

214

"I'm going to take out the trash," CJ said, squeezing my shoulder and heading outside.

With the kids both in bed and my sisters all cried out, I was exhausted. I wanted to talk to Claire about projecting and continuing to hold onto our mom and Holden and couldn't deal with it tonight. I had nothing left inside of me to give. It had been such a long couple of months.

As CJ's trash run stretched out, I began to get worried and got a flashlight. I headed out into the back yard and saw that the shed light was on.

"CJ?" I called out, trying not to yell and scare him.

Music was coming from the shed door, which was bizarre since it only held old shovels and bags of soil. I pushed the door open and gasped.

All of the clutter that had filled the shed since my parents divorced was nowhere to be seen. Twinkly lights were stapled to the wooden walls along with the ceiling and the couch from CJ's apartment was pushed against one wall. On the other wall was a small entertainment center and a TV. In the center of the room was a coffee table piled with snacks. CJ sat on the couch, smiling at me.

"What is all of this?" I squealed, walking over to him in a daze.

"I knew that we weren't going out tonight, I still wanted you to have a real Valentine's Day," CJ said, leaning forward to press play on the remote.

Princess Bride had been queued up and began to play.

I smiled at him. "Wow, babe."

"Pretty good, right?" he said, clearly impressed with himself.

I nodded. "Oh yeah."

"That's not all. I have chocolate 'lovers kisses,' sandwiches, and chips from Jimmy Johns."

My current favorite lunch place. He always knew exactly what my stomach needed.

"I love you. Do you know how much I freaking love you?" I asked him.

He wiggled his eyebrows. "I don't know. You might have to show me."

I wiggled my eyebrows back. "As you wish."

<u>Claire February 2018</u>

"It's good that you are starting this now. I had the three of you so close in age that I was drowning in photos. I always wanted to have these beautiful albums for each of you. I only got as far as organizing them into big boxes," my mom told me, flipping through snapshots of Noah on his first hayride.

"We love those boxes. Every time I look through them, I feel like I find something new. Something I forgot. It always feels like a little message from you."

As I searched for my favorite photo of Noah sleeping for his naptime scrapbook page, one fell out of the pile and onto my lap. It was Noah, and Holden passed out on the couch. Noah's hand was tucked under Holden's cheek as he cuddled his dad's neck and Holden's arm was wrapped around him even in his sleep.

I wiped a tear off my cheek.

My mom leaned over to see and gave me a sad smile.

"I wish I could say that missing him would get easier."

"It's just not fair. He was such a good dad, and it's not fair that we only got him for such a short time. Why couldn't I see him in high school? If we had dated through college, we might have gotten married sooner, we might have had Noah sooner. I could have loved him for longer."

My mom shook her head. "That's not how it works, sweetie. If you had fallen in love sooner, then you would have been given a different child. Souls come to you at very specific intervals in time. You would have had children; it just would not have been Noah. Your time together was predetermined, it was carefully planned out. I am so sorry that it wasn't as long as others will have."

I nodded. When I thought about not getting to love Noah, I felt guilty for wanting Holden. Becoming parents together was one of the things that made us, us. Loving Noah with Holden was worth all of the heartbreak I had to endure. It didn't make surviving afterward any easier.

"I think he would have been such a good dad forever. Not just a baby dad, you know? I think he would have been a baseball coach, the kind of dad that stayed up late building Lego sets with you and reading your math book so that he understood your homework. He was so damn good. And still seeing him and being able to see part of it and taste a little bit of it is unbearable."

My mom patted my hand. "The seeing him part is probably not helping. I don't say that to hurt you. I know you feel like saying goodbye is impossible, it's not. While he is still here, you are never going to be able to let go of what might have been."

"It's not just me, Mom. I want Noah to remember him. He was the best. He deserves to be remembered. I want Noah to love him like I do."

"He will, honey. What you are doing isn't the right way. This has to be the way that he remembers him," she gestured to the photo album in my lap.

"It's not fair," I said, wiping more angry tears off of my cheeks and chin.

"No, it's not fair. And it's not fair to Noah either. If you keep Holden here, when he does eventually move on it will be even harder for Noah to understand. It's already confusing him."

I nodded. I knew, I had seen the way he looked at him and struggled with what was happening.

"Sweetheart, you have to let him go."

218

I agreed with her while everything inside of me screamed that it wasn't time. It couldn't possibly be time. I wasn't done loving him.

***

Being back in the forest that she died in wasn't helping Kadence feel safe or ready to move on. I had only seen this place in a vision, and I still had goosebumps and wanted to look over my shoulder.

"It wasn't always scary," Kadence told me, slipping her hand into mine.

"No?" Terry asked, looking around, unsure.

"No," Kadence smiled. "We used to have tea parties out here. We used a stump as a table and would make little cakes out of mud and pine needles. It smelled good. I always got so dirty though, and my mom didn't like it."

"Did you ever bring your mom here? She might have understood," I told her.

She shook her head. "No. And when I wanted to stop being friends with Emily, she was so confused. I was afraid to talk about it, and I think she didn't want to know."

"Your mom could see that you were scared?"

"My mom had found one of the letters, and it made her so mad. Daddy didn't really understand what it was. I told her that Emily and I wrote them. I don't know why I lied."

I rubbed her back. I understood. Lying was sometimes easier than admitting what was happening. As much as you know that what is happening isn't your fault, it's impossible to see outside of the guilt and shame. Telling her mom would have made it real. Having to tell meant having to face what she went through.

"What did the letter say?" Terry asked, slowing as she sensed we were close to the murder site.

219

"It said that I was beautiful and perfect. It was one of the nice ones. She didn't find the other ones," Kadence said, squeezing my hand and stopping when we came upon a big rock.

"What other ones?" I asked.

"The ones about wanting me to take off my clothes at the playhouse or telling me they wanted to see inside of me," Kadence said, in a matter of fact voice that was entirely toneless.

"Why are you still lying?" A small voice asked from behind us.

I jumped, and Kadence pinched her lips together in fear. Emily revealed herself from behind a tree. Of course, she would be attached to this place as well. Murdering someone did a number on your soul.

"Why do the letters upset you so much?" Terry asked, and I recognized her therapist's voice.

It comforted and terrified me. Either way, I was happy to have her here with me.

"Because she's lying about what they said. They would never ask her to take her clothes off or to touch herself. She lied to get them into trouble and hurt my family. Why would she do that to me?" Emily asked, her voice rising and trembling.

"Who would never ask her?" Terry asked.

Emily's eyes flashed, she was still human enough to still want to protect whoever it was. In her growing fury, she turned to me.

"Did she tell you that she did it? That she took off her shirt and was touching herself? My mom said that only dirty girls did things like that," Emily said, her aura fluctuating and radiating black from within her.

Kadence began crying, and Emily forced a vision to us.

Kadence was rubbing her tummy, looking unsure, when Emily pushed the playhouse door open.

220

Kadence jumped, and her eyes darted to where her shirt was lying on the floor.

"What are you doing?" Emily asked, almost laughing.

"Um," Kadence's bottom lip trembled.

Emily looked at her shirt, and her face shut down. "What are you doing? Is it another letter?"

"I know you told me not to open them anymore. This one promised that if I took my shirt off and touched myself that he would bring me a brand-new princess dress. He said he had one that looked just like Princess Ariel when she gets married," Kadence sputtered, holding her hands out to Emily and begging her to understand.

"Why would he ask you to do that?! He could get in trouble for that. You could get in trouble for that."

Kadence shook her head. "No, I'm not doing anything wrong. Maybe he wants me to undress because I am going to put on the new dress."

Emily laughed and it aged her in a way that gave me chills. "Don't be a baby Kadence. Only dirty girls do stuff like this."

Kadence pulled back and away from the vision. "I'm not dirty."

Emily stepped closer to us, her fury making her firm and solid in our world. She pushed Kadence gently on the chest and smiled when she saw that her hand made contact.

"Yes, you are. This is all your fault. If you had just thrown the letter away, none of this would have ever happened."

"You are just sad he didn't love you as much!" Kadence exploded, pushing her back and crying.

"Shut up," Emily said, looking shocked.

"I didn't want him to love me. I just wanted to be a kid," Kadence said, crying and wiping her face.

That seemed to be the last straw, it wasn't just that she was second best. Kadence didn't even want the love in the first place. She jumped on Kadence, screaming and pulling her hair.

"Stop!" I said, realizing I was crying as well.

I went to grab Emily off of Kadence, my hands went right through. Emily's laugh echoed in my ears, and I realized she was able to project to her victim and no one else. She was solid to everyone but me.

"Let me go! Claire! Help me!" Kadence screamed, pushing Emily away just as Emily slapped her across the face.

"Stop it!" I screamed again, my hands going through them over and over.

I had to get to Kadence. I had to protect her. My vision started blacking out as I tried to meld into whatever dimension Emily was hiding in. I grabbed onto Emily and was thrown into one of her memories.

Crying was coming from the bathroom. Did Kade hurt herself?

"Kade?" I pushed the door open slightly.

Someone was standing behind Kade, they were both looking into the mirror. Tears were on her cheek, and she was trying to look away. He-no, don't look at his face. It can't be him.

"What are you doing?" I asked.

His hands were inside of her pajamas and moving around. He swung around and knocked Kadence into the sink. A huge breath escaped from her like she had just fallen off a scary ride at the carnival.

"What are you doing?" I asked again, my stomach was queasy.

He looked at me, and I can't see his face because he shouldn't do that. He can't do that. He slams the bathroom door in my face.

"Claire!" Terry ripped me from slipping through by slapping me across the face and shaking my shoulders.

It felt like being doused in cold water, and I jolted back into myself. Emily was thrown from Kadence and abruptly disappeared. Kadence was huddled on the floor crying.

"You can never follow them. Never. They don't have the power, you do. Your pain and your fear for Kadence is what allows Emily to take solid form. It's based on emotions. Don't let her pull it from you and use it. You have to keep a handle on yourself. If you don't, you will lose yourself, and I can't go in after you," Terry told me, holding my face and forcing me to look at her.

I nodded, crying, and apologizing. The same thing had happened with Barbara and Len last year. Our fear gave them their power. I couldn't let Emily do the same, I couldn't let her hurt Kadence again.

We had come here to try to find Kadence's hair, Emily's trophy, so that we were able to free her. Instead, I had just put her through even more humiliation and hurt.

"I am so sorry. You don't have to come back. I can keep you safe," I told Kadence, pulling her into my lap.

She glared at me for half a second before dissolving in my embrace. I stood up and carried her back to the car, making promises and hoping that I could keep them.

***

A 911 text from Ash usually meant that she had found yet another online sale and needed me to talk to her and her credit card down, but it still could be important.

"Hey, could you watch Noah for a minute? Ash texted me that she had an emergency, so I want to walk down really quick," I told Terry.

Noah yelped from his highchair and tried to throw a Cheerio to where we were standing by the stove.

"Of course," Terry laughed.

The walk to Ash's was short, and I knocked before pushing the door open. She had lived in the same apartment building for most of her life and knew her neighbors so well that their door was rarely locked. It looked like Ash's mom was running errands, so I headed straight to her bedroom.

"911?" I asked.

At the sound of my voice, Ash jumped up and ran over to hug me.

"A happy 911?" I said, laughing.

"Ben proposed!" Ash said, her eyes wild with disbelief and elation.

It took me a second to process her words before I forced a smile to my face.

"What?"

She thrust her hand out where a princess cut ruby adorned her third left finger.

"Isn't it beautiful?"

The ruby was perfect, at least he had gotten that right.

"How did he do it?" I asked, needing something else to say.

"We went out to dinner. You know he had been weird and moody the last couple days. Nothing new. Except it was because he was afraid of spilling the beans! He had them put the ring it in my dessert and then got on his knee in front of everyone. It was perfect."

I nodded. Ash always talked about how she would have hated a public proposal. This was as cliché as it could get. I guess when you're convinced it's never going to happen, you'll take whatever you are offered.

I squealed with her and listened to her already endless wedding plans while feeling wooden inside. It wasn't just that I was barely ready to talk about Terry's wedding, at least her and CJ were meant to be together. It made it easier to focus on them because they really deserved to be happy together.

This was never going to work out. I loved Ash so much and wanted her to be happy. However, Ben had made a career out of disappointing her for the last ten years. I was going to be her maid of honor, and all I wanted was to talk to Holden and have him promise me that even if it was a terrible ceremony, he would dance with me at the reception. I knew that was not going to happen.

Ash wasn't going to be happy, and neither was I.

***

Kadence's hands danced with the paper dolls I had made her, singing in a little voice. She was narrating a story for Noah and he was completely entranced with her. Suddenly, she stiffened right before my phone rang. I gave her a strange look and answered the unknown number.

"Hello?"

"Is this Claire Shaw?" an unsteady voice asked.

"It is. Can I ask who is calling?"

"This is Cynthia Morton. Kadence's mom."

I froze. Kadence looked down and started putting her dolls away. She wanted nothing to do with contacting her family yet, it was too much to even overhear our conversation. I walked to the kitchen and sat at the table.

"What can I do for you?" My heart hammered in my chest.

After seeing Kadence being assaulted by a faceless man in Emily's vision, I had been calling Cynthia constantly. She always pretended to be busy, and this was the first call she had returned. However, from the tone of her voice I knew this had nothing to do with my stalking.

"I don't even know where to start. The cops have been no help whatsoever."

"I'm so sorry. Cases like this are already complicated, when they are closed its more about saving public face."

"No, I had to call them again."

"Why?" I asked, my skin feeling like it was full of static.

If I didn't know better, I would have said that it was the feeling of foreboding. The future leaning against me heavily.

"I went outside to garden this morning and saw Jaime bringing something in from her clubhouse mailbox. It was a letter, just like the letters that Kade used to receive."

"What letters?" I asked, she had never confirmed to me that they existed.

"You know what letters," Cynthia whispered, sounding defeated.

"Why didn't you tell me before?" I asked, sitting heavily.

She began to cry. "I found them right before she died, and she told me that they were nothing. I wanted so badly to believe that. And she started having accidents, and I knew what that could mean. I was afraid to ask. I was afraid of what she might tell me. And then... and then she was killed, and I found hundreds of those disgusting letters. I showed them to the police, and they said it wasn't enough. It was only evidence of how I had failed my daughter."

"What did Jaime's letter say?" I asked, feeling sick.

This was more than just a letter. This was Kadence's stalker coming back for her sister.

"It asked her to come to the Simmon backyard so that he could give her a special present. She went ballistic when I ripped it in half. I guess these letters have been coming to her for half a year and she believes they are friends. We never told her the details of her sister's death. I have no idea what to do. The police said that since none of the letters were threatening all they could do was 'keep abreast of the situation.' Which basically means, they are worthless until my daughter is dead."

Cynthia's words broke into sobs for the next few minutes.

"Can we meet tomorrow? I would like to meet Jaime. I think we have a few things we need to talk about," I told her, hoping that me being in contact with Kadence would bring her peace and not cause her to write me off.

As I hung up with Cynthia, the house was too quiet.

"Noah?" I went into the living room, where he had been playing with Kadence.

Kadence's spirit had retreated to wherever she hid when she was overwhelmed, and Noah was nowhere to be seen. I felt a breeze and saw that the front door was standing open. Fear jolted through my body, waking up every single one of my senses.

"Noah!" I screamed, running out to the front door.

Noah was crawling across the grass, reacting to black sparkles swirling around the front gate. Emily stood outside the warding, playing with the air and whispering to my son.

"Get away from him!" I snatched him up, breathing hard and glaring at Emily.

She glared back at me. "What's wrong, Claire? I just wanted to play."

As she dissipated, it took me a few moments to get ahold of myself. I wanted to be angry with Kadence for leaving him and couldn't quite manage it. I was the one who had walked into the other room. I wanted to destroy Emily's very essence for threatening my child. I wanted to wash my hands of the situation.

Kadence was nowhere near ready to move on. Emily was only getting stronger. Jaime was running out of time.

Chapter 10
Terry March 2018

It was funny having a baby shower for Macy after the baby was already here. However, we had planned the party before her C-section, and it seemed like a silly reason to say no to gifts that she really needed. It just became a great way for her friends and family to meet the baby all at once.

"Thank you," Macy said, wrapping a Boppy pillow from Missy around her waist and laying a sleeping Carla against her stomach.

"How is breastfeeding going?" Missy asked.

Macy shrugged. "I think I'm doing it right. It's still a learning process for both of us."

Missy patted her shoulder and kissed the baby on the forehead gently.

"Who's next?" Claire asked, bringing another sparkly gift bag over to Macy.

"That's mine," Britney said from across the room where she was chatting with Kate.

I froze a little bit, Macy just smiled over at her. She coaxed a tissue paper encased package from the bag and tried to open it without tearing anything. Mom had always tried to save the tissue paper, and it was a habit Mac had picked up unconsciously. There was a huge rainbow stack next to her.

"Wow. This is beautiful," Mac said, pulling out a footprint mold set.

"I know you're not super crafty. This is all in one. You mix it with water, pour it into the mold, and just press her feet into it. You're not going to want to forget those little toes," Britney said, smiling at Carla.

Mac smiled back at her and there was a snap of electricity in the air. Everyone went on with their business and the party, yet, I felt Claire freeze as well.

Things still hummed between them. Macy's life was kind of complicated right now. It was still clear that she and Britney were still connected and there was some unfinished business there. Yet, Mac was a mom now.

She put the mold back into the bag and moved onto the next gift.

I walked over to where Britney was standing, offering cake as I went.

"Hey, you. Long time no see," I told her.

"I know. I heard that you and CJ are engaged? Congrats. He is quite a fox."

I grinned like an idiot. "Yeah, he is. How are you doing? Are you still in school?"

She nodded. "Yep. I will be a sophomore next year. I am thinking of changing my major, though. I was going for business, but whenever I am in an econ or business law class, I kind of want to die. I have really been enjoying my biology classes, so I might head in that direction."

"Well, good luck," I touched her back lightly as I slid past her and was surprised by the intensity of the vision seeping from her.

Being here was hard. She was still at home in these walls. Throughout her and Macy's junior and senior years, they had hung out here almost every single day. It was difficult to feel like an outsider when she knew where we kept the spatulas and that there were cookies hidden behind the multigrain bread in the pantry.

Being around Mac was hard because her new life didn't change how she cared about her. She had cried herself to sleep for months and knowing that she was sleeping with guys again broke her heart. She had made mistakes too. She knew how hard it would be for Macy once she went off to school, and she resented the fact that she couldn't just be a college student. She hadn't returned her calls and partied instead, pretending like she was single. She hadn't crossed any physical lines. Her emotional lines didn't even exist anymore.

Britney wanted more than anything to make it work, to help take care of Mac. When she looked at Carla, she didn't feel resentment, she felt a surge of devotion for this little person who was made up of everything she loved about Mac.

She wanted to start over and make this work. Britney froze as if she sensed the vision and turned towards me.

"Brit," I rubbed my arms, unsure of how I wanted to proceed.

She nodded.

"I waited a long time to go after CJ. Too long. To feel the way I did and watch him live his life without me, it was excruciating. I'm glad I took the chance I did. You know what I mean?" I said.

A grin slowly stretched across her lips, and she held my hand. "Yeah. I know what you mean."

***

"What are we doing here?" Kelsi asked, looking scared for the first time in weeks.

I had to admit, staring up at the imposing walls of the jail made me afraid as well.

"I keep telling you that you have to trust me, that I am taking the same chances that you are. That's not true and I'm sorry. You know my history, you looked me up. I had a patient who killed her mother and abusive boyfriend. My family was involved."

Kelsi nodded. "You saw what was going to happen."

"I did. I ignored the truth because I didn't want it to be her. I was so used to dealing with abusive

231

assholes that I blamed the whole thing on him and ended up not being able to save her mom. I tried to protect my patient and ended up aiding her in the murder."

Kelsi's mouth dropped open.

"I didn't do it on purpose, and for a long time, I thought that didn't matter. It did. What Gina did to me almost destroyed me. I almost quit altogether. I'm glad I didn't. If I had, we never would have found each other."

Kelsi looked at the door. "So you're ready to face your monsters too."

I nodded. "I'm ready."

I wasn't sure that Gina would even see us, but within a half-hour, she was being led over to a table in a room that was unbelievably cold considering the number of people meeting with their loved ones at other tables.

"This is a surprise," Gina said, sitting across from me and looking at Kelsi with questions in her eyes.

I couldn't believe how much her appearance had changed. She had gained at least 10 pounds in muscle, and her hair was full and long now. It seemed that jail agreed with her.

"You look well," I said.

She smirked at me. "I'm going to be here for the rest of my life. I should probably make the best of it."

I looked at my hands, unsure of where to start now.

Gina sighed. "What do you want, Terry? You already know everything. You already testified against me. I am never going to walk free again. What else could you possibly want from me?"

I took a deep breath. "I just want to know why. You know that I saw what was going to happen. You can deny that you meant for it to happen, we both

232

know better. I saw it. I saw it months before you did it. And you knew it. Why did you make me feel crazy? Why did you involve my family when I was in a coma?"

Gina shrugged. "I can't really expect you to understand what living in that kind of hell was like. Lucas was still beating me every single day. I went to your house because I had nowhere else to go. Then your sisters wanted so badly to help me."

Anger flared in my stomach. "That's bullshit, Gina."

Her eyebrows shot up, and I saw a peculiar look flit across her face. She was still trying to be my patient. She was still trying to make me feel for her.

"Gina, you were my patient for a long time. That means I know that you are aware of the programs out there to help you. You came to me and got me involved, I tried to find a way to save your mom, and you let me talk to your brother and bring up all of that old crap. He killed himself because of it. I fought for you. And you still killed her."

Gina's eyes flashed. "She was suffocating me, Terry."

"No!" I smacked my hands on the table, crying now.

Kelsi rubbed my back.

"No, just stop. Lucas hit you. I get it. I saw the hospital records. Gina, you killed your mom. The person who gave birth to you and took care of you. You put a pillow over her face and pushed down until she died. Lucas didn't do that. You did. And then you bought a gun and brought it home. Lucas was after my family because of you. You got my mom killed, you almost killed me. And when you came home that day, my sisters could have died. You hurt so many more people than just your family, you almost destroyed mine."

Gina was crying now, but I didn't feel it. It was all a game. She was sick. She always had been.

"Lucas was a jerk, an abusive dickhead. That's true. Yet, you are the only murderer here. You were the real monster. I feel sorry for you."

"Do you want me to apologize? Is that what you need?" Gina asked, throwing her hands up.

I looked at her and looked within myself. I felt nothing towards the whole situation. A million pounds had lifted off my shoulders. I didn't need her to say that she was sorry. She couldn't possibly mean it. I just needed a chance to be heard.

"No. I think I'm finally done."

As we made our way out of the jail, I collapsed into the driver's seat.

"That was intense," Kelsi said, making me laugh.

"It was. I feel better."

"Ter, if you can confront someone who did… all of that to you. I think I'm ready. That could have ruined your career. Still, you didn't give up. You came back even though there were rumors and you kind of had to start over. I can do that."

"Are you sure? Because I told you that we can't prosecute them without physical evidence. This would be a civil suit, this would be you going after them personally," I told her.

"I'm ready. I have to file a formal complaint with the police. It's the only way to find out if Guy still has the video."

"No time like the present?" I started the car and looked at her for confirmation.

She nodded, and we drove to the police station. I didn't know what would happen after Kelsi made her official report, but I did know that we would get through it together.

***

I couldn't get over how much baby Carla looked like Noah.

"And she has little toes just like you did. Can you believe you were this small?" I asked Noah as he crawled next to his cousin and stared into her face.

Seeing them together, my heart yearned for a future I had never envisioned for myself. This is what I wanted more than anything. The more I wanted it, the more I wanted it as just Terry.

I was afraid of what our gifts would mean for these little souls and how their lives would be harder because we were different.

I wanted to be a mom. I wanted little ones to hold in my arms that were the universe's design of me and CJ. I wanted the minivan and the soccer games, the macaroni art and sticky kisses. I just wanted it without the visions and the past hanging on every moment of our lives.

I was sure.

***

Patients had brought me gifts before. Sometimes they were strange, ultrasounds to tell me they were staying with their husband after all. Keys for their new apartment three towns away. Paintings, journals, even a cactus. A bottle of wine from a teenage patient was new.

"Kelsi?" I gave her an arched brow.

She laughed and handed it to me. "My mom bought it."

"What's the special occasion?" I asked, hoping this was not goodbye because her mom hadn't changed her mind.

235

"Guy's locker was searched. His phone was inside and covered in the warrant. The video was there, and links to several sites he had uploaded it to."

I covered my mouth with my hands, trying not to yelp.

"We did it. It was submitted to my lawyer and we served him and Shannon with subpoenas. The hearing is in a few weeks."

I leaned forward to hug her. "I am so damn proud of you."

I knew that this wasn't the end and that Kelsi still had a lot ahead of her to face and to be brave for. However, these were the moments in this field you had to hold onto. These were the seconds you had to look back on when you felt like you had nothing left.

Claire March 2018

"What was your favorite animal today, little man?" I asked Noah as he wrapped his chubby arms around my neck.

His favorite thing to do right now was cling to me like a little monkey. His legs were tightly wrapped around my waist, and he was so high on my chest that our cheeks were smooshed together.

"Foosh," he said, his words garbled in his exhaustion.

"I liked the fish too," I gently peeled him off of me and laid him in his crib. I pulled the stuffed tiger he picked from the zoo gift shop out of our diaper bag and placed it next to him.

We had a long day at the zoo, and he was so tired that he was already sleeping with his hands tucked under his chest.

"Are you here?" I whispered into the room.

After marrying, Holden and I had brought Noah to the zoo for the first time. He had carried him in a front pack and kissed his head throughout the day. Holden loved the elephants and made as many of the noises as possible to make our son giggle. Today, I had taken him alone.

I had felt Holden with me every step. When he first passed away, I relished in that feeling of accompaniment. Now it was beginning to feel more painful than not having him there at all. It was feeling him so close to my heart and not being able to touch him.

He always used to make himself known when I was back at home and alone, now he was keeping himself away from me. He was here and wouldn't let me see him. It hurt too much.

***

237

I knew Ash inside and out. I knew that brown and red were her favorite colors. I knew that she loved rap music and cursed like a sailor when she drove. I knew that she dreamed of a huge wedding with a ridiculous dress, so much family she couldn't greet them all in one night, and a cake that could be featured on Food Network. I knew she also loved Ben and would take him any way that she could.

So here we were, waiting in line at the courthouse for them to be married by a justice of the peace.

"Are you sure I look okay?" Ash asked, smoothing her cream-colored bandage dress. Her hair had been curled into loose waves, and her makeup was immaculate.

We didn't have time for a bachelorette party, but I did insist on a day full of pedicures and salon time before she took the leap. We wore matching burgundy nail polish, and she had talked me into way smokier eyes than I was used to. The entire time she talked about her plans for the future and I had to fight feeling like this was a last of sorts.

"You look beautiful," I told her genuinely, not being able to deny that her happiness was giving her a glow.

"My mom is going to freak," she said, rubbing her hands together nervously.

Ash's mom has never approved of Ben and wouldn't have consented to a wedding. So, they decided to elope so that they didn't have to deal with their families trying to butt in. I wish she saw that their families not supporting their relationship after almost ten years was a huge red flag. She just saw it as a reason to have a romantic adventure and painted them as a couple that had to fight for what they had.

Her mother was not going to happy. However, she knew that she would have to get over it in order to have her daughter in her life.

"Yes. Then she is going to plan a huge reception barbecue and life will go on," I told her, holding her hands to still them.

"Ready?" Ben asked, coming back from paying their fee.

She nodded, and I followed them into the room. I was Ash's witness, and Ben had picked a friend. The same friend that had been caught with cocaine four years ago, landing them in jail for the night.

Watching them say their generic vows, the suffering in my chest so strong it could have existed on its own. This wedding was so unlike mine. Regardless, I was still being ripped back to my own special day. As much as I hated Ben, I wanted Ash to have the same experience that I did. I wanted her to have flower petals in her hair and being able to dance to 80s music in an overpriced dance hall. I wanted to toast her and watch her throw her bouquet. I wanted her to have the wedding she deserved. I wanted her to have the husband that she deserved.

The ceremony was over in minutes, and she and Ben headed to their honeymoon in the San Juan Islands. He had balked on a wedding but agreed to an Ash-funded trip as long as it included a winery tour. The next few days would be full of her having to babysit him as he drank too much and she was talking about it like it was everything she had dreamed of.

As I drove home, the leaden feeling in my stomach intensified. It reminded me of how I felt when Emily and Kadence fought in the forest. Their fury combined with my gift and made them solid, made them real. The memory swirled in my mind, combining with my grief and creating a plan.

I didn't have to be alone. I couldn't have Holden the way that I wanted him, and I couldn't make him real for the rest of the world. Still, I could make him real enough for us.

***

I knew that everyone was not going to agree to my idea about Holden. I never thought Terry would fly off the handle the way that she did.

"This is wrong, Claire. And you know it."

"No, it's the only way…"

"What about Noah? How is he going to cope with this? He can't think that this is normal. You are just afraid of him moving on, the supernatural is unknown."

"You're wrong. I am not afraid of the supernatural, the unusual. I am afraid of the normal days," I said, angrily wiping tears from my cheek and trying to quietly shut the door where Noah was sleeping.

"What do you mean?" she asked, trying to reach out to me and I smacked her hands away.

"The supernatural almost makes sense. The ghosts and spirit figures are here because their story still needs to be told. They are scary because they are so done with being ignored by the masses. I get that. That makes perfect sense. The day just being perfect and then falling apart makes no sense to me."

She stared at me at a complete loss for words.

"Do you remember the day that Mom and Dad separated? We were gardening. Dad was so focused on trying to turn that muddy patch over by the shed into a vegetable garden. He tilled the soil there and even put up this ridiculous chicken wire fencing. All-day Mom seemed made of static and vibrated with sad purpose. Then, that night we heard them fighting."

She nodded, swallowing hard. "I remember."

"The next morning, they came into our room and told us that they weren't going to be together anymore, and that Dad was going to live somewhere else. I remember thinking that he looked shocked. His face was all puffy from crying and he just got his stuff and waved goodbye to us. I will never forget his face that night. He was stunned. It just being a normal day and Mom pretending like everything was fine before pulling out the rug betrayed him. He was just planting the garden and then everything changed."

I sat next to her. I knew it was hard for her to not take Mom's side on this matter because she saw her grieve in a way that no one else did. She couldn't argue this one with me though. She remembered that day and I was right. Dad wasn't perfect, and he was awful to Mom for a lot of their marriage. He was still completely sideswiped by her decision to end their marriage. He took a long time to fully let go of the idea of their life together.

"And then… that morning with Holden. We were giving Noah a bath. We used that lavender soap, and we were both getting over a little cold. Holden put a handful of bubbles on my nose and kissed them off. Then he put Noah and I down for a nap together and kissed me. He told me he had to go run some errands with Macy. When I woke up, the police were calling me and asking me to go to the hospital. It was like I was still asleep, and it was just this awful dream. Because there was no warning. It was just a normal day."

"Claire, I can't even imagine what you are going through. It doesn't justify this. This is not the right choice."

"And you can't make this choice for me," Holden said from the doorway.

I jumped, wishing he hadn't overheard our conversation before I had a chance to try to talk to him.

Terry looked at both of us and slowly made her way out of the room.

"Please, just let me try to explain," I told him, standing up to cross the room over to him.

When he didn't answer, I took that as an agreement.

"I can do this. I can make you solid. We can exist together like we did before."

He slowly shook his head. "No, we can't."

"You won't even think about it? You won't even try?" I yelled, balling my fists.

"No, Claire. I agree with Terry. This isn't the right way."

"I don't think you understand that this feels like you are leaving me. I never wanted to fall in love. I fought it, you bastard," I screamed at Holden, pushing his hands away when he reached for me.

"Claire…"

"No! You found your way inside of my heart, and I changed. I wanted all that ridiculous crap I never wanted. I want hardwood floors with you and to go through the boxes of baby photos we got from your mom's attic. I wanted it all, and I put in my all, despite how scared I was. And still, you're gone. And I'm alone."

Holden forced his arms around me, holding me as I completely fell apart.

"Claire, I have wanted all of that for us since high school. It was always you. I wanted to buy a house and build you an easel so that you could finally learn to paint. I still want it all. It makes this impossible. I need to do this because you deserve better than half dreams. You deserve it all."

"You don't get to choose for me," I said, feeling bitter and heartbroken.

"No, but I do get to choose for me," he said softly.

He gently kissed my forehead and then disappeared.

I wanted to scream. I wanted to hit the floor with my fists until my knuckles broke apart. I wanted to hurt physically the way that my heart raged inside. I wanted to hurt Holden for making me love him this way and then not wanting to make this work.

As much as I wanted this to work and be the solution I had been looking for all year, I knew he wouldn't change his mind. Because I believed him, I always did once he made a decision. He wasn't going to let me keep him. He was going to force me to say goodbye.

***

Before putting the charm around the house, my dreams were terrifying adventures of dancing with shadow figures as they held me down and fed off of my energy. Since our house has been ghost-free, I just dreamed of empty darkness and woke up still feeling drained.

That was before Kadence moved in. Kadence had been having nightmares and was able to pull me in when she felt trapped. Emily was getting stronger and had finally found her.

I was in her nightmare again. Kadence was fighting now, refusing to be caught up in the murder in the same way again. Emily still succeeded in killing her each time. I didn't want to watch these dreamed-up scenarios but was desperate for clues on how to help her.

Emily had used a chair this time, choosing to bludgeon Kadence each and every time. I watched from the window of the playhouse as she walked in,

243

carrying something tightly in her hand. Her hands were shaking. As I tried to step in closer, a branch snapped under my foot, and she froze. She turned slowly, pinning me with her eyes angrily.

As my eyes ripped open, I saw that I wasn't in my room anymore.

"Where are we?" I asked, seeing Kadence beside me.

She looked groggy as if she was still trapped in her dream.

"I needed to... come here. You needed to see," she said.

I turned and was frightened to see that we were back in the forest, this time, the dew under my feet convinced me that this was real. I had no idea how I had gotten here and hoped I hadn't driven in a half semi-conscious state. A light popped on and I could see the playhouse light had turned on. I walked with Kadence, holding her hand tightly.

When we reached the door, she pulled her hand free.

"You're not coming?" I asked.

Kadence shook her head. "No. This is for her."

I pushed the door open. Emily was behind a little table, prying something up from the ground. She looked up and jumped.

"What are you doing?" I asked.

She hid her hands behind her back. She looked so small and so very tired of reliving this moment over and over. I sat in front of her.

"Who are you protecting?" I whispered.

Emily looked down, seeming defeated.

"I love him. He was my best friend. Before Kadence, he played with me every single day. He built this playhouse for me. Then, he stopped coming because he said that being around her was too hard. I didn't know what that meant. Lewis didn't want to be my brother anymore."

"Your brother?" I asked, shocked.

I tried to pull a poker face, not wanting to show my cards and scare her off.

"Why did he try to do those things to her? It made my mom so sad, and my dad yelled all the time. It was ruining everything."

I put my hand on her knee as she trembled. "Sometimes people are just made broken. I don't think he wanted to hurt Kadence. He might not have been able to help it. He might have needed help."

Emily nodded. "I tried to help him. If Kadence was gone then he would be safe and could get better. Then Mom and Dad wouldn't send him away."

I sat back, and Emily's eyes pleaded with me.

"Kadence wasn't just gone, Emily. You killed her. She didn't want what he was doing to her. She was a scared little girl, and she trusted him. And she trusted you."

Emily's face was a mess with the tears mixing with her snot and dirt from the ground.

"We had a sleepover. Kade went to the bathroom, and I heard her crying. I opened the door, and he had his hand in her pajama bottoms. She was so sad, and he was angry at me for not knocking," she shook her head.

"I am so sorry."

"I should have told," she said, breaking completely.

"Then why did you do it?" I asked, wanting so badly just to understand.

"Because I loved him. I didn't want my family to be broken."

We sat in silence as she cried herself out.

"Will she ever forgive me?" Emily asked.

I thought of Kadence waiting outside. She had said this was for Emily. She had already forgiven Emily. She had still loved her. She just wanted to move on.

"I think you need to forgive yourself. You were a little girl too."

Emily finished prying the board from the ground and handed me a little metal box hidden underneath. I opened it and saw a chunk of brittle hair with a wisp of skin attached to one end. I had to bite back my vomit and shut the lid tightly.

She couldn't make what she did better, and she could never really apologize for stealing Kadence's life from her. Maybe she could help Kadence make it to heaven, it was the only gift left to give.

"Will it hurt?" Emily asked me, her body already dissipating in rays of black and gold swirled together.

It looked like the universe was still balancing the anger in her heart with her regret and sins.

"I don't think so. I think being stuck here hurts more."

She closed her eyes and tried to let go. It was close, but the gold won out in the end.

I walked out of the playhouse with the box in my hands.

"Is it what we needed?" Kadence asked, looking at it with fear.

I nodded. "We just have one more thing to do."

Kadence held my hand again, ready to go home. "What?"

"We need to find her brother. We need to make sure you find justice and your family gets the answers they deserve."

Kadence looked up at me. "I know where he is. He never left."

I should have known better. When something like this happens, the land itself seems to remember. The people who had to cover this up for the last five years would have sensed the shift in the air when it was disturbed. They would have noticed the light on in the middle night.

They would be praying that they reached him before we did. Emily's brother might have been targeting Kadence, and Emily did kill Kadence. Emily's killer was still out there. He had seen us in the backyard that night. He saw the box in our hands. He knew that it was all going to fall apart again.

Chapter 11

I had heard about the video. I had seen that night through Kelsi's eyes in our shared vision. Seeing the actual video and hearing the laughter in the background was almost more than I could take. After filing her report, the cops had cause to search Guys phone and had found the video. It was enough to file charges against him and Shannon.

Both parties had agreed to a closed hearing, and I was allowed to come as her emotional support. She had been doing amazing. She was watching the video with a straight face, strong and beautiful. Her hands were trembling and gave her away. I encased them in my own.

"Okay," the judge said as the video ended. "Would either party like to say anything before I make my decision on sentencing?"

Kelsi's lawyer stood up.

"Yes, your honor."

Kelsi stood up and made her way to the middle of the room where a small podium was waiting.

"Over the course of the last year, I have changed my mind about who I am as a person. When I first started my senior year, I thought I was the new girl and that I needed to lower my standards as a person to fit in. I kissed a boy I barely knew because I wanted one friend to make my high school experience easier. And that kiss led to what you just witnessed. I then decided that I was a mistake of a person, and the only way I could hide from that embarrassment and shame was to cut myself. I was pushed around all day at school and came home to slice at myself to get away from a situation I thought I had created."

Kelsi's mom wiped the tears from her eyes, and I leaned over to squeeze her shoulder. She wasn't sure that she trusted me, but after learning that Kelsi was going to fight for herself, she had warmed up to me again.

"Then, with the support of my family, I had gotten help. I had gotten the same help that Guy and Shannon should have gotten before they decided that putting people through this was acceptable. I learned that only weak people needed to hurt people this way to get through their own day. I learned that I wasn't a victim and that I didn't deserve what happened to me. I discovered that I deserved justice because I get to decide who I am and how the rest of my life unfolds. I learned that sometimes I have to stand strong so that no one else has to go through what happened that night. Thank you."

Kelsi stood up straight, looked right at Guy, and folded the paper her statement was written on. He looked away first. She sat next to me, and the judge called a recess. We were scheduled to come back later that afternoon to end this once and for all.

I didn't know what was going to happen. It could be a slap on the wrist, a fine, community service, or even a short jail sentence. Regardless of what happened today, Kelsi would not be bringing this experience with her to college. Whatever happened today she would leave this courthouse the person was supposed to be, walking with her head held up high.

***

My mom hadn't been with me during any of the wedding planning, but the big day was coming up and I needed her today. As always, when my heart really called to her, she found me.

"Did you always know I would feel this way someday?" I asked her as she finally appeared and sat on my bed next to me.

I was writing my vows and all of the talk about the future was choking me as I felt trapped in the past. I wanted to be focusing on what made us great and the life that we would have together. Instead, I was desperate to cut the psychic part out of me so that I could become someone new. I felt like I was betraying my mom and needed to be with her.

She nodded. "I did. Still, I think that you're missing a big part of the picture. I'm not hanging around because Claire is keeping me here. I am here because we have unfinished business."

I looked at her in shock. "What do you mean?"

"Really think about it, sweetheart. You are feeling suffocated by visions of the past. But Terry, you honestly can't picture not having these gifts in your life. You just want to focus on the future. And it's the only thing I have left to give."

I froze as the implications of her words sunk in.

"Where would my gift go? I don't think I can have both."

She held my hand. "You can. I don't think you want both. And that's okay. However, it is a gift, which means you need to give it away. To who, that is really up to you."

Tears filled my eyes as I realized that once my mom gave me her gift, she would move on. I hadn't been given a chance to say goodbye to her before she was buried, I was the only person who could truly say goodbye to her forever.

"I don't know how to live without you," I told her, throwing myself into her arms.

"My sweet Terry. You already are. That's the point. You can't live in the past. You need to focus on what's ahead. And I can help you with that. It was always the plan. I saw the future through you, and now I finally know why."

When I finally sat up, we held hands, and my mom looked at me for an eternity. She memorized my face and I did the same.

"I will never stop loving you. You know that, right? Love doesn't die with a person's soul. It just lives in the people left behind. Nothing could change how much I care about you girls. You were my reason for living. Our story doesn't end with this life. Forever isn't enough," she told me, her voice choking.

I nodded, unable to talk. In a jolt of fiercely burning electricity her power begin to course through my veins and wrap itself around my entire being. I saw our past and a love so strong that I thought it would rip me apart. Her fear every time we were sick. Her pride when we won awards or learned how to whip the perfect meringue. And the clarity of her grief in leaving us before we got to finish our walk of life together.

Her devotion still tingled in my hands as hers left mine and the shine of where she was going blinded me. And then I was alone.

As I climbed the stairs, I found my sisters sitting in the living room together. Macy's eyes darted around my head, and as she saw mom's aura mixed with mine, she covered her mouth with her hand.

I didn't want to be the one that told them that she had moved on, but I needed them to understand. I knew the person who I needed to give my gift to. It would be the only way Holden could move on.

***

I wanted to savor every single moment of today, it was already going way too fast. This morning I woke

251

up early and just laid in my bed alone. CJ had stayed the night at his mom's house, and it would be the last night we would spend apart from each other. The last day of being just us before we became *us*.

I missed him already.

I met my sisters in the kitchen and Claire made us chocolate banana oatmeal before driving to the venue. I made it before every big dance during high school. My mom always said I needed to have something filling yet not bloating. This was the first time that Claire had made it for me, and it already had me teary-eyed.

The botanical garden we chose had a smaller reception space equipped with a bridal suite. It was Claire's biggest reason for supporting this choice. Claire did my makeup and Noah crawled around our feet. She chose cream eyeshadow blended with gray and a sweep of green eyeliner. For my lips, it was always red. Macy did my hair in loose waves and intertwined braids in a floral headband. Carla nursed from a front pack and was too cute for words in her mini flower girl dress. Lucy arrived with the dresses about an hour later, and we spent the next two hours helping each other get dressed.

Carla's head was adorned with a thin floral headband to match her cream lace flower girl dress, and she had a miniature corsage that matched the one attached to Noah's shirt. Noah was wearing the same outfit as CJ and his brother Joey. Cream slacks, a white shirt, suspenders, and bare feet. CJ picked white spider mums as their boutonnieres.

My dress was the last touch. As Claire zipped me up, it was hard not to choke up.

"Ter," Mac said, wiping her makeuped eyes discreetly.

I watched myself in the mirror, examining my dress from every angle. I didn't feel like myself, I was a fall goddess. At the same time, I had never felt more comfortable in my own skin.

"I'm seriously hot," I said lightly, crossing the room to touch up my lipstick.

Claire laughed and squeezed my shoulder.

"Do you think it's okay that I asked Britney? Should I have asked Alex instead?" Macy asked Claire, adjusting Carla's headband.

She hated it already and was determined to taste it instead of wear it.

Claire shook her head. "Do you want to be with Alex, or do you want to be with Britney? It's really as simple as that. Things will be complicated. If you're happy, they are infinitely easier."

Macy smiled to herself. "Then I'm glad she's here."

I watched them interacting so easily with each other and was so incredibly content. I wished my mom was here, but Claire being the one to tie me into my dress didn't feel wrong. We were right where we were supposed to be.

"Are you ready?" our coordinator said, poking her head into the room.

Everyone looked at me. I nodded. I had been ready since ninth grade, since that first formal dance when I slow danced with CJ for the first time. He had always been it for me.

CJ's brother was able to attend the wedding and escorted Macy and Carla down the aisle before Claire walked down with Noah. Macy wore a red bridesmaid's dress that flowed around her feet and had a daring slit up one leg. She had baby's breath and tiny red roses braided throughout her hair and a shade of maroon lipstick that only she could pull off.

Claire called dibs on yellow and looked beautiful in a form-fitting gown that tied around the waist. She had a small sunflower in her hair and carried an yellow Starbucks cup to pay homage to my favorite coffee buddy. Noah walked next to her and stared suspiciously at every person he passed.

I couldn't choose between my sisters, so I chose Lucy as my maid of honor. She walked down alone, looking beautiful in the orange dress and orange carnations in her hair. From the way she was checking out the crowd, she wasn't planning on walking out alone.

"Thank you for asking me to escort you," my dad said from next to me, holding his arm out for me.

I choked back my tears for the thousandth time and kissed his cheek. This wasn't a day I had ever imagined him being part of. It wasn't something I ever thought he would want to be part of. I was so glad to be proven wrong. Here he was, supporting me barefoot and happy. It was perfect.

When we talked down the aisle, I locked eyes with CJ. I saw his world tilt and freeze just a little bit. I loved that I was capable of doing that to him. I grinned at him and walked towards my future like it was the only thing I had been put on this earth to do. And then he relaxed because this was the good part.

A vision swept over to me, connecting us like an invisible tether. I saw everything. My missing front tooth in elementary school and how I had gotten more freckly every summer. I saw the way he looked at my legs when I wore my first bikini, I saw myself crying on his shoulder after my heart had been broken for the first time. I saw him holding my hand when I told him my parents were divorcing, kissing for the first time on his backyard swing set, going to Prom, kissing me on the cheek after graduation.

I saw him taking me by the waist and laying me down in the pine needles. I saw us fumbling in his backseat to 90's R&B and laughing when we bumped our teeth together. I saw us fighting, and the time I slapped him in tenth grade. I saw us making up, making it better. Becoming stronger.

My gift danced with my mother's and the future began to whisper to me. I saw him imagining me with a swollen belly and giving our child butterfly kisses. Our tiny apartment with my Princess Bride above the bed, but I only had to turn over to wake up to beauty. Him building a treehouse for our kids in our first family home. Dancing in the kitchen and swinging on a porch wing together at night with beers in hand. I saw him loving me forever. And I held onto it and gave it back to him.

My dad shook his hand, and then I was holding CJ's. I became his.

***

We only had two days for our little honeymoon in Seattle. We did all of the touristy things that we always talked about and never got around to. We had cheesecake at the Cheesecake Factory. We drank Starbucks in the original café and kissed on the Space Needle. We had an enchilada in the Elvis room and bought souvenirs in the Ye Olde Curiosity Shoppe. Yet, my favorite part of the trip was when we ignored our itinerary and spent an entire day in bed instead.

It was an amazing trip, yet, I already missed my sisters and the kids.

"We're home," I called, pushing into the front door with my suitcase.

Claire gave me a hug; fear was written all over her face.

"What happened?" I asked, the worst swirling around in my head.

255

Noah had an accident. Carla was sick. Noah and Carla had both been hurt somehow.

"I just got off the phone with Cynthia Morton. Jaime didn't come home from school today."

"Holy shit."

"I told her to come over. We were going to meet today anyways so that I could talk to her about Kadence. This makes it even more important."

"I think we should ask Krista to come over as well," I said, trying to formulate a plan in my head.

"Why?" Claire asked, looking horrified.

"Because it looks like her son is back in town. She might be the only one who can get through to him."

"Cynthia, you must know that this is crazy," Krista said, standing up with her eyes bulging.

I took a deep breath, expecting that reaction. However, Cynthia was sitting calmly, looking at her hands. Telling someone that I knew what happened to their child because I could see their spirit was never easy. I didn't expect either one of them to believe me, I just needed them to hear me.

"Is she here?" she asked.

I looked into the kitchen, where Kadence was peeking around the corner.

"She is."

"Enough!" Krista screamed, covering her ears.

Cynthia pinned her with her eyes, the anger in her eyes making my stomach flip flop.

"What are you afraid of Krista? That I will find out what your family is hiding?"

The coldness in her voice gave me goosebumps.

"Can she hear me?" Cynthia nodded.

"Yes, she isn't ready to talk yet," I told her, my stomach clenching as she processed that painfully.

"How do we find Jaime?" Cynthia asked.

Macy sat up, straighter. "I can see auras. If you have something of hers, I can follow the trail."

"Let's do it," Cynthia said, digging in her purse and handing Macy a small yellow rabbit.

"Wait!" Krista said, her face pale and waxy.

"For what? For another one of my children to die?" Cynthia screamed back at her.

"You don't understand," Krista replied, tears in her eyes. "He is all I have left."

Cynthia's face drained of color as it all fell together. Terry and I had found out that Emily's brother was the one who had been molesting

257

Kadence. We wanted to expose him but had nothing. Without evidence, there was nothing we could do. Krista admitting the truth made evidence irrelevant.

"You knew," Cynthia said in a strangely flat voice.

Cynthia's throat tightened as she struggled to swallow that. Her hands tightened, and she took quick puffs of breath through her nose. This family was supposed to be her friends. She had trusted them. And Krista had known all along. If we hadn't been looking for Jaime, she might have killed her right in front of us.

"I am so sorry. I didn't know until that night. Emily was trying to protect him. She didn't know what she was doing."

"Emily… Emily killed Kadence?" Cynthia looked like she was going to pass out.

I held onto her arm, trying to steady her.

"Who killed Emily?" I asked.

Krista shook her head. Terry reached out slowly and gripped her arm. In her anger, she projected the vision for all of us. Cynthia gasped as it stole through her mind.

"What have you done!" Lewis screamed into Emily's face, holding up her bloody hands.

Emily looked like she was going to throw up.

Krista walked into the room, her husband trailing behind her and cursing. He always hated to be woken up in the middle of the night. When she saw the blood on her daughter's hands, she ran to her, terrified.

"What is going on?" she asked, grabbing Emily's hands and searching for a wound.

"It's not her blood. Its Kadence's," Lewis said, his face a picture of grief. He sank to his knees.

"Emily?!" I yelled, so confused. "Is Kadence hurt?"

Emily's mouth gaped, and she was unable to speak.

"Emily!" Darryl came up from behind her and slapped her across the face.

"I killed her," she said, finally coming back into herself.

"What?" I asked, sinking to the floor.

"What the fuck are you talking about?" Darryl asked, gripping her shoulders so hard I heard them crack.

Emily stared at her brother and it all fell together. A few weeks ago, Emily told me she that caught him with his hand down Kadence's pants during a sleepover. Lewis denied it, saying that Kadence had an accident and he was helping her change. I didn't want to believe it. I wanted to think that it was a mistake.

From the look on Lewis's face, he had lost more than just a family friend. He had lost someone he shouldn't have been around at all. There had been signs, the way he watched the girls playing outside. The letters I found in his room. But he was my baby. There was no way he could be capable of that. My stomach heaved, and I tried to breathe through it.

"I didn't want you to send Lewis away," Emily whispered.

I gagged. She had been protecting her brother. She had killed a person, a child. My babies.

"What have you done to us!" Darryl screamed into her face, shaking our daughter over and over.

Suddenly I heard a huge tree branch snap. It took me a few minutes to realize that it was simply Emily's neck.

Cynthia screamed, pulling away from the vision, and breaking the connection. Krista was completely useless now, sobbing on the ground.

"Please don't take him away. He is all I have left."

I looked over to where CJ was hovering, he looked helpless and scared.

"Can you call the police? We are going to look for Jaime."

I held my hand out to Cynthia and Macy gripped the bunny.

"Can you see it?" Terry asked.

Macy's eyes looked glazed over and she nodded.

When we left the living room, Cynthia didn't look back to check on her old friend. There was nothing left we could do.

***

The aura was fading but led us back to the clubhouse at the Simmon house. Cynthia seemed to be able to sense Kadence's presence in the car and was impossibly calm under the circumstances.

"What do we do if we find them?" Macy asked us.

I turned towards her and pulled a gun out of my purse.

"Where the hell did you get that?" she asked, pressing herself into the seat.

"Cabela's. I bought it after… Lucas. I had a permit and took classes."

Terry and Macy stared at me. When Cynthia started fidgeting, they nodded to me, and we went straight to the backyard. The gun was back in my purse, I was glad that I had brought it. I refused to ever be caught off guard ever again.

"Is this where she died?" Cynthia asked, looking sick.

I shook my head. "No one died in the clubhouse. Kadence died in the forest, and Emily was brought out here afterward."

Terry shivered and pushed the clubhouse door open. Macy screamed when she saw a tall teenager

260

lying face down in a spreading puddle of blood. I covered my mouth and kneeled down to roll him over. It was Lewis, Emily's brother.

"Where is Jaime?!" Cynthia said, her hands going to her face in panic.

"He's still warm," I told my sisters and picked up a letter lying next to him.

Macy took it out of my hands gently. "The aura on this is stronger. She was just holding this."

As her eyes took on a stronger glaze, we followed her, leaving the car behind this time.

***

It only took us an hour to find Jaime at the park, the same park where Terry had tried to hide from us last year. It felt like a lifetime ago. Cynthia saw her daughter and screamed. I held onto her arm to keep her from running over to her.

Emily's father, Darryl, was holding Jaime next to him. It seemed like he was talking to himself until he saw us walking across the field. Jaime was dazed and her head rolled around. I would bet that she was drugged to keep her calm and limp.

"How did you find us?" he asked.

He pulled a knife out of his jacket pocket and laid it across his lap.

"My sister followed Jaime's aura," I told him, too terrified to lie.

"What?" he asked, shocked.

"That's why we came to talk to you. We're not reporters. I guess you know that. We are psychic and met your daughter and Kadence."

He nodded, accepting the impossible easily. Because this whole situation was impossible.

"I knew you knew. I just didn't know how."

"There's no reason why you need to hurt Jaime. We can all just walk away from this," Terry said, trying out her therapist voice with her hands up.

She was saying surrender with her hands, but it felt like a signal to me. Darryl was too far gone. Our only chance was to call Kadence, to bring her here. To give her a chance to help Jaime, to give her a chance to confront the man responsible for covering up her murder.

"I don't think so. Lewis made that impossible."

"Where is Lewis?" I asked, wanting to hear his side of the story.

"You don't have to worry about my son. I already took care of him," Darryl said, looking at his hands.

"What do you mean?" I asked, terrified.

A man with nothing left to lose was the worst kind. The scariest.

"It was him. He was after Kadence all those years ago. And it broke Emily's heart. When Emily... did what she did, I went a little crazy. I was shaking her over and over, asking her how she could have done that. I killed her; I didn't mean to. I couldn't believe it. My wife was destroyed, I told her that it would be okay. My brother is a police officer. He would help us. And Lewis could go onto college and have his life because we had already lost a child."

"It didn't stop?" Terry asked, our skin cooling as Kadence approached.

"No, he came home from break and saw Jaime playing in the street. I found one of his letters in his bedroom. After everything that happened, he was doing it all over again. When you guys got close, I knew it was over. When I found out that Jaime went missing, I knew it was him."

"What did you do?" I asked.

262

"I saw the clubhouse light on. He had the nerve to bring her there. So, I killed him. I already killed one of my children, I thought it might be easier this time."

He put his head in his hands, still holding the knife. Terry glanced over to me and stood up straighter. I looked beside me and saw Kadence, watching him cry. She looked so scared but strong. I projected her presence and heard Cynthia gasp.

"Mr. Simmon?"

He froze and slowly looked up, locking eyes with Kadence in disbelief. I trembled with the effort of projecting her in this kind of state.

"You killed Emily?" she asked, tears in her eyes despite what Emily had done to her.

His mouth dropped open. "She killed you."

"Because she was sad. Because your family was falling apart. Because you didn't protect her. You wanted to hide it and told everyone I was lying. Now you are trying to do it again."

"No, I'm not," he said, standing up.

"Yes, you are. Are you going to tell everyone what really happened? What your son did?" she yelled.

He looked down. "I couldn't. It would destroy us."

"There's nothing left to destroy," Kadence said, splaying her hands and bawling.

"I can't," he said again, shaking his head.

Kadence's aura darkened. She had been in the in-between for years. Because of what this man did she had danced with more shadows in her afterlife than she ever did here on earth. Darryl might have had nothing left to lose, but Kadence was not going to lose her sister to the darkness.

"You owe that to Emily. I won't let you hide it this time. I will stay with you forever. I will make you crazy."

My skin broke out in goosebumps as he finally looked up with the emptiest eyes I had ever seen.

"I'm already crazy."

As he brought his knife to his neck, I was barely quick enough to reach out to Kadence. I covered her eyes before his blood sprayed forward. His body slumped to the ground, and Jaime slid to the ground. Cynthia rushed to her daughter and pulled her into her arms.

"Jaime? Baby girl, can you hear me?" she said, lightly smacking Jaime's cheeks.

Her eyes were still unfocused, she struggled to come back at the sound of her mother's voice. Kadence pulled from me so that she could go to them. She kneeled next to them, and Cynthia looked up with tears in her eyes.

"You saved her," Cynthia said.

Kadence put her hand against her mother's cheek, and Cynthia leaned into it.

"I miss you. I love you," she whispered to her.

Kadence leaned down and kissed her sister's forehead before letting the projection drop and dissipating.

"Will she be okay?" Cynthia asked, crying.

I nodded. "She will. She's ready to move on."

***

"Do I deserve forgiveness?" Kadence asked, eerily close to the same questions Emily had asked me only weeks before.

"Why wouldn't you?" I asked her, sitting across from her with the gravestone between us.

"I made him do that. I was so angry for Emily. And now her whole family is gone," Kadence said, wiping her tears.

I held her hand. "You didn't do that sweetie. It was his own guilt. He couldn't handle what he did to his

264

family. He didn't try to protect either one of his kids. That's what destroyed him."

Kadence nodded and looked at the box in my lap.

"Are you ready?" I asked, already knowing that I was going to miss the sound of her running up and down the stairs and laughing with Noah.

She took a deep breath and closed her eyes.

I opened the box and gently took out the hair that kept her tethered here. I dug a small hole in front of her gravestone with my fingernails and placed it inside. Afterward, I said a prayer and covered it. Kadence was finally where she belonged, all of her.

I was never going to get used to seeing this kind of beauty, in seeing this snippet of whatever laid before us when we moved on. Kadence's skin glowed gold, and she finally smiled and sighed, free of every single hurt she had carried with her during her small number of years on this earth.

She was brilliant and opened her eyes to smile at me once more before dematerializing into complete radiance. I was moved and crying from exhilaration. This was right. This is why I was put on this earth.

Spirits weren't supposed to stay here and be locked in the life they left behind. They were supposed to reach the next destination. It was the point of faith in the first place, what you earned for living a life that made you proud.

This beauty, this peace. I wasn't allowing Holden peace.

***

I had never been more grateful that Terry let me keep this room than I was right now. Because I couldn't do this unless I was able to wrap myself in these memories. I sat on my bed and waited for him. Something told me he would know I was here.

"Do you think that you'll ever be able to write anywhere else?" Holden asked.

I opened my eyes and saw him standing next to my desk.

I shook my head. "No, I think this is my forever home."

He smiled at me and sat on the bed across from me.

"Noah is asleep upstairs. I watched him for a while. He's pretty perfect, isn't he?" Holden asked me.

I nodded, my throat tight. "Yeah, he is."

"I kissed him goodnight, and he smiled. I could feel his cheek on my lips. Thank you."

I nodded again.

"It's the last time I will feel him, isn't it?"

A tremor escaped my throat. "Do you think that I am giving up on you?"

He shook his head. "Never. I think that you love me."

As he held my hand, I struggled to get my tears under control.

"Can I hold you one last time?" I asked him, feeling desperate.

"I thought you would never ask," Holden said, leaning forward and pulling himself on top of me.

I wanted to devour him and keep him a part of me forever. I felt the muscles in his shoulders beneath my hands, I kissed him until my lips were bruised, and gave him everything inside of me.

"I love you," I whispered, breaking.

"Love you most."

We laid together afterward and he kissed my forehead. He was laying behind me, our fingers intertwined. I was aware of the light in the room changing and forced myself to turn and look him in the eyes. Because as much as I didn't want to say goodbye to him, I couldn't let him do this alone. I knew he didn't want to leave me behind, but he deserved this bliss. He deserved heaven.

We held hands as the light stole over his body, and when he finally closed his eyes, I kissed them. And then he was gone.

Chapter 12
Claire July 2018

Terry was sure about giving her gift away, but it wasn't until today that she felt ready to say goodbye. Holden really being gone forced us all to let him go for real and it was a black time for everyone. She was right, this was the next step. This would change our family forever, and we were ready.

"Are you sure that you are okay with this? That he would be okay with this?" Terry asked me, looking down at Noah.

I watched him look up at us.

"He is a Shaw."

Missy, Macy, and Terry held hands while Noah and I sat in the middle of them. Gifting a psychic gift wouldn't always hurt. Still, it might be painful for someone so small. Terry closed her eyes, and after a time we saw something resembling thread make its way from her heart and swirl around in the air above us before finding Noah. It gently weaved itself into his chest. He looked up, surprised.

Terry and Macy opened their eyes, and we tied our gifts together, projecting. Noah was so young when Holden died that he didn't have much to remember on his own. With Terry's gift, he would be able to see him forever through our memories.

I saw him drinking mocha with Terry and surprising her with flowers. I saw him tickling Macy and covering her with a blanket when she fell asleep on the couch. I saw him kissing my pregnant belly and whispering to Noah through my maternity shirt.

Noah smiled in complete awe and laughed.

About the Author

Nita Farris is the author of the Shaw Sister Trilogy. She is a freelance writer, author, and preschool teacher based in the Pacific Northwest. Keep an eye out for her debut young adult novel, to be published in the summer of 2020!

Learn more about Nita Farris at nitafarrisauthor.com or follow her on Instagram at @nitafarrisauthor

Books by Nita Farris

The Shaw Sister Trilogy
Sneakers in the Shadows
Sneakers on the Dashboard
Stranger in the Shadows
Screams in the Forest

Note from the Author

If you enjoyed this book or any of the books in the Shaw Sister Trilogy, please take a few minutes to leave a review on Amazon or Goodreads. Reviews are so important to indie authors, help keep us relevant in search results, and lets Amazon know that our book is worth promoting to other readers. Thank you so much for your support!

Made in the USA
Columbia, SC
21 August 2022